A HAND OUTSTRETCHED

LIGHT AT EMPIRE'S EDGE

KIRSTEN PANACHYDA

WORDS AMONG LIONS LLC

For my dad, Larry Weidemier
Because I've always been able to count on your love and support, and
because you've always modeled a life of learning and interest.

And for my mom, Carol Weidemier
Because you've loved me for myself and nurtured me in my passions,
especially for history and reading. And most of all, I'm grateful you
introduced me to our Savior.

I love you both; talk to you soon.

CHARACTERS

Tiann (Tee-AHN) An Iceni girl

Prasudoc*- (pra- SOO- dock) Iceni chief

Boudica*- (BOO -di- kah) Iceni queen

Iceni*- (eye-SEE-nee) Celtic tribe in southeast Britain, present-day Norfolk

Mara*- (MAH-ruh) daughter of Prasudoc and Boudica

Aife*- (EE-fuh) daughter to Prasudoc and Boudica, heir

Shal- (shall) Iceni royal advisor, Druid

Caradoc* (ka-RAH-dock) rebel who waged guerilla warfare against the Romans for 8 years after the Claudian invasion

Goram- (GOR- um) Iceni horse trainer

Devyn- (DEH-vin) Young Iceni warrior a year older than Tiann

Teth- (teth) Brigantian warrior

Brigantes*- (brig-ANT-ees) northern tribe

Cartimandua*- (kar-ti-Man- doo- ah) queen of the Brigantes

Venut*- (VEN- ut) chief of the Brigantes

Shinoc- (SHIN-ock) a spy

Coritani*- (kor-i-TAHN-ee) neighboring tribe

Costri- (KOS-Tree) warrior in charge of escorting Tiann

Amlethius- (am- LEETH- ee- us) Roman commander of a *castra* (small outpost on a road)

Cattia- (KAT- ee- uh) Celtic woman captured by Romans from Gaul

Vidia- (VID- ee- uh) romanized Briton woman

Servius- (SUR- vee- us) Roman, guest of Amlethius

Fein- (fane) Brigantian boy who tends horses

Nuallen- (noo- AWL- len) young man from the far north, student of Shal

*Indicates characters and people based on historical figures

PART ONE

CHAPTER
ONE

Tiann clung to Mara's sweaty hand as they ran. Around them, children laughed and shrieked, scattering in every direction, dodging cooking fires, looms, and irate mothers. Why had Tiann agreed to be Mara's partner? The younger girl couldn't keep up. If only Tiann could let go and run by herself. She'd easily beat them all to the goal and win the game.

She pictured herself holding the large white shell above her head in triumph. Those boys who had mocked her for being left behind by her father, for having no mother, would look her in the eye and admit she outran them. But could she win while hauling the slower girl along?

Mara tugged. "This way."

Tiann resisted, intent on reaching the hideout by the stables.

"Trust me," Mara pleaded.

Tiann allowed herself to be pulled the other way, although she could not see a hiding place. She stumbled as the ground dipped.

Mara yanked her down into a shallow bowl in the earth. "Lie still." The girl combed the grasses up around them, making the spot as invisible to pursuers as it had been to Tiann. Mara caught her eye and grinned.

Tiann smiled back with admiration. She found the queen's daughter mild, a little boring even. So quiet she barely made a ripple in the bustle of the royal household, Mara disappeared and reappeared, as if by magic. But Tiann was lonely and over-whelmed since coming to live with Boudica, the queen, and her family. Mara offered Tiann companionship and acceptance without hesitation. And maybe that quietness hid a quick mind.

Tiann lifted her head to see if the chase had passed yet.

Mara stopped her. "Listen," she breathed, pressing Tiann's ear to the ground.

The sound of footsteps thumped up through the dirt and grass. A moment later a shout sounded from the direction of the paddock. The hideout Tiann had been heading for, she realized.

Mara wiggled her eyebrows in mirth, and Tiann almost laughed out loud.

She pressed her ear to the earth again. The vibration of running faded. "Now?" she whispered.

Mara nodded. The girls pulled their feet under them and crouched, ready to spring. The shell gleamed on the wall, waiting for Tiann to snatch it to victory. Just as she tensed her muscles for the attempt, Mara clamped a hand on her wrist. Irritated, Tiann yanked free, but then she heard it too and felt it through the earth. Thundering hoofbeats heading straight for the village.

She lifted her head now, watching the horse and rider. Glancing at Mara, she read in her crinkled brow the confirmation of her own impression—this was not one of their people.

They forgot the game. Mara sprang up and ran. Taken by surprise, Tiann lagged, catching up just as they reached the inner courtyard.

The rider threw himself off his horse and ran into the hall.

Mara reached out a hand, and Tiann grasped it. This time she followed without protest. The two girls passed through the court-yard to the back of the encircling buildings. Mara turned at the cookhouse, set just outside the ring to prevent the spread of accidental fires. The girls crept along the side of the building.

Tiann had never explored the outer ring, but Mara clearly had, moving unerringly between the front of the cookhouse and the back of a structure adjoining the hall. She ducked under a plank laid between two windows midway up the walls. Puzzled, Tiann squatted next to Mara, who put a finger to her lips. In a moment voices sounded from the open window of the larger building.

"Tell us what's happened."

Tiann caught her breath when she recognized Boudica's voice. She heard Prasudoc giving an order, then the chief's heavy footsteps toward the queen. Were she and Mara eavesdropping on the royal chambers?

"I've asked for some food and watered mead to be sent for you."

"Thank you, Chief," said a third voice, unfamiliar.

"What has happened? Is Caradoc nearby? Has he won?" Boudica's questions came sharp and fast.

Tiann's heart thudded. Caradoc!

"No. No, Lady." The stranger's voice was heavy, and Tiann could hear the protesting creak of a stool as someone sat. "We lost the day. The Romans—they don't even fight like people. They move together like great beasts. In the mountains in the west, we could fight them like men, but on the field . . ."

"Yes," Prasudoc said. "We've heard of this. Like many fortifications moving against the enemy."

"But where is Caradoc now?" the queen demanded. "Is he putting out the call?"

Her da had spoken of Caradoc in the evenings with the other warriors around the fire in the months before he'd left. She had let their words drift around her, uncaring. Until the night Dahad pulled her onto his lap, as though she were still a baby. Told her she was going to live with the chief, Prasudoc, and his wife, Queen Boudica. That she could play with their daughters, Aife and Mara. Told her he was going away to fight. With this Caradoc. She was glad he'd treated her like a baby, because she had pressed her face into his neck and cried like one. She had pleaded for him to take her along, not to leave her behind. He had only tightened his hold until her tears ran through his beard.

"Lady, he has fled to the north. His wife and children were captured."

Another stool creaked, and Prasudoc spoke, his voice muffled. "What about his men? And . . . ours?"

"Killed or captured. Before he rode north to the Brigantes, Caradoc sent me here. Your men were slain in the last defense of his family. He honors them. He says keep their memory alive and wait for the fighting season to come again."

Over Tiann's and Mara's heads, a shutter banged open. Tiann jumped, and Mara clamped a hand over her mouth so fiercely that Tiann tasted blood.

A bell rang, and footsteps approached the cookhouse window. "Bread, meat, and mead, Lady." Something scraped along the plank overhead, then the cookhouse shutter closed again.

Mara's hand lifted from Tiann's mouth. The small girl reached to hold Tiann's shaking shoulders. Didn't Mara understand? Da was one of their men. One of the men Boudica and Prasudoc had sent. One of the men with Caradoc.

Tiann shoved Mara off and stumbled out from their hiding place. When she began to run, Mara's hand gripped her own, and once again Tiann allowed herself to be led, eyes blurred.

Tiann ran and ran, clinging to Mara's hand, ignoring the stitch developing in her side. Her sobs heaved for breath, and the wind whipped the tears in her eyes. Mara tugged, trying to stop her, but Tiann jerked her hand free to keep going. Instead, she crashed into muscle and bone. Strong hands grasped her upper arms and steadied her.

Tiann looked up into the stern face of Shal, druid and royal advisor. Gulping, she stepped back, lifting her hands to scrub at her cheeks, wiping her dripping nose on a sleeve. She knew she ought to apologize for her discourtesy, but could only look at him, mute, gasping from her run, throat tight with tears.

"Pardon, sir," Mara squeaked out. "We . . . we were playing . . . and Tiann didn't see you. Pardon."

Shal looked down at them, a concerned smile softening his expression. "Now, now, what kind of game is this? Has someone hurt you? Are the big boys chasing you?"

"No, sir," Mara answered, when Tiann stood silent, looking up into Shal's face. "Tiann can outrun any of them anyway. We just . . . We just—"

"What is it, child?" Shal cut off the breathless excuses, his gaze intent on Tiann. "Something has wounded your soul. What is it?"

"My father . . ." Tiann strangled over the words. "My father . . ."

Shal knelt, his arms sliding around her sweaty, shaking body. "My da is dead! My da is *dead*!" She shrieked the words.

Shal held her tight, rocking her as she cried. A keening sound rose from him as they swayed. He held out an arm to include Mara, and Tiann saw tears flowing from her eyes as she crept close and put her arms around Tiann.

When the tears spent themselves, Shal leaned back and patted her hot, sticky cheeks with his sleeve. He rose to his feet and took the girls' hands. "Let's go splash some cool water on those faces."

Tiann allowed herself to be guided by his large hand around hers, expecting to be led back to the courtyard. A hint of unease crept into her, remembering how she had spied on the royal chambers. Surely she would be reprimanded, maybe even punished, for this infraction. But Shal did not turn back toward the bustle of the village, instead marching past the horse paddock.

Soon they came to one of the boundary stones of the settlement. Tiann had been warned when she first came to stay in the royal village that children were not to venture past them. She glanced up at Shal, wondering if she ought to mention the rule. Deciding against it, she gripped his hand more firmly and hurried her steps to match his longer ones. She had already broken the rules today— what did it matter? Really, with Da gone, what did anything matter?

The trio skirted the barley fields and headed toward the forest. Not pausing, they plunged into the green darkness. Tiann had never seen such a wild place. Even when her father had taken her from their farm to the royal village, they had kept to well-traveled tracks, brush cut back and path worn level. Shal seemed to travel a path only his eyes could see, pulling them around obstacles of boulders and fallen tree limbs. The world was cool and damp, as though the sun that shone hot on the rows of crops had been traded for a different one here. This filtered light grew moss and mushrooms and ferns. The damp deadfall under her feet smelled mysteriously of both decay and life.

They came to an outcropping of boulders twice Tiann's height. She craned her neck to look up and saw the top of an oak towering beyond.

Shal let go their hands, stepping toward the largest of the rocks, then disappeared. Tiann saw her amazement reflected in Mara's face. A moment later, Shal stepped back into view, gesturing them forward. Tiann peered around him and perceived an opening between two boulders, camouflaged by ferns and a trick of the light. With a glance back to make sure Mara was coming too, she inched between the rocks. They felt smooth in the narrow passage, bare of moss, as though countless bodies had brushed against them.

She stood in a small clearing of sunlight, carpeted with delicate moss. The spot was nearly a perfect circle, thirty paces across, with a spring near the northward edge. To the east loomed the ancient oak. To the west, many paces of thick bramble blocked Tiann's view to the other side.

Shal touched the fingers of his right hand to his forehead, then his chest, and bowed. He gathered up the girls' hands again and led them to the spring. "Sit down, my daughters," he instructed. From a niche in a rock he drew a clay cup, which he wiped with a cloth drawn from an inner pocket of his robe. He dipped it in the spring, then turned toward the oak, lifted it, and poured the water out. Refilling it, he handed it to Tiann. "Drink, child."

Tiann raised the cup to her lips but lowered it before taking a sip. "Sir?" She felt foolish questioning him, but fear pushed the words from her mouth. "Isn't this a holy spring? I mean, perhaps I should not drink—I'm just a girl, and I have been punished many times for breaking rules." Maybe Shal didn't know about her naughtiness, the times she had disobeyed her father, the way she had pouted and cried when he'd left. In this place with its green hush, she did not want to deceive.

Shal put his hand over hers and lifted the cup back to her lips. "It's all right. What purpose could be more holy than to soothe a throat aching from the tears of grief?"

The water was so cold it sent a shiver through Tiann as she sipped, then gulped the mineral elixir.

"What purpose could be more holy," Shal continued, "than to wash the eyes that will always hold the shadow of loss?" He dipped his cloth into the water and brought it to her face, wiping her forehead, her eyelids, her cheeks. "What could be more holy than a heart that beats with a friend's sorrow?" He offered the cup to Mara, then ran the cloth over her face as well.

A great tiredness overtook Tiann. Shal cupped his left hand behind her head and placed his right palm on her forehead. He laid her back on the springy moss. "Rest now, daughter."

Mara lay beside her and snuggled close. As Tiann's eyelids drifted shut, she saw Shal sit nearby, with his back leaning against a large stone, keeping watch.

When she woke, the oak was on fire. She sat up, startled. The sun had lowered and now blazed across the bramble, lighting the ancient tree scarlet and gold. Glancing around, she saw Mara still asleep, one hand under her cheek. She met Shal's eyes, and he smiled, then rose to bring her another cup of water from the spring. He gently shook Mara's shoulder. She sat, hair tousled, the imprint of her hand on her face.

"Sir," Tiann said, "it is so late. Mara and I will be missed. Her parents . . ." Her voice wobbled. "Her parents will be searching."

Shal looked at her, and her eyes filled once again. He reached out and wiped away a tear with his thumb. "All right, children." He held out his hands. "Let's go home." He squeezed her hand as though he could feel the pang in her heart. She looked up at him. "Home," he repeated firmly.

Tiann lingered just inside the hall. She wanted to bolt, to hide from the noisy throng of family groups reconvening after the day's activities, but her gnawing stomach held her in place. She watched the great bowls of stew coming past her on their trip from the cookhouse to the long trestle tables. She had snatched a leftover hunk of stale bread that morning before running to the woods, but birds had discovered the berry bramble.

She scanned the scene, trying to gauge how she could scavenge a trencher of that fragrant stew, full of venison chunks from the day's successful hunt, thick with barley, and steaming the scent of herbs. She knew she could approach one of the fathers and ask for a place with his children. She also knew the rest of the evening would be passed enduring pitying glances, head pats, maybe tears from the mother, and awkward silence from the other children. Much better to snatch some bread and run.

She jumped when a hand slipped into hers and tugged. "Come on," Mara said. "I've been looking for you."

Reluctantly, Tiann followed. She had been avoiding Mara since the night, a moon ago now, Shal had led them to Boudica's chamber. He had spoken in low tones to the queen.

She had looked at the girls without speaking for a long moment. "I will not punish you this time. But no more spying and no more disappearing." She laid a hand on Tiann's head. "My heart grieves for you." Her voice was gruff. She'd turned away, and Shal had led them out.

Since then Tiann had kept to herself, exploring, afraid the torrent of tears would overtake her in the presence of others. She passed the boundary stones with hesitation at first, but when no one stopped her, she became bolder. She spent her days in the otherworldly forest, pretending that as long as she was there, Da still lived and would return any time now. Sometimes she thought she felt him behind her for a long breath, but when she whirled around, she was still alone. At dusk she slipped back to the village, tried to get dinner without speaking to anyone, and curled up in one of the open-sided animal enclosures to sleep. She couldn't bear sleeping on her pallet in the communal area where eyes watched and tongues whispered.

Now, Mara pulled her to the far end of the hall, toward her own bench with the rest of the chief's family. Tiann hesitated, aghast. Boudica and Prasudoc had not invited her to approach, let alone sit with them.

The queen reached for the salt bowl and saw them standing hand in hand. Her eyebrows lifted, and her hand hovered. She nodded, then turned to whisper to her husband.

He looked up from his food and cleared his throat. "Please join my family for the meal, ummm . . ."

"Tiann," Mara supplied, scooting to her place and dragging Tiann with her.

Boudica gestured for another trencher to be brought and ladled a generous helping herself.

Tiann ate her fill, warmed inside and out. When she finished, she moved to bring her trencher to the common washing barrel.

Mara stopped her. "Put it with ours. You will eat with us from now on." She looked to her mother for confirmation.

Boudica's eyebrows lifted again, but her mouth quirked with affectionate amusement.

"Yes, you will eat with us. And I suppose you might as well share Mara's sleeping chamber too."

That night Tiann lay curled on a pallet, feeling the warmth of Mara's back against her own. The movement and conversation in the adjacent hall tapered off, leaving only Mara's light, even breathing and the occasional shuffle and huff of a hound rearranging himself. For the first time in weeks, Tiann drifted to sleep with a full belly and dry eyes.

Tiann woke to a foot nudging her hand and something tickling her face. She opened bleary eyes to see Aife, Mara's older sister, bending over her.

"Huh," the bigger girl said, tossing her russet-colored braid away from Tiann's cheek and straightening up. "You're still here. Well, you might as well come help me with my chores."

Next to her, Mara struggled to a sitting position. "Don't be a pig, Aife." She rubbed at her eyes, then stretched upward with a mighty yawn. "Tiann's not going to do your stupid weaving for you. She's going to spend the day with me, aren't you?"

Tiann glanced up at Aife, who looked annoyed, then at Mara. She nodded. Aife might hold a grudge, but Tiann would worry about that later. She longed to be with Mara. Her champion. The one who cried with her. Her friend. She couldn't think why she had avoided her company all those days.

Mara flopped back with another luxuriant stretch. "Well, that's settled. Tiann is with me." With an indignant swing of her braid, Aife stomped out. Mara giggled, then sprang to her feet, pulling Tiann up with her. "Come on. Let's find some food."

TIANN AND MARA spent the next five days running free. In the mornings, Mara wheedled some bread and cheese from the cookhouse, then they were off. Their favorite activity was visiting the horses, begging for chances to ride. Tiann would never have dared to even pat the royal animals, but the trainers loved Mara.

Tiann had only ever ridden the small workhorses her da had kept, and the bigger animals scared her. But today she would ride one.

Mara laughed at her and coaxed her up. "You'll see—they are good beasts, aren't you?" She leaned into the flank and rubbed the mare's nose.

Tiann perched uneasily in the saddle.

Mara patted her foot. "Really, they are well trained. You'll find their gait much smoother than a pony or a workhorse."

She was right, and Tiann soon enjoyed the ride. When they were done, she slid down and rubbed the mare's nose as Mara had done.

"What's her name?" Tiann asked the trainer who came to lead the horse away.

"That's Gwyndolyn." He smoothed her mane. "Named after the widow of an ancient king. She ruled after him until her son was old enough."

"I like her."

Gwyndolyn lowered her head and blew down the front of Tiann's tunic.

"She likes you too." He laughed and pulled the reins. "High honor, that. Now she'll always be asking for you."

Mara came running up, breathless. "Did you see me ride the stallion? He wanted to pull, but I held him at a walk. Tiann, are you listening? I said . . . Oh!"

"What?" Tiann turned from watching Gwyndolyn.

"You're smiling." Mara grabbed her hand. "Come on—let's go see if the hunters are back yet."

THEY SPENT the afternoons lazing in secret spots, inside the hollow of a spreading bush or where a curve of the palisade hid them from view. They smuggled their blankets out under their tunics and made nests for themselves. Sticks and braided-grass twine became little people populating an imaginary village. The girls wove small baskets and blankets, also out of grass, to furnish their play homes. Then they made the figures into warriors, with stick horses and spears.

Those harvest days were hot and still. One afternoon, tired of playing, they lay back on their blankets. Tiann stretched, drowsy with heat and the activity of the day.

"Tiann? Do you ever think about that day . . . what they said when we were listening at the window?"

"Sometimes." She didn't want to think about it. For the first weeks, she couldn't stop crying, so she'd hid from everyone. But these past few days with Mara had been different. Her thoughts dwelled on other things—the horses, especially Gwyndolyn—and their secret make-believe world.

Mara propped herself up on an elbow. "I mean, of course, the worst part, the most important part, was about your father. But there was more. About Caradoc. And the Romans."

"I don't understand any of it. All I know is Da went away to fight with this Caradoc and got killed."

"I don't know either. Caradoc isn't Iceni. And I don't know why my father didn't go, or his regular warriors. My mother shushed me when I asked her and told me not to talk about it. I thought maybe your da had told you something."

"No. Only that the chief and queen were sending him and it was important." Tiann wasn't sleepy anymore. "Come on—we should get back."

THE NEXT AFTERNOON, thunder boomed in the distance and the wind lashed the trees and hay. All available hands joined the harvesters in the frantic work. When the first fat drops fell, a halt was called, and everyone scurried toward the shelter of their dwellings. Mara and Tiann found the main hall full of people and hounds shaking off and trying to find a place to settle. In the corner by the looms, Aife looked around, probably for someone to boss.

"Quick," Mara whispered. "Before she tries to make us weave!"

They ducked and slipped through the crush of wet people toward the far curve of the hall. Crouching behind the long table where the royal family sat for meals, Mara grinned and slid her fingers into a notch in the floor. Lifting a narrow hatch, she gestured Tiann down a ladder, then followed, pulling the hatch closed. The bustle from above muffled. The darkness was almost complete, but Tiann could feel air moving against her cheek. Mara scrabbled at the wall, and then came the click and scrape of flint as she tried to strike a spark.

"Do you have a torch?" Tiann asked. "Here, hold it. Let me light it." She had been in charge of the fire when she lived with Da, but she had never seen Mara do so much as poke a log. The torch flared to life, and a tunnel appeared, sloping downward away from the hall above. Support timbers two paces apart rose to the low ceiling. Tiann put a palm to the wall, and when she drew it back, it shone a dusty white in the torchlight.

"Chalk," Mara whispered. "It's an old mine. Follow me, and don't fall down the shaft." She took the torch and shuffled down the passage.

Tiann stayed close, fingers clutching Mara's tunic. When Mara stopped, Tiann bumped into her. "Don't push me into it either!"

"Sorry." Tiann peered over her friend's shoulder. A square black hole in the tunnel's floor plummeted to blackness beyond the reach of the torch. Mara edged around the shaft, feet sideways. Tiann took a deep breath, willed her knees not to shake, and imitated her. Past the dark cavity, the tunnel narrowed, and soon the girls had to duck.

"Here we are." Mara straightened as the passage widened into a circular cavity.

Whole tree trunks supported the ceiling here. A breeze blew through the chamber, making the torch flicker. Across walls and wood, carved shapes danced and swirled. Mara lit the wicks of two oil lamps hewn into the wall, then smothered the torch in a pile of sand. She settled down on the floor, leaning against the wall, and smiled at Tiann.

"What is this place?" Tiann paced around, tracing the spirals and waves with her fingertips.

"No one knows. It's not part of the mine. I followed Shal down here once. He was furious. Mother made me stay in my chamber for two days when he told her. But later she told me that the ancestors dug the shaft to mine flint for their tools and weapons. This chamber, though, is a mystery. Maybe the ancestors just needed a place to get away from older sisters." She stuck out her tongue in the direction of the tunnel.

Tiann laughed and sat down next to her. "Aife is not so terrible. I wouldn't want to weave all day either."

Mara looked chastened. "Yes—she used to be more fun. She's a wonderful rider, actually. She misses the horses. She won't have to keep weaving forever—it's just part of her training. She's happier outside."

"Does she ever come down here with you?" Tiann kept her voice neutral, stifling a pang of jealousy.

"No. I don't know why I never showed her. I guess because she is the heir. She's not supposed to get into mischief. Mother would have to punish her more. I'm sure they will tell her about this place eventually though. When the time is right." She leaned her shoulder into Tiann's. "Besides, I come here to be quiet. To dream. I can do that with you. Aife talks too much."

Tears pricked at Tiann's eyes, and the dancing spirals on the walls blurred and swam. She blinked hard, then reached over and squeezed Mara's hand. "I'm glad you showed me."

They sat quiet together, and Tiann thought back on the events that had brought her to that moment: the sight of her father riding off, the moment she learned of his death, the unmoored weeks of grief, Mara marching her up to the chief's dining table. The easy rhythm of their days since then. Just like the running spirals circling the ancient timber supports, one led mysteriously to the next.

Mara stirred, stretching her legs and wiggling her toes. "We should go back up. I'm getting hungry." She relit the torch and blew out the flames in the small oil wells.

Tiann stood and let her eyes linger on the space. She didn't want to leave and rejoin the bustle in the hall. But her stomach grumbled, and Mara's torch was receding into the tunnel. She looked around one more time. *I'll come back.*

CHAPTER
TWO

Harvest days grew shorter, and the outbuildings filled with sacks of barley and pulses. The hunters ventured out every day, keeping the cooks busy salting and drying meat. When traders visited, the stewards inspected the oils, spices, or cloth on offer. Some they bought, trading livestock, jewelry from the metalworkers, or coins.

Tiann noticed Gwyndolyn's coat becoming thicker and rougher.

"She's getting ready for the cold," Goram said. The wizened horse trainer always had time for Tiann's questions and knew every answer. Even the most fitful young stallion stood still for Goram while he untangled a burr from a mane or picked a rock from a hoof.

One dull gray morning, flakes of snow drifted on the breeze. Tiann shivered on her way to the hall from the paddock where she had been helping to thatch a shelter for the horses. Blinking against the brightness of the central fire, she noted the chief's family already sat at their dining table for the morning meal. She hurried around the perimeter of the space, sliding onto the bench she shared with Mara just as a bowl of broth was passed to them.

A hunk of barley bread sopped in the hot liquid warmed her from the inside. She ate hungrily, watching the antics of the newest litter of puppies born to Prasudoc's favorite hound.

Over the busy din in the hall, Tiann heard a side door crash open.

"Chief! Lady!" a voice cried out, pitched to carry.

Heads swiveled and conversations stopped midsentence. Tiann craned her neck to see a warrior she didn't recognize pushing people aside to approach Prasudoc and Boudica.

"That's Ian," Mara whispered in her ear. "He's been gone since last harvest."

The newcomer reached the table and stood, panting. Sweat streaked his face despite the wintry morning, and Tiann smelled a reek of horse and unwashed man.

"They are on their way. A patrol of twenty men. There is a junior officer. Moving fast from the west—probably within the hour."

For a breath, silence hung in the hall. Then Boudica sprang to action. Rising, she clapped her hands for attention. "The Romans are heading here for a visit. Let's give them what they expect. Armorers and warriors, with the chief. Stewards and cooks, with me. Trainers and grooms, with Aife. Everyone else, see to your own."

The hall burst back into life as all dispersed, shoving the last of breakfast into their mouths and gulping drinks to wash it down.

"Where is Shal?" Boudica scanned the crowd. Turning to Mara and Tiann, she commanded, "Tiann, you're the fastest. Go find him and warn him. Mara, come help me. Hurry!"

Tiann ran from the hall.

Where could he be? Tiann stopped to consider. *Didn't I see him this morning? At first light? Where was that?* It came to her with a jolt. On her way to the paddock, she had caught sight of his tall figure in a gray cloak, striding toward the edge of the cut barley field. The oak circle. West of the compound. The Romans might even pass him on the path.

Tiann didn't understand the queen's command, but she obeyed its urgency.. The cold stabbed at her lungs as she bolted toward the fields, but she tried to ignore it and control her breathing. She did not pause as she passed the boundary stone. When her foot caught an unseen rise, she stumbled forward, arms swinging, and used the momentum to spur her feet faster. Snowflakes landed on her eyelashes, and she blinked them away Her breath blew out in great white puffs. Just as she left the fields and the forest loomed ahead, Shal stepped into the open. He raised his hand, smiling a greeting, but then frowned as she lurched into his arms.

"Child, what is it?"

"They are coming. The Romans. From the west. The queen sent me to tell you."

"Thank you." Shal gathered his robe and tucked the loose ends into his belt. "I must run. Can you keep up?"

"Yes, sir." Tiann fell in with him, surprised that his pace pushed her limits. They ran without speaking back to the hall. As they entered, Boudica rushed to him.

"Shal. You're here. I put a bundle for you near the entrance to the tunnel."

Shal strode to the front of the hall and disappeared behind the table.

Boudica turned to Tiann. "Thank you. Thank you for finding him. Mara is in your chamber. Go change your clothing."

Mara sat on a low stool, struggling with her hair. Tiann looked at her in astonishment. Instead of her usual belted tunic and leggings, or braccae, Mara wore a long pale-green Roman-style gown with a darker green shawl. A slender silver clasp held it at her shoulder, rather than the thick twisted gold circle pin she favored on her cloak. Her hair was twisted into loose braids, which she attempted to secure at her nape with a matching decorative comb.

Seeing Tiann, she stopped her efforts. "You're back. Did you find him?"

"Yes, I found him. I think he went down the tunnel to hide. What in the world are you doing?"

Mara's hands returned to her hair. "Can you help me with this?"

Tiann examined the comb, then gathered the braids into a knot and awkwardly stuck it in.

Mara gave her head an experimental shake. "It will do. Now for you." She shook out a similar outfit in blue. "Put it on."

Tiann complied, shedding her familiar clothes and wiggling into the dress. She tried taking a few steps. "How do you move in this? Or ride?"

"I don't think you're meant to. Roman women don't run or fight or ride. They stay home, and when they have to go somewhere, they are carried in a box."

"Well, why are we dressing like them?"

Before Mara could answer, Tiann heard the main doors open, and the hall fell to a hush. She pulled back the hanging covering the opening to the bedchamber and peered into the wide space. The room was as still as a stone carving. At the far end, against the backdrop of the gray sky and swirling snowflakes, stood soldiers, with helmets and breastplates gleaming.

Boudica entered the hall from the royal chambers. She wore a dress like Mara's, but the greens were reversed. Her mane of fiery curls was braided and coiled and held with a silver filigree headband. She wore no torc at her throat.

Her appearance seemed to break the spell that held everyone still. The room buzzed with whispered conversations as the soldiers strode inside, boots clattering.

Tiann hissed over her shoulder, "Come, we should go out. Your mother is there."

"I can't."

Tiann turned back to her friend. Mara sat on her pallet with her knees drawn up under her chin. She lifted a face full of panic to Tiann, eyes welling.

Baffled, Tiann squatted beside her. "What's wrong? Are you hurt?"

"I can't go out with all those people."

Tiann sat back on her heels. Mara was afraid? Mara, who rode stallions and explored tunnels? "But you're always in the hall with everyone."

"But I know all our people! And I don't have to talk—no one makes me. But I don't know these soldiers. What if one of them asks me a question?"

The door hanging moved, and Aife slipped into the chamber. "We need to join Mother . . ." Her eyes lit on Mara, and she paused, kneeling down beside Tiann.

"Oh my darling, don't cry." She peeled Mara's hands from their grip on her knees and pulled her sister close. "It's all right. It will be all right," she crooned, rocking the younger girl. "Tiann and I will stand in front of you, and if anyone needs to talk, we will do it." She fixed a steely gaze on Tiann. "Won't we?"

Tiann shook herself free from her astonishment. "Yes . . . yes! Of course we will. You won't have to speak to anyone."

Mara lifted her head and swiped her hand across her face. She searched each of their faces, then nodded.

"Come then, sister." Aife rose and held out a hand to Mara.

Tiann stood, and together they pulled Mara up.

Aife stole a look into the hall. "We will just slip out and make our way toward Mother." She held them back. "Father is walking in . . . Let's go now."

Tiann gave Mara's hand a reassuring squeeze as the girls emerged from the chamber.

The group of soldiers—Tiann counted ten—marched into the hall, led by a short, stocky man wearing a helmet with a prominent black crest. He stopped before the royal family, his eyes sweeping from Boudica to Tiann and Aife, with Mara behind them, and finally to Prasudoc.

"I come from governor to make greeting." His words sounded strange, spoken with halting pronunciation. He removed his helmet and inclined his head to the chief.

Tiann felt a flush of embarrassment for him when he ignored the queen. She peeked at Mara to see what she thought of his poor manners, but Mara's eyes were round and staring at the man's helmet. Following her gaze, Tiann noticed that the crest flowed into a long tail at the back. *Maybe she's wondering why the man wants to look like the back end of a horse.* Tiann felt a giggle bubble up in her throat. Her breath chuffed out of her involuntarily.

Aife gave her a swift, sharp glance. Then looking straight ahead, she pinched Tiann's upper arm until tears sprang and all traces of laughter fled. Both grateful and resentful, Tiann rubbed at the spot under her blue shawl. An ugly mark would emerge there later.

Prasudoc tilted his head in response but did not extend his arm in greeting. He spoke in smooth, fluent Latin. Tiann recognized the word for welcome. Her puzzlement increased. The chief spoke words of welcome, but he did not treat the soldiers like they were welcome. He withheld his arm, and Boudica had not yet said a word. The warriors had not brought cups of mead to the Romans, as they would to others of their rank. Yet the visitors had been allowed entry to the hall without surrendering their weapons, like allies. Were these the soldiers who'd fought against Caradoc? No, no. If they were, wouldn't Prasudoc and his men cut them down? But they were Romans, just like the ones who'd killed Da. And Shal was hiding. The soldier with the helmet no longer seemed funny, and Tiann's stomach felt sick.

The group in the center of the hall shifted. Two soldiers advanced, carrying a chest, which they opened before Prasudoc. Tiann glimpsed rich fabrics, a bronze mirror, and several small glass bottles sealed with wax.

Prasudoc thanked the commander, turned to Boudica, and said in Iceni, "Gifts from the gracious governor."

Boudica clasped her hands together as though overwhelmed and inclined her head toward the Roman. After another brief exchange in Latin, Prasudoc, two of his warriors, the Roman leader, and two other soldiers retreated toward the royal apartment. The other soldiers took seats at one of the long tables used for meals. Boudica went to the door and gestured for a waiting group of women to enter.

They carried jugs of wine and platters of bread. Boudica took a jug and nodded to Aife, Mara, and Tiann to do the same. As the platters of bread were laid in front of the soldiers, Boudica began filling their cups. Burning with shame for her queen, Tiann followed her example. Aife's face was flushed and her expression cold, but she moved from cup to cup gracefully, never making eye contact, a younger version of her mother. Mara stayed close to her older sister, pouring with fierce concentration that kept her shaking hands from spilling the red liquid.

The soldiers ate and drank, talking amongst themselves without acknowledging those who served them, except for a cup waved aloft to demand more wine. Boudica most often responded to this unspoken demand, hovering near the table with her wine jug, moving the platters to ensure each man had access to the bread. One soldier jabbed his companion with an elbow, making a jest with a crude gesture, then looked at the queen and laughed.

Boudica's fingers whitened on the jug, but her face remained impassive.

After an hour, Prasudoc and the Roman leader reentered the hall with their men. The chief led the way to the high table, and Boudica hurried to join them there. Instead of taking her place beside her husband, as Tiann expected, she filled the cups with wine and stepped back. Aife carried a bread platter and laid it on the table. The Roman leader sat in the queen's chair, setting his crested helmet on the seat next to him.

New platters appeared, piled with meat and fruit along with more bread. Boudica led Tiann and her daughters to stand along the wall behind the table where the Roman soldiers now lounged, sated, still talking but more subdued in the presence of their commander. Tiann's stomach grumbled, and she wondered why they did not also sit and eat at the table with Prasudoc. She did not dare to break Boudica's tense silence or even whisper a question to Aife and Mara. A bead of sweat trickled down her back, making the uncomfortable dress stick to her skin.

When the men at the high table had finished eating and drinking, they stood. The leader called a command, and the soldiers jumped to their feet and assembled in neat rows. Boudica nodded toward one of her warriors, who stepped forward to pull open the heavy doors. Out marched the contingent, their boots loud, their gear jangling. When the doors shut behind them, the room held its breath for two long moments. Then Boudica turned, strode to her seat, wiped it with a cloth in exaggerated movements, and sat down. A ripple of relief and mirth swept through the Iceni, and people shifted into action. Someone brought the queen a cup, and she poured herself wine. Prasudoc pushed the platter of food toward her.

Aife, Mara, and Tiann sat at the table vacated by the Romans. For a few minutes, they munched on the leftover bread, but then

Tiann could stand it no longer. "Aife, why were they here? And why did your mother act so strangely?"

Aife finished chewing and swallowed, considering Tiann. "First of all, they are not gone, so keep your voice down. They are setting up their camp next to the paddock and will be here overnight. Second, Mother has reasons. She always does." She put another piece of bread into her mouth.

"Don't be mysterious. She hasn't been here long. She doesn't understand," Mara said. "The Romans think of us as allies. Father made an agreement with them to protect us. They think we are becoming Roman. So when they come, we show them what they expect to see. We dress like them. We act like them. Their women are not respected. Someday we will drive them out, and they will see that women can fight. Then we will burn these awful dresses."

"But for the queen to serve those rude men!" Tiann protested.

"Don't be a fool." Aife brushed breadcrumbs from her fingers. "She was listening. She and Father speak Latin as well as the Romans. He listens to the leaders, but she learns even more by listening to the underlings, especially since they think we can't understand them. I'm learning Latin too."

"Does Shal need to stay in the tunnel until they leave?"

Mara's face grew serious. "Yes. The Romans hate the druids. In the West, where the tribes are still fighting, the druids help them. They unite the tribes to fight together. And some of them" —she lowered her voice to a whisper—"are not like Shal. They have arguments about what to do when they capture a Roman. Some of them practice dark sacrifices."

"Hush!" Aife scowled at her sister. "You speak too much about things you should not."

Mara subsided, and Tiann pondered what she had learned. Her impressions were right. These Romans were treated as friends but were not. She felt a little better, knowing that the people who had killed her father were not well loved by

Prasudoc and Boudica. Still, here they were, taking advantage of Iceni hospitality, forcing Shal into hiding, expecting the queen to pour their wine and accept their rudeness. The leftover bread tasted like dust in her mouth. She choked down her last bite and stood.

The afternoon passed quietly, with most of the household staying indoors. The warriors played games of chance, looking bored and restless. When people left to use the privy or see to outside chores, they went in groups of two or three.

Tiann caught glimpses of the deserted courtyard, still collecting drifting flakes of snow, when the door opened. Though she chafed under the confinement and inactivity of the day, she derived a grim pleasure knowing the soldiers would have a cold night in their tents. When the time came for the evening meal, the Roman leader joined them again, but not the other men. Platters of bread and wine were sent out to their encampment. Iceni warriors accompanied the women who carried the food from the hall.

Tiann remembered the disrespect the soldiers had shown to the queen. She was glad the warriors were there to discourage such behavior, although she knew the women could, and would, fight to defend themselves if it came to that. But in front of these Romans, they hid their strength.

After serving the meal to the men, the women sat at separate tables to eat.

"Don't Roman men and women eat together?" Tiann asked Mara.

Boudica overheard her question. "Yes, sometimes." She leaned closer to her daughters and Tiann. "Their nobles have large parties where they eat and drink too much. The noblewomen can come if they are with a husband or male relation. There are also women who mingle among the men just for their pleasure.

"We, however, are not considered noble by that one." The

queen slid her eyes to the Roman commander, who was laughing and thumping Prasudoc on the shoulder.

Tiann wrinkled her nose as his elbow upended his wine cup.

"And we don't want them to think of us as the other type of women. So we stay apart," finished the queen.

Tiann was relieved when the commander rose at last, thumped Prasudoc once more, and made his unsteady way to the doors. Cold air blasted in, and he pulled his cloak tighter around himself, ducking his head against the wind. When the doors shut, the chief came to Boudica and settled on the bench across from her.

He smoothed Aife's hair and smiled at Tiann, then reached over and pulled Mara into his lap. "You all played your parts admirably today. But I hated watching you do it."

"They will be gone tomorrow. It's almost over," Boudica said.

"For now." Prasudoc gave Mara a kiss and set her down. "We should sleep. My head is pounding with trying to keep up with that Roman's drinking. It was a good idea to have my pitcher well-watered."

Tiann hurried to the bedchamber, looking forward to shedding the Roman dress. Mara came in a few minutes later, carrying something bundled in her shawl. Her face shone with excitement.

"What is that?" Tiann tried to wiggle out of the dress without tearing the seams.

"It's a secret." Mara put the bundle on her sleeping mat. With a flourish, she pulled away the shawl. There sat the crested Roman helmet. "Remember how that man had too much wine? He must have forgotten his helmet. It was still on the seat next to Mother's. Look at the tail! It's exactly the same as the stallion." Mara put the helmet on and pretended to gallop and rear.

Tiann laughed. "Let me try." She took the helmet and tried it on. It was too big and wobbled on her head. Also, the leather lining smelled like it had been soaking up sweat for two lifetimes.

"Well, the tail looks better on the stallion's backside than it does on that man's head." She took it off and handed it back to Mara. "You should put it back."

Mara looked stubborn. "No, I want to take it to the stable tomorrow and show Goram. Maybe he can collect the tail hair from the horses when he grooms them, and I can make a hat for myself."

"Why do you want to look like a Roman?"

"I don't. I want to look like a horse!" Mara lay down with the helmet beside her.

THE DISTINCTIVE SOUND of Roman boots thumped on the floor. Tiann scrambled from her pallet and peered out past the door hanging. The Roman leader stood with Prasudoc and Boudica near the royal family table. Red-faced and shouting, the leader gestured toward the seats, while Iceni warriors edged nearer to their chief. The rest of the Roman soldiers stood in a block in the center of the room. No one had bothered to close the doors, and gray dawn leaked an icy draft into the space.

Aife caught Tiann's eye from the edge of the room. She made her way to her and slipped into the chamber.

"What's happening out there?" Mara's voice trembled.

"I'm not certain. He's talking so fast, and he is so angry. But I think he said something about a thief. Let me listen." Aife cocked her head by the hanging, trying to hear. "Father is saying his people do not steal."

Tiann sat down next to Mara. "Do you think . . ."

Mara turned wide eyes to her. "No, it can't be that . . . He left it there! And I was going to put it back after I showed it to Goram!"

Aife whispered from the doorway. "Now he's saying that Romans execute thieves if they aren't citizens. I can't believe

Mother is holding her tongue. As if an Iceni would steal something from these Romans!" She listened again. "Now he's threatening to have his men search everywhere until they find whatever is missing."

Mara's eyes filled with tears as she clutched at Tiann's arm. "What have I done? What if they search and find Shal? They will probably take him away and distrust the Iceni. I've dishonored my tribe by stealing and making Father a liar. And they are going to kill me."

Aife turned to the girls on the bed. "What are you talking about?" Her eyes fell on the tail of the helmet trailing out from under Mara's bed covering. With a swift step, she covered the distance to the girls and whipped back the blanket. "Mara! What . . . Why . . . How could you!"

"I didn't mean to steal," Mara said. "What am I going to do?"

Aife sank onto the floor and stared at her little sister.

Tiann looked from the terror on Mara's face to the anguish on Aife's. Surely the Romans wouldn't put a young girl to death. But she wasn't so sure. Boudica and Prasudoc would protect Mara. But what would happen then? A dizziness overtook her, and she closed her eyes. Against the inside of her lids, a scene played out.

Warriors charge forward. Boudica tears the sides of her green dress to the thighs and throws the silver headband to the floor. Her hair flames in the sunlight as she screams and runs, sword in hand. The Romans form into their neat rows. Their leader spins around, holding Mara by the hair, and casually slices his dagger across her throat before joining his men. A soldier falls before Boudica's sword, but then the one next to him sinks his blade into her side. Blood washes over the scene. The redness spreads and spreads, and Tiann is falling . . .

"Tiann!"

Someone was shaking her. She dragged her eyelids open and saw the ceiling, then Aife's face leaning over her. "Are you all right?"

"Yes . . ." She pressed her hands to the floor under her and sat up with care. A dull throbbing pulsed behind her eyes.

"What happened?" Mara asked. "You just crumpled."

"Mara!" Tiann lurched toward her and pulled her close. No. Not Mara. These Roman monsters would not kill her like they did Da. *I won't let it happen.* Tiann backed away, and before the other girls could speak, she snatched the helmet, stood, and walked past the hanging into the hall.

Refusing to think, Tiann pushed her way through the murmuring Iceni toward the raised voice of the Roman leader. His back was to her. She met Boudica's eye as she willed her quaking legs to carry her forward. The queen stared at the helmet, then at her face, shaking her head. Tiann kept moving in defiance of Boudica's unspoken command, hurrying the final span in a desperate rush before her courage failed.

"My chief." Her voice came out as a hoarse whisper, interrupting the Roman's tirade.

The Roman leader and Prasudoc turned to her, and the murmuring in the hall stopped abruptly. Tiann could not think of another word to say, so she held out the helmet and waited.

THREE

The Roman glared at her and grabbed the helmet. His face turned a deeper shade, and he barked an order to his men in the middle of the hall. Boots thumped toward her, and before she could even turn her head, rough hands seized her arms. Boudica made a quick protesting movement, but Prasudoc drew the commander's attention, saying something in a soft tone. The leader made a slashing movement with his hand and growled another order. The two soldiers holding Tiann's arms spun her around and marched toward the doors. Her bare feet tripped as she tried to keep up, and they dragged her for a few steps until she regained her balance. She craned her neck to look back and saw Prasudoc hold Boudica, preventing her from bolting after them, whispering in her ear.

Tiann turned forward again, seeing a blur of shocked faces. When she passed the doorway to her bedchamber, she saw Mara and Aife watching. Mara wept, and Aife looked grim, her arm around her sister.

Tiann's skin rose in goosebumps in the cold courtyard. She still wore only the long, loose tunic she had slept in. A tide of people came out of the hall behind her, talking again, concern and confusion in their tones. A few of the women sobbed. She stubbed her toe on a rock, and the painful shock of the impact on the numbing appendage jolted through her. For a moment it distracted her from the headache, which still throbbed.

The soldiers pushed her to her knees in front of the large hollowed stone where barley was ground into flour. One held her arms behind her back while the other pushed her head down on the stone. The rough surface bit into her cheek when she wrenched her face sideways to see. Now the talking rose to outraged cries. She could see Prasudoc speaking to the commander with broad, urgent gestures. The leader seemed to listen, the rage fading from his face. He waved his hand to the soldiers holding her and issued an order. The hand on her head lifted, and she cautiously straightened her back. Blood trickled from the cut on her cheek.

The soldier took hold of her right arm and wrenched it forward until it lay across the stone. The other man continued to hold her left behind her back and pressed a firm hand on her right shoulder. His hobnailed boot came down heavily across her bare ankles, and his knee pressed into her back. The soldier gripping her arm across the stone drew his gladius from the scabbard at his side.

Horror rose in Tiann, and she struggled, but the men held her like iron bands. Something gave way in her ankle with a blinding crunch, and she sagged from the agony. Her vision blackened at the edges.

Boudica's voice cut through the clamor of the watching Iceni. "My chief, please tell the honored commander that the girl is my slave. She was very expensive and is well trained. If she cannot work, I will be very displeased. I will request the governor make compensation so I can buy a new one."

Is that what I am to the queen? A slave who requires compensation if I lose a hand? Did Mara seek me out not as a friend but for a slave?

She watched Prasudoc convey the queen's message in Latin to the commander, who raised his hand to the soldier with the gladius. The crowd went silent as he paused, considering. Finally, he tilted his head to Boudica and spoke.

Prasudoc translated, "He will not take the hand but will issue a symbolic punishment instead. He does not wish to deprive the king's wife of the use of her property."

The soldier replaced the gladius and removed his dagger from its sheath. He held Tiann's arm up. With no hesitation, he made a cut encircling her arm just above the bones of her wrist. Then he cut a large X on her forearm. For a moment, Tiann watched the blood welling up from the wounds on her arm, feeling nothing. Then her arm burned with searing pain. The soldier holding her from behind let go, and she slumped to the ground, retching.

"Please ask the commander and his men to come into the hall and eat before their journey." Boudica's voice moved away. Footsteps headed back to the hall. "Someone see to the slave."

The sound of the crowd faded, and the hall doors thudded shut. Tiann lay on the cold, hard-packed earth, her ankle and arm unformed masses of pain. She heard herself moaning. Someone laid a hand on her hair, and she opened her eyes and jerked away, afraid it was a soldier. The movement focused the pain into exquisite torment, and she screamed.

"Shh . . . shh . . . Hush now, little one." It was Goram. He spoke to her like she was one of his spooked horses. "Easy now. I'm going to lift you." He cradled her in arms knotted with muscle, as if she were an injured foal.

Even with his gentleness, every step jolted her with new spasms of agony. He carried her to the stable, instructing one of the boys to lay a horse blanket across a bale of hay. He laid her down with care, then folded another blanket and placed it under her leg to take pressure off her ankle. "Push my medicine chest over here and then get water," he told the boy, his gruff voice a contrast to the tender touch of his hands as he lifted Tiann's arm into his lap. From the chest, Goram pulled a soft cloth and a length of bandage. He dipped the cloth in the water and cleaned the wounds, then wrapped her arm in the bandage. "I don't want to do any more until we have proper medicines. When the fiends have gone." He spat onto the floor.

Goram stayed by her side, wiping her face and offering her sips of water. She concentrated on continuing to breathe and sometimes tried to move to make herself comfortable, but nothing helped. Her arm and ankle throbbed, her head still hurt from … *what? A dream?* … and her back ached from where the soldier had leaned on her with his knee. Her stomach felt both sick and hungry. Blood seeped from the bandage and dripped onto the straw-covered floor. All was quiet except the buzz of flies and the horses' occasional nickers.

Tiann woke from a restless doze at the sound of footsteps tramping past the stable.

Goram hurried to the window. "They are leaving." The marching faded. "I'll be right back, child." He slipped out the door.

Tiann didn't want him to go. Her throat ached with thirst, and shivers shook her. She closed her eyes, wanting to find relief in more sleep. Instead, she saw the dagger slicing her skin. With her good hand, she tried pulling the horse blanket around her shoulders, but the effort jostled her ankle, and she gasped against the pain.

When the door opened again, relief filled her. She peered

against the glare of daylight, but it was not Goram who came toward her.

Boudica rushed to her side, with Shal close behind. She laid her hand on Tiann's cheek. "She's freezing. We need to get her to the hall."

Goram spoke from behind them. "We can carry her in the blanket. I think that will hurt her less. Careful now."

He and Shal lifted the ends of the blanket until she hung swaddled in its folds. They made a slow procession from the stable, through the courtyard, to the hall, with Boudica admonishing the men to tread gently. She led them to her own chamber in the royal apartment, motioning for two of her women to follow.

"Lay her on the bed. No, wait. Hold her a moment more."

From her makeshift hammock, Tiann watched her cross to the chest of goods the Romans had brought. She lifted out the glass bottles, then gathered an armful of fabric, trailing it across the floor as she hastened back to the bed. She dumped it down and smoothed it out. "Now, lay her down. They hope their gifts will buy our loyalty—rather, let them bring comfort to the one their cruelty has wounded."

Shal and Goram lowered her, and Boudica removed the horse blanket from under her. In the place of its coarse texture, silken cloth embraced her aching body.

"Let me see the medicines they brought," Shal said. He and Goram looked over the glass vials from the chest, conferring about each one.

"Well? Will any of them help?" Boudica demanded.

"Lady, I believe for the wounds on her arm, we would be better with our own treatments," Shal said. "Send someone to my chamber for yarrow, mallow root, and calendula. I'll need hot water and bandages."

Boudica motioned to the women, who left the chamber at a trot.

Shal knelt beside the foot of the bed. "Daughter, I need to feel this ankle. It will hurt."

Tiann nodded and gritted her teeth. She gathered the soft cloth in her good hand and clenched her fist around it, determined not to cry out. Still, tears sprang and trickled down her face as he probed the bones.

"I think there may be a medicine I can use for this," Shal told the queen. "One of those vials contains a powerful drug from the East. I have never used it, but I learned of it from a trader a few years ago. It can dull her pain while I set the bones back where they belong. If I do not set them, she may never walk properly again. But the process will be delicate and painful."

When the women returned with the supplies, Shal unwound Goram's bandage from Tiann's arm. It stuck to the wound, which bled afresh when he pulled it away. He mixed some herbs into water and set it over the brazier to steep. Boudica moved closer and touched just above the gaping skin. Then she hurried from the chamber.

She just wanted to make sure it would mend so I can work. Checking on her property. Tiann's chest ached. She wished Da would come into the room and wake her, as though from a bad dream. He would gather her up, blankets and all, and sit by the fire and sing in his husky voice. All this pain and terror would fade away in his tight embrace, and his heart would be a steady thud beneath her ear. Da loved her. *Who will love me now? A slave. A marked thief.*

When Shal was satisfied the herb mixture was ready, he gestured to Goram to help him move the basin close to the bed. "I'm going to clean your wounds. It may sting." Goram held her arm still while Shal dipped a cloth in the pungent water again and again, wiping the dagger cuts with painstaking thoroughness. At last he sighed and sat back. "It looks clean. We will dress it with the mallow root and hope it heals without heat or discharge. You will always carry the scar, I'm afraid." He removed a few shriveled brown roots from the packet of supplies and placed them in a mortar bowl. "Goram, did they include olive oil in their gifts?"

The horse trainer rummaged through the chest, returning with an amphora, stopped and sealed with wax.

"Maybe." He held the vessel over the brazier until the wax softened. Removing the stopper, he sniffed the contents, then tipped a drop onto his finger and tasted it. "Yes. This is one Roman gift I like." He handed the amphora to Shal.

"This bottle is destined for better things than your bread, my friend." Shal poured oil over the roots and mashed them together with vigor. He brought the paste to the bed and spread a generous amount over the wounds, then bandaged Tiann's arm. "We will change the dressing every day, daughter. The herbs will clean it, the root will help it heal, and the oil will keep the bandage from sticking."

Her arm did feel better—the throbbing lessened. But she felt wrung out and limp.

"May I have some water?" Her voice came out in a croak.

"Yes! I'm so sorry, child. I should have realized." Shal filled a cup and slipped his hand under her shoulders to raise her so she could drink.

For a moment she closed her eyes and rested against him, imagining he was Da, that he loved her. Then he laid her back down.

"I'm afraid the really hard part is coming next, daughter. I'm going to give you some of this medicine. I hope it will do as I've heard and make you sleep without pain."

Shal unstoppered one of the small bottles and poured a few drops of a dark, viscous substance into her cup, mixing it with the rest of the water. Lifting her again, he held the drink to her lips. "Drink it all now, child."

She gulped the bitter substance, trying not to gag. Shal filled the cup one more time so she could swish the foul taste away. Still, her teeth felt sticky, and the drug lingered at the back of her throat. A strange fuzziness developed around the edges of her thoughts. Her body felt heavy then, as though it floated. Shal lifted her leg, and for the first time she saw her ankle and foot, purple and black, angled all wrong. Then Goram positioned himself at her knee, and she couldn't see it anymore. A blankness closed in on her mind, and she sank into it.

"Hold her still," she heard Shal say.

And then, nothing.

"MOTHER, MAY I SEE HER?" The voice fell into the blankness like a pebble into a still pond. *I know her. She sounds sad. I don't want her to be sad.* Tiann tried to raise her eyelids, but they felt leaden and crusted. She licked her lips and tried to speak.

"She's still sleeping. Shal doesn't know how long the drug's effect will last."

That voice . . . flaming hair and a green dress and a gold torc . . . I am awake. I'm thirsty. Where is Da?

"Let's leave her to sleep now."

No, don't go. Please stay. Tiann lifted her hand to entreat them, and jagged pain shot up her arm. She gasped, sound forcing out through her parched throat at last.

"Mother! She's waking!"

Mara. You are Mara, my friend. Alive. Or not my friend? I don't remember.

A cool hand rested on Tiann's cheek. "Tiann, it's me."

She is crying. Don't be sad. You're alive. Your mother is alive. Tiann dragged her eyes open to look at Mara.

"Mother, her eyes are open."

"I'll get Shal." Boudica rustled from the room.

"Thirsty," Tiann whispered.

Mara hurried to bring her water.

Tiann shifted to lift her mouth to the cup. "My leg . . . I can't move my leg!"

"Peace, child." Shal strode into the room. "Your leg is bound down so you couldn't move it if you wakened suddenly." He slid an arm under her shoulders and supported her so she could look.

Thick layers of cloth wrapped her leg and held it straight with wood splints. Padded with cushions, the whole limb was held to the bed with more strips of cloth.

"You will need to keep it still so the bones stay in their places while they heal." He took the water from Mara and offered it to Tiann.

After she drank, her eyelids fell again. The smooth fabric under her smelled of the woods near the oak circle. With the hand of her unbandaged arm, she stroked the softness, and she drifted into the green scent.

The next time she floated to the surface, someone was bathing her face with cool water. From nearby came the rhythmic sound of something being ground with a mortar and pestle, and the scent of herbs grew strong. She opened her eyes, lashes wet and no longer crusted to her face.

Aife wrung out a cloth over a basin, and Shal stood with his back to her, wielding the pestle. The brazier lit the room with a soft glow.

"May I have some water?"

Shal turned around, his face crinkling into a smile. "Ah, you're back. We've been keeping some broth warm for you, haven't we?"

Aife ladled a cupful from the pot beside the brazier and

carried it to the bed. She sipped it first. "Just making sure it's not too hot. If I prop her with cushions, can she sit up?"

"Yes." Shal turned back to his task while Aife arranged Tiann into a half-reclined position. "After you've had your broth, we will change the bandages on your arm."

Aife spooned the rich, salty broth into her mouth with a brisk efficiency. The warmth soothed Tiann's throat and settled with a comforting heat in her belly. When the cup was empty, Shal unwound the bandages from her arm. They came away covered with oil and herbs and blood, and Aife held out a washbasin as he peeled off each one. He took his time cleaning every bit of the wounds with clean cloths and herb-infused water. Aife's face paled as the angry cuts lost their oily covering of herb paste, but she met Tiann's gaze. "Hold my hand. You can squeeze as hard as you want."

Shal examined the scarlet ring around Tiann's arm and the carved X. "The wounds are still seeping but not bleeding much." He sniffed at the skin. "There is no smell of sickness. I believe these will heal with good care." He smiled up at Aife. "You may tell your sister. I will finish here."

Aife nodded. "Tiann, Mara wants to tell Mother and Father what happened with you. When Shal says you are ready and not too tired." She bit her lip, then cleared her throat. "To say it seems so feeble, but . . . I want to say . . . thank you." She leaned over, kissed Tiann hard on the forehead, then spun and rushed from the room.

Shal's deft hands spread a new batch of oil and medicines on her arm and coiled fresh bandages around it. The throbbing continued, but his touch was so light he added hardly any pain with his ministrations.

"Are the chief and queen very angry with me?"

Shal's brows snapped together. "Angry? Yes, they are in a rage. But not with you. Why would you think this?"

"I am causing so much trouble. Perhaps I will not be able to work for a long time."

"Child, they are pleased to take the trouble over you. We all are. Besides, I do not know the whole tale, but I believe there is more behind your actions than we all saw, isn't there?" He fastened the end of the last bandage and tied it off. "I think you will find the chief and lady very ready to listen to what you and Mara have to say. Rest now. I will tell them to wait an hour and then come to speak with you."

Tiann dozed on and off, but could not banish the anxious thoughts assailing her about the coming conversation *What if I was very foolish? Maybe I caused extra trouble instead of protecting Mara.* But she kept picturing her friend's terrified face, kept seeing the images from her vision of blood and death. *Did Boudica mean it when she told them I am her slave?* Tears pricked her eyes. Da had been proud of his status as a landowner and warrior. He would be saddened if his daughter was brought so low.

A firm knock sounded, and the door pushed open. Prasudoc strode into the room, followed by Boudica, Aife, and finally Shal and Mara. The younger girl clung to Shal's arm until she saw Tiann. She let go and darted past the others and knelt beside the bed, burying her face in the cushion next to Tiann's head.

Mara's muffled sobs sounded next to Tiann's ear, and she reached over awkwardly with her good hand to pat her hair. "Shh, shh, Mara. I'll be all right."

Prasudoc pulled an armless chair over for Boudica, then stood behind her, his hands on his wife's shoulders. "Well, young women. It's time for you to explain today's events." Aife began to speak, but the chief held up his hand. "No. Mara first, I think."

When Mara lifted her head, her eyes were puffy and her face blotched. Her hair hung in untidy tangles. Still, she stood and squared her shoulders. "Mother . . . I mean, my queen, my chief." She heaved a deep breath. "I took the helmet from the hall. I brought it back to my chamber. When Tiann realized the danger to me and that Shal might be discovered, she brought the helmet out to you. She took my blame."

Boudica sat straight as a spear shaft, eyes fixed on her younger daughter.

Aife stepped forward. "May I speak?"

Prasudoc nodded.

Aife shifted her feet, looking at her parents' faces. "I don't know everything that happened. I only knew about the helmet when the Roman was yelling and Mara was scared. Tiann grabbed the helmet and went into the hall without explanation, after . . . well, I'm not really sure what happened to her. But she was not asked or coerced. Only her courage motivated her."

Shal's head swiveled toward Tiann. His eyes questioned her, and she dropped her gaze to her bandaged arm. A patch of blood mottled the cloth. She focused on it, tracing its shape. She wasn't sure what had happened to her either, but she could tell Shal knew *something* had. But she didn't want to speak of it, not in front of Mara. Her friend had barely made it out of her chamber when the Romans had arrived. How would she react if she found out Tiann had seen her death, and the queen's, at their hands? No, Tiann would wait until she could ask Shal her questions in private.

Boudica spoke at last. "Why did you take it, daughter?"

"Tiann told me to put it back, but I wanted to play with it. I wanted to show Goram so he could help me make a horsetail hat."

Boudica bent her head and clenched her hands in her lap. "I have been wrong. I tried to keep you from fear, but I see I have not made you afraid enough. We are not playing a game with these Romans. The pretending we do—it is deadly serious. It's the difference between slavery and freedom. The difference between slaughter and life."

At the mention of slavery, a lump rose in Tiann's throat. Did she dare ask the queen about her own status? "My queen, I heard you in the courtyard . . . That is . . . my father was a warrior and a farm holder, but you told the Roman that I am . . . I am wondering . . ."

Boudica rose from her chair, crossing to sit on the bed. She placed a gentle hand on the fingers protruding from the bandage. "You heard me call you a slave. No. No, my dear girl. I know there are Roman laws about destruction of property. I hoped by making the commander think he would get in trouble with the governor, I could keep you from being punished. It worked—but not as well as I'd hoped."

The tightness in Tiann's chest released. She tilted her head to look at Mara. "You are my friend, after all." She regretted her words when fresh tears streaked down the girl's face.

"Yes. Yes. Friends."

Boudica considered the two of them, biting her lip. "Tiann, your mother was my childhood friend. Your father died in our service. Now you have placed yourself in harm's way for my daughter. Husband"—she stood and took Prasudoc's hands in hers—"Tiann belongs to us."

"This is a weighty matter, Lady."

"I do not say it lightly. And I think Mara should be the one who binds her to us. Shal, can you advise us?"

The older man stepped from the corner where he had observed. He pushed his sleeves up to his elbows, then tugged them back down. He laced his fingers, standing with head bowed, while Boudica waited for his response. Tiann looked up at Mara and Aife, trying to read in their faces what was happening. But they looked as bewildered as she felt, Aife's brows drawn together and Mara biting her lip, both looking from Shal to their parents and back again.

Shal lifted his head and nodded. "I cannot tell what the consequences would be. But it seems that an act born out of love and loss and sacrifice must be good. But the girls must be willing—they must understand what it means." He laid his hand on Tiann's head. "Chief, Lady, you and your daughters should go discuss the matter. I will stand for Tiann and talk it over with her."

Prasudoc inclined his head to his advisor. He offered his hand to Boudica. "Come, daughters. Let's go talk. And, Mara, perhaps now you will finally eat something, yes?" The chief shepherded his family out of the chamber.

Shal dragged the chair Boudica had vacated over to sit by Tiann. "How are you feeling?"

"Well enough, sir."

Shal's lips quirked. "You forget—I am the one who dressed your wounds and set the bones in that ankle. I want to know."

"I . . . it hurts. Sometimes I think my arm is the worst part, but then it's my ankle. And my head."

Shal's fingers searched her skull. "Did you hit your head when you fell?"

"No. It hurt before. Before the courtyard. And then when I woke up after the medicine, it was hard to think or remember. And my head started hurting again, but in a different way."

"I think the headache now is from the drug I gave you. I wasn't sure about the dose and maybe gave you too much. But I still think it is better to suffer this now than to have been awake while I tended your ankle." Shal pushed his sleeves up, fiddling with the fabric. "Tiann, what happened right before your head started hurting?"

Will he believe me? Tiann closed her eyes. It was easier to talk about it if she didn't have to look at him. "We were peeking into the hall. The Roman was yelling, and then Aife came in and told us it was about a thief. I knew Mara had taken the helmet. I felt like . . . like the room was moving. Not turning exactly, but going away from me. A little like when I am very, very hungry. So I closed my eyes, hoping it would pass. But instead I saw the court-yard. The Roman had Mara. He held her by the hair. They were facing away from me. He pulled out his dagger. The queen screamed. She tore that green dress so she could run, and she threw the silver thing from her head on the ground. She had a sword."

Tiann opened her eyes and stopped to take a breath. Shal brought her a cup of water, and she sipped at it. Her heart pounded.

"Child, I know this is hard. I know you want to sleep. But I need to hear the rest before you do. Can you finish?"

She nodded. "The Roman, he turned around. He cut Mara's throat and dropped her. The queen put her sword in one of the soldiers. But another soldier put his sword in her. And then there was just red everywhere, coming from everywhere. I heard my name and opened my eyes. I was back with Aife and Mara. But I knew the Roman must not hurt Mara. So I took the helmet out."

Shal tugged at his sleeves again, pushing them up and smoothing them down. "I will need to think on this for a while, child. But I believe you had a true vision of a might-have-been. I cannot say if it is all over now that we are traveling a different path because of your actions. And I do not know whence it came." He stood. "Now you should sleep. The body knits itself when it rests."

"Please, sir, wait. What did the queen mean when she said Mara should bind me?"

"Ah. The queen believes you should belong to her family. She wants you and Mara to consider becoming blood sisters. This is a very special relationship, because it means not only would you be adopted into the family, but you and Mara would be bound. You would defend each other as you would your own selves. Do you understand?"

Tiann nodded. Shal smiled down at her and laid his hand on her head. He left the chamber, shutting the door behind him.

Tiann settled her head into the cushions, looking at the flame in the brazier. The glow blurred as her eyes filled with tears. A family. A new father. Sisters. A mother. *I never had sisters and I don't remember my mother. Would Da be sad if I had a new father?*

FOUR

Tiann hobbled toward the paddock, using the walking stick one of the warriors had cut for her. Her progress was a slow shuffle and hop. Her ankle, which Shal had sternly warned her not to use, hampered her, as did her wounded arm, which could not hold a twin walking stick. Puffing with exertion, she reached the fence and leaned on it.

The paddock was set up with obstacles. Goram held Gwyndolyn on a lead and ran beside her as she trotted through the course, alternately jumping over logs or brush piles. He brought her around three times, then pulled her up. Seeing Tiann watching, he led the mare to the fence.

"Ah, it's good to see you back at the paddock. Gwyndolyn's been missing you. Here now, she's done a fine job with those obstacles and deserves a treat. Give her this." Goram pulled a dried apple from the pouch at his waist and handed it to Tiann. "Hold it in your hand with your fingers flat."

Tiann set her stick against the fence and balanced on her good leg. She held out the apple. Gwyndolyn's soft lips nuzzled against her palm, making Tiann laugh. "She likes it!"

"Oh yes, she'd eat the whole store we gathered last autumn if we let her." The trainer rubbed the mare's neck. "But we mustn't let her. Too much would make her terribly sick."

"How did you learn about horses, Goram?"

"Oh, just like you, I suppose. Every time I could escape chores, I'd be off to the stable or paddock. Soon, they started giving me chores like keeping the stalls clean. Then more and more. Now, this wasn't here, you understand. No, I lived east, near the sea, among the marshlands. The horses we had were ponies with large, wide hooves. One day Shal came walking into our village. He stayed for half a moon. In the evenings he told stories, and during the day he visited the artisans and the workers. He asked who the horse expert was, and everyone pointed to me! He came back the next year and asked if I wanted to come to serve the chief and queen, training their horses. That clever druid brought one of them. This one's grandsire. One look and I packed my things." He smoothed the mare's mane.

"Do you miss your home?"

"My parents had gone on by that time. Like yours. It seemed good to make a new life. And that horse! I had never seen the like. I couldn't say no. But I miss the sea, being inland here. The smell of it coming in on the wind, the sound. I miss the gallop through the shallows, all the salt and grit flying up at me. When they need men to journey to the villages near the sea, I always volunteer, unless one of the mares is ready to foal."

"I've never seen the sea," Tiann said. "I would like to."

"Maybe when you're well enough, I'll need an assistant on one of those journeys." Goram winked.

"I'd like that." Tiann stroked Gwyndolyn's soft nose. "Goram, do you think your parents would have felt bad if you got new parents? After they were gone, I mean."

"Hmm. I don't know. Maybe if I was trying to replace them,

like they weren't really gone. Or if I forgot them. But I think they would have been happy if I had people who loved me after they were gone. Who I could love too."

"Did you have people like that?"

"Not an exact mother and father. But like in pieces. Boudica's parents, who were chief and queen when I first came here—they took care of me, made sure I had a good place to sleep, and clothes, and training. They checked up on how I was doing. There was an old woman, a cook, who coddled me and gave me extra honey cakes. She would throw her arms around my waist—her head only came to my shoulder—when I came back to the hall for the evening meal. Then she would laugh, push me away, and say, 'Go wash all that horsiness off you and come back for a real hug.'"

Tiann smiled at the thought of Goram as a young man, spoiled and bullied by an elderly cook. "Thank you. I think I understand now."

Goram handed her the walking stick. "You go on and get ready for tonight. Don't worry about your da. He'd want you loved."

TIANN EASED herself onto her bed. The exhaustion of just walking to and from the paddock frustrated her. Boudica had asked the carpenter to make a bed frame for Tiann, so now she didn't need to struggle up and down from a pallet on the floor. She lay back on the soft coverings. The cloth had come with her when she had moved back to the chamber she shared with Mara. Aife had been set to hemming the unfinished silks and linens into bedclothes, bribed with the promise that she could choose some of the fabric for her own bed as well. Tiann pressed Mara to choose something also, but she would not.

Tiann's eyes lingered on the garment hanging from a peg on the wall. The striped cape hung in folds over the long tunic, which had been embroidered with the symbols of the Iceni and the royal family. The seamstress had asked her if she had any personal designs she would like to include. She'd asked for her father's symbol of the owl, and then thinking of the carvings in the tunnel room, she asked for a design of three interlocking spirals. These now embellished the neckline and sleeves. The outfit, completed with braccae just visible under the long tunic, reminded Tiann of the oak circle—shades of green and yellow and rich brown. She had never worn such fine garments.

Mara came into the chamber with a twitch of the door hanging. "Oh, Tiann, here you are. I was hoping. Do you need to rest, or can we talk?"

"Don't be silly. Of course you can talk to me." Tiann wished Mara would stop being so apologetic and careful with her. "I want to talk to you too."

Mara sat on the edge of the bed. "May I go first? It's important."

"No. I'm going first. Mara, it is not your fault what those Romans did to me. I'm not sorry I brought the helmet out that day." Tiann sat up and tugged her friend close. She held her in a hug, ignoring the discomfort in her arm. "Please stop acting like I'm a clay pot you can break. We're still friends, aren't we?"

Mara's shoulders heaved, and she snuffled into Tiann's shoulder. "Yes. We're friends. Forever. I wish you hadn't been hurt like that. I'll never forget when they . . . and I've never really thanked you." She leaned away, eyes wet. She rubbed her sleeve across her runny nose. "So I want to say that first. Thank you."

Tiann opened her mouth to tell her *Never mind. Don't worry about it—it was nothing.* But Mara looked at her with intent anxiety. It wasn't nothing. It was big and important.

"You are welcome."

Mara sighed and closed her eyes. When she opened them again, she smiled. Tiann felt a smile lift her own mouth as well.

"What was the second thing you wanted to say?" Tiann asked.

"Well, about this ceremony. You only have to do it if you want to. I know Mother thinks it's our destiny. But I talked to Shal about it, and he says it's a choice. It's our choice. He asked if it was what I want. No one had asked me before that! I do want to be your blood sister"—Mara squeezed her hand—"but I thought maybe nobody asked you either. It's a very serious thing. And I don't want you to think you have to."

"I guess no one did ask me, exactly." Tiann thought about it for a moment. "But I do. I do. I want to be your friend *and* your sister. I don't know anything about destiny. I think it's more like something we get to have. Like a gift."

When dusk had fallen, Boudica, Prasudoc, and all the royal household came to fetch Tiann and Mara. The queen led the procession with Mara, followed by Tiann and Prasudoc, who placed his large hand under her elbow. Watching Boudica's erect posture with her magnificent hair cascading down made Tiann straighten her own back as best she could, gripping her walking stick. She determined to limp as little as possible. Shal met them just outside the hall. He held a torch, and everyone lit theirs from his flame. Shal led them all out of the courtyard into the clearing between the horse paddock and the fields. Stars blinked into view.

Shal stopped the silent procession with a raised hand. Tiann looked up at Prasudoc's face. The flames from the torches cast wavering shadows across his eyes, making him seem unfamiliar.

Shal walked forward to the edge of the forest. He turned back to the waiting crowd and raised his arms, holding his torch high.

"People of the Iceni. Tonight we celebrate the making of a blood bond between Mara and Tiann. This is a solemn undertaking. Will you support this bond and light their way?"

"We will," the assembly responded. The people carrying torches moved to form two lines between Shal and the royal family.

Boudica, Mara, Prasudoc, and Tiann passed between the rows of torches while the people murmured blessings. To Tiann's surprise, Aife and Goram stepped out of line and walked behind them.

Shal turned and led them into the forest, leaving the light of the many blazing torches and the stars. Despite the solemn pace, Tiann still stumbled, trying to keep up.

Prasudoc tightened his hold on her elbow. "Easy now, my dear. We will go at your speed." His voice was warm and reassuring in the dark.

The forest took on new mystery, lit only by Shal's torch. Wild shadows leapt, and the green scent carried an undercurrent of musk. An owl hooted in the distance, and Tiann thought of her father. *He is part of this. He is part of me.*

When they reached the opening to the oak circle, Prasudoc slid between the rocks first, drawing her after him. Emerging, she saw Shal lighting torches set into stands ringing the area. When he finished, he went to the spring and lifted the cup from its spot in the hollow of the rock. He filled it and drank, then gestured for the others to come forward. When they had all sipped the water, he dipped the cup once again, lifted it toward the oak, and poured it on the ground.

"Tiann, Mara, please come forward."

Tiann moved to Mara's side, missing Prasudoc's comforting hand under her elbow. She didn't know what would happen next.

For the first time, she wondered what the "blood" part of this bonding meant. She stepped forward, heart pounding, planting her walking stick to steady herself. Her body quivered all over, and she thought she might burst into tears.

Shal seemed to tower over them. "You have agreed to become bonded. Is this true?"

"Yes, sir." Mara's voice filled the night.

Tiann gulped. "Yes." Her response sounded like a squeak in her ears.

Shal bent to her and touched her cheek. "Don't be afraid, child. It is still us. We are being very serious, but we are still the people who love you. You know us." He straightened but kept a hand on Tiann's shoulder.

"Who stands with Mara?"

Boudica, Prasudoc, and Aife surrounded Mara. "We do. She is our daughter and sister."

"Mara, hold out your hand." Shal removed a small silver knife from its sheath on his belt. "A blood bond means you are united. You agree to support, defend, and, if necessary, shed your own blood for each other. This small hurt is a symbol of that commitment." He made a tiny nick on Mara's palm, just below her thumb. A drop of blood welled up, showing black in the dancing torchlight. Mara cupped her hand to keep the droplet from falling to the ground.

"Who stands with Tiann?" She felt as though her chest was being squeezed. Who could stand with her? Her mother had died in childbirth, her father far away in battle, and she had no brother or sister.

She felt a presence at her back. "I do," Goram said. "I would be as a father to her."

"I do," Prasudoc echoed.

"I stand as a mother to her," Boudica said. "In honor of my friend."

"I would be a sister to my sister's sister," Aife added.

"And I too." Shal smiled down at her. "You have lost your dear father, Tiann, and we can't replace him. But we would like to be your family."

Tiann's tears dripped off her chin onto her fine tunic. Unable to speak, she nodded and leaned against Goram. He patted her head and whispered, "He'd want you loved."

"Tiann, please hold out your hand."

She obeyed, no longer afraid. "You have already shed your blood for Mara." Shal unwrapped her bandage a bit. "These scars are not a sign of your shame but of your honor and love." He made the slightest cut on the healing wound. He reached to Mara and pulled her hand to Tiann's arm and laid it across the cut.

Tiann searched Mara's face, seeing a solemnity there that matched her own wonder.

"My sister. You are my friend and my sister." Mara threw her arms around her and would have knocked her down if Goram had not stood behind her. Tiann laughed, tears still pouring out of her eyes. The sound came out as a choking kind of snort, and Mara laughed too.

"Come now, children. Let's rinse you off with water from the spring." Shal gave a deep chuckle. "I believe the rest of the household is impatient for our return, so we may celebrate!"

When they emerged from the forest, all Tiann could see was the cluster of blazing torches. A shout burst from the darkness behind the flames, and a chattering mass of people surrounded her, hugging her, kissing her cheeks, and patting her back. Prasudoc kept her steady with his firm hand under her elbow. When it seemed every Iceni in Albion must have greeted her, two burly warriors swept her from her feet, linking their arms to form a carrying chair. She was glad she had walked under her own power to the ceremony, but grateful for the rest now.

Solemnity gone, they made their way back to the hall with

talking and snatches of song. Mara skipped along just ahead of Tiann, looking over her shoulder to grin at her in her human litter. Spilling through the great double doors into the hall, men and women spread out, fixing the torches to brackets in the walls until the space was twice as bright as any other evening. As the warriors carrying her set her down in her seat at the head table, Tiann looked up to thank them.

"Ach—no trouble, sweetie. Make sure you get plenty of that roast boar—you're light as an oak leaf. And when your leg is better, we'll expect you out on the training grounds. You'll want some growth to be strong then." The man winked and withdrew.

Tiann settled back into the cushions on her seat—another provision Boudica had ordered once Tiann had healed enough to rejoin household activity—and surveyed the festivities. To her left, a cask of mead was being broached. To her right, half a dozen people gathered with bone flutes, lyres, and hand drums. Coming through the doors, the cooks puffed under the weight of the long plank they carried, loaded with a whole roast boar, vegetables, and bread.

Mara plopped down in the seat next to Tiann, breathless from helping the cooks. "It was all I could do not to snitch bits of that meat. It smells so good. I've hardly eaten anything today. I was so nervous. What about you?"

Tiann's stomach gave a loud grumble in response, and both girls fell into a fit of laughter. The musicians striking up soon drowned them out.

Mara leaned toward her and shouted, "I'll go get us food. I'll be right back." She flitted toward the gathering crowd at the trestle table in the center of the room.

The smile felt like it would never leave Tiann's face. Her fingers joined the rhythm of the song, tapping on the table to the beat set by the hand drums. Mara returned with a trencher piled high. The two girls gorged themselves, savoring the rare treat of roast boar, the result of a lucky hunt two days before. The cooks had even made use of the precious stores of honey and spices, concocting a sweet, sticky porridge sprinkled with exotic flavors bought from merchants traveling from far-off lands.

When they had eaten beyond their fill, Tiann and Mara lounged with their seats pushed back so they could lean on the wall behind them. Tiann's injured ankle rested on a cushioned stool. She fidgeted with her walking stick, rubbing her thumb along the smooth surface of the wood. The music grew livelier. The large center table, with the wrecked remains of the feast, was moved to the side to make room for dancing. Devyn, a gangly boy with a flute, capered to where Tiann clapped along with the tune. He danced an enthusiastic step then bowed to her with a flourish. Tiann laughed and applauded as he danced away again. The hall vibrated with song, conversation, and the swoosh and thump of dancing feet. Faces shone with laughter and perspiration.

Tiann's eyes lit on a scuffle near the doors. At first she thought it was just some boys engaging in one of their endless wrestling games, but the sound of angry voices drifted over the merriment. She sat up straighter, nudging Mara.

Mara squinted where Tiann was pointing. "I don't know who that is with our warriors. Look, he's wearing the badge of another tribe."

People gradually became aware of the conflict, and conversations ceased as attention turned toward the heated exchange.

"Traitors! Collaborators!" the stranger shouted at the red-faced warriors. "How can you host those brutal interlopers? Trade with them, take their bribes? You're lower than they are! Cowards."

"Shut your mouth, you Brigantes scum," bellowed one of the warriors, approaching with fists raised. "How dare you speak of Iceni courage?" He swung, and his fist connected with the stranger's nose. Blood gushed. The man staggered back, then lunged forward, taking a wild swing.

"We know those Romans were here." Blood and spittle flew out of his mouth. "They were here for two days—you fed them and toadied to them and sent them on their way." He swung again, making contact with his opponent's chin.

The warrior grabbed his arm with the next swing and spun him around, twisting the arm behind his back. "Where were you Brigantes when Caradoc was making his stand? When we—"

"That's enough." Boudica's voice roared. The music trailed to a stop and silence ruled for a moment. Striding to the two men, the queen pushed between them. She quelled her warrior with a look, and he stepped back, but his hands remained clenched. "I don't believe we invited any representatives from other tribes to this celebration. But perhaps we can escort you to our table, where the chief and I can receive you properly." She nodded to her warriors, who surrounded the man and pushed him toward the other end of the hall. Boudica put a restraining hand on the warrior who had struck the stranger and spoke to him, but her voice was quiet and Tiann could not hear what she said. He gave a curt nod and stalked out of the hall.

The stranger was shoved into a seat at the other end of the table. Tiann stared at him, fascinated. He still cursed Prasudoc, Boudica, and the Iceni, although in lower tones. His beard was divided into two long tails, with a shaved stripe down the center of his chin, unlike the Iceni men, who wore their beards full and short. His hair was cropped and stood up stiffly from his head.

Boudica and Prasudoc approached the table, and the man lurched forward, as though he would attack them, but the warriors forced him back into the seat.

"Who sent you here? Was it Venut? I can hardly believe your queen would countenance having you in her service."

"Ai, Venut is my lord. Cartimandua has become as bad as you

lot." The man's teeth, chin, and beard were gory from his nose-bleed. He sniffed and made a choking sound, then spit out a gob of blood.

Boudica, face impassive, gestured for one of her women. "Get the man a cloth and a basin of water." She stood over the man. "Now you listen to me. I know Venut is an honorable chief, despite his wife —"

"One-time wife," the man muttered.

Boudica raised an eyebrow. "Is that so? Intriguing. Nevertheless, I will speak to you out of regard for your chief." She paused as the cloth and basin were delivered. While the stranger wiped his face, she continued, "Your spies did not see with eyes that look behind things. In fact, they saw with Roman eyes, the things we displayed for their benefit."

"You let them maim one of your own! Our man saw it!"

Boudica winced and lowered her head for a moment. Then she straightened and turned to where Tiann was watching the exchange with Mara. "Daughter, come here."

Tiann approached, trying to limp as little as possible.

Boudica put her hands on Tiann's shoulders and gazed into her eyes. "Would you be willing to tell the man about your injuries?"

"I will if you ask it, Lady. But . . ."

"What is it? You may speak your mind. This is your story, and you can decide who hears it. You are not bound to obey. I'm not commanding you."

"Lady"—Tiann struggled to find the right words—"he insulted you and our tribe. He came to our celebration and began a fight. Why do you care if he knows what really happened? How can we know if he will even understand?" She felt her face flushing with her own boldness.

Shal moved to stand beside the queen. He smiled as though

Tiann had just proved the fastest in a race. "These are good questions. You are reaching to know what is behind things."

Boudica nodded. "Yes, you should know why I ask it. The Iceni have . . . well, a complicated kinship with the Brigantes. Do you know of Cartimandua and Venut?"

Tiann shook her head. In truth, she felt ignorant and foolish. She had never considered whether her people had contact with other tribes beyond the merchants and traders who traveled throughout Albion.

"They are the queen and chief of that northern tribe. Venut has always been wary of the Romans, even before they came with their armies. Cartimandua, on the other hand, welcomed them. She enjoys their luxuries."

Behind her, the stranger made a sound like a growl and then spat on the ground.

Tiann thought of the bitterness in Boudica's voice when she had dumped the rich fabrics onto the bed to make Tiann comfortable while she recovered from her injuries. "Bribes," she had called them. Maybe this Cartimandua was more easily bought.

The stranger's voice drew their attention. "It's gone beyond that now. She prevented us from joining the fight with Caradoc. Sent all us warriors off with some story about a band of Picts raiding in the North. Later we found out the summons had come, and she never told the chief."

Tiann's eyes burned. If more warriors had fought with Caradoc, could he have won? Could her da have been saved?

"Iceni warriors were there." Tiann's voice crackled. "My da was there."

The stranger looked up at Prasudoc. "Is this true? We heard the Iceni did not send warriors either."

"Yes, it is true." Prasudoc sat heavily opposite the stranger, still being held in his seat by the warriors, although now with less force. "I did not go, nor any from the royal household who would be recognized. But loyal warriors from the outlying villages answered the summons and agreed to go, Tiann's father among them. Only one messenger returned."

"We have been playing a risky game with the Romans," Boudica interjected. "We are not strong enough for them yet, so we maintain the appearance of friends and allies. Meanwhile, we train. We gather weapons and information. Tiann knows more than most how dangerous this game can be." She put her arm around Tiann and asked, "Well, child? Are you willing to tell about your wounds?"

Tiann's mind went blank, her mouth dry. She tried to swallow, but her tongue was heavy. She reached for a cup from the table and gulped, realizing too late it was not hers and contained the fiery mead favored by Prasudoc. She sputtered, but at least the drink loosened her tongue.

She pulled back her bandage enough to show the angry-looking scar and explained what happened that day. "They also hurt my ankle when they held me still." Tiann didn't look in Mara's direction. This stranger didn't need to hear about how she had feared for her friend, about her red vision. Boudica wanted him to understand what had happened, so she would tell him. But after all, he had ruined their feast. She didn't need to let him look into her heart.

The stranger leaned toward her. There was dried blood in the bare patch in the center of his beard and on his lips.

Impulsively, she held out the cup of mead to him. "I am Tiann."

He took it, his eyes studying her. Then he drew a long swallow and handed it back. "I am Teth. Thank you. And what about your da?"

"He told me he must go fight with Caradoc. But he was killed helping in the escape."

Prasudoc jumped up. "But you should know all this. Caradoc would have told Venut himself. He was fleeing to you for refuge."

The stranger dropped his head into his hands. A low keening sound seeped from between his fingers, making Tiann's nape shiver.

Mara knelt in front of him, pulling his hands away from his face. Boudica moved to stop her but checked and waited. The man raised wet eyes to look at Mara. "The witch turned him over." His gaze never left Mara's face. "Caradoc came to us just at dawn. He was not wounded, but two of his men were. They were exhausted, hungry. She fed them food and sweet words, then gave them her own apartments to rest. Before darkness fell, the Roman demons were there, bowing and bringing her gifts."

Tiann gasped. "Like here? Did Caradoc hide in time?" She thought of her own frantic race to find Shal and warn him.

"No. No, not like here. It wasn't pretense. She sent for them. Cartimandua, she—" His voice choked off into a sob. "She sold him. Caradoc didn't even have time to strap on his sword."

Boudica clutched at the table as though to steady herself. "Is he dead then?"

"No. They killed his men. But they took him away in chains. They sent him to Rome."

Boudica moaned, and Prasudoc put his arm around her. She turned into his bulk, burying her face in his neck.

"Word came that they forced him to walk in chains through the city, in one of their triumphal parades," the man continued. "But they allowed him to speak before his execution. He impressed them, I gather. They didn't kill him. The report is he's still there, living with his wife and children."

Boudica lifted her head with a noise that sounded like a strangled laugh. "He always did have a golden tongue. Still, for him—a chief of noble blood—walking in chains through the enemy city . . ." Her voice shook. She pulled away from her husband, planting her feet and clenching her fists. "Never. I will never see the Iceni brought so low."

Tiann felt a thrill run through her at the queen's words. Unthinking, she held out her hand to the queen. Boudica squeezed it once, hard. Then she swept away, clapping. "Music! Tonight is for the Iceni!"

PART TWO

FIVE

Tiann laughed as Devyn waggled his expressive eyebrows over the elk-bone flute. She dug her toes down to the cool, wet sand under the surface warmth and clapped along with the rest of the group to the merry tune. She didn't know where he got the energy to dance about. Everyone else on this journey to visit outlying Iceni villages sprawled out around the fire, resting. After today's long push for the sea, she herself was happy to collapse onto her outspread cloak.

Devyn finished his capering and sprawled, grinning, next to her. She absently picked a splinter out of her palm, garnered when she had helped gather firewood from the last bit of scraggly forest, half a mile from their resting place.

"Did you hurt yourself? Let me see." Leaning forward, Devyn took her hand and inspected it.

She looked down at his bent head, the wavy dark hair springing in every direction, his cheek just beginning to be obscured by a beard. Did she look as different to her childhood playmate as he did to her? She felt an impulse to touch that bristly new growth, and jerked her hand out of his, self-conscious.

"Come on." He jumped up again. "You can wash it in the sea."

She ignored his hand waiting to pull her up. "I can just rinse it off. My waterskin is still half-full."

He bent and lifted her up under her arms, then swung her in a circle. "Not like this water! This water is magic!"

Tiann stumbled as her feet returned to the ground, but he caught her around the waist and urged her to where the surf made foam on the sand. When the cold swept up over her ankles, she stopped, protesting, but his arm around her was firm, and she stepped forward until the water wet the bottom of her rolled-up braccae. She shivered, wanting to lean into his warmth. The strange sea scent mixed with his, musky from the day's journey, with lingering hints of forest and wood woodsmoke.

He let go of her and leaned down to cup some of the water. He tasted it. "See? It's salt." He held out his dripping hands. "Taste it."

She turned away. Bending, she touched the water and brought her fingers to her mouth. Salt. She straightened, looking at the blue vastness before her. "Is it all salt? All the way to other lands? Why is the inland water not salty?"

"I don't know. Those are questions for Shal. Why is anything as it is? But when I was here last year, I fell down a ravine. Probably not looking where I was going." His grin flashed on the edge of her vision as she squinted harder toward the sea. "I'm sure you cannot imagine it. Anyway, I gashed my shin. Goram told me to soak it in the salt water. When I first went in, I thought he was playing a trick on me. It stung like fire. But the pain subsided, and the water felt good. And the wound healed clean and fast."

She glanced down to his legs, bare like hers, with boots left on the sand and braccae hitched up. How many times had she watched those feet, those legs, on the training field while they sparred with staves? For years he had given away his next move with his feet until one of the warriors took him in hand and trained the bad habit out of him. After that, she'd never bested him. Her limp hampered her natural speed just enough to put her at a disadvantage with a bigger, well-trained opponent.

"Go on, then. Put your hand in."

Tiann leaned over again and submerged her hand in the eddying water. He was right—it stung. But she left it there, squatting to a more comfortable position. She kept her eyes on the sea, noticing now that the water was not just blue but variegated shades of green, gray, black, and gold.

Devyn squatted beside her. "Last year when I saw this for the first time, I could hardly believe it, even though Goram had been talking about it since we were children. That a person could see so far. The sound and smell of it. I sat right down in the water, soaking that leg, and I felt like something in me unknotted. I didn't even know I was tied up before."

The sun descended behind them. Tiann pulled her numb, wrinkled hand out of the water and stood.

Devyn examined her palm. "Ah, see—the salt water has made the skin release the rest of that splinter." He gently plucked the bit from her hand.

"Thank you." Tiann searched her mind for something else to say, for a way to pull away and go back to the rest of the party. "I wish Mara could have come to see all this."

Devyn's mouth crooked a smile quite unlike his grin. "Yes. But then again, no." Lifting her palm, he brushed his lips against it. "Salt." He dropped her hand and strode back to where the fire leapt.

Tiann trailed behind, fingers closed protectively over the small wound. Skirting the group around the fire, she headed to where the horses made black shapes in the waning light. "Aiee," she called.

A graceful head rose from grazing the seagrasses along the edge of the dune. Gwyndolyn nickered a greeting, ears tilting forward.

"There now, my friend." Tiann stroked the rippling coat on the mare's neck and checked her halter and line, making sure it was long enough to allow the horse to move without tripping. "Are you settling in for the night?" She stayed until the light was almost gone, soothing her rumpled emotions with Gwyndolyn's undemanding companionship.

A celebratory shout from where the fire glowed drew her back. Ignoring Devyn watching her approach, she gathered her boots and cloak and sat beside Goram. "What is the excitement?"

Goram jerked his head toward two men just visible outside the fire ring. "They've caught a couple big cod. It's almost too late in the season. We'll dine well tonight, with more than barley and onions to fill us." He smacked his lips.

Tiann tried to hide her disappointment. Dried cod made a regular appearance in stewpots and travel pouches. She much preferred dried venison. "Hmm."

Goram laughed. "Just wait, my girl. Pulled straight from the water, cleaned, and cooked over the fire—it's a completely different food."

The sand was losing the warmth of the early spring day, so she used the edge of her cloak to wipe the rest of the granules from her feet, then slid on her boots. Her braccae were still damp at the bottom, so she unrolled them and stretched her legs toward the fire. Soon the smell of the barley stew mingled with the thick scent of fish over coals raked from the fire. Tiann thought it was nothing like the pungent odor that hung over the village when the cooks simmered the cod stew over the central hearth in the winter.

The meal, eaten from a scavenged piece of driftwood washed in sea water, was as Goram had promised. The fish, smoky and salty, tasted a bit like the fresh trout she sometimes ate in summer, but was firm, filling her mouth with a satisfying richness. Even the plain barley mush tasted better to an appetite sharpened by travel, new sights, and a splash of salt water for flavor.

When the cooking was done, they built up the blaze again. The flames danced over Devyn's face as he played his flute across the circle from her. The plaintive tune sang of the ancestors and their passing. As the last note died away, one young man, a bard in training, picked up the theme and chanted the story.

Tiann gathered her cloak around her. She traced spirals and intertwining knots in the sand, the shapes stored in her tactile memory from the stone tunnel. Heavy lidded, she nestled into the sand until it conformed to her body, her pack under her head. In the distance, the seabirds squabbled over the scraps left from cleaning the fish. The night faded into rush and ebb of sea and flicker of flame.

A LONG WHINNY roused Tiann from her relaxation. She sat up, shaking sand from her cloaked shoulders. The whinny sounded again, far down the beach. *Is it Gwyndolyn? Did she break her picket line?* Tiann rose, moving from the fire. Away from the golden warmth, the night vibrated with a blue clarity. The full moon, a hand span above the horizon, cast a yellow stream upon the sea and lit the land enough that boulders cast shadows on the sand. She walked, clutching her cloak around her, the hair from her loosened braids wisping against her cheeks.

In the distance, she heard galloping, and she broke into a run, fearing the horse would injure itself. Reaching a headland, she slowed, but the shore stretched empty to the north, and the sound had faded. She glanced over her shoulder toward the camp but pressed on. *I can't get lost if I keep the sea in sight.* She followed the curve of the land until she could no longer glimpse the light of the fire when she looked back. Here the forest crowded the dunes, looming black to her left. She kept walking, straining her ears for the horse.

Stamping hooves and an equine snort snapped her head toward the trees. *There! Are the branches moving?* "Aieee . . . Gwyndolyn, is that you? Come out, and I'll give you a piece of apple when we get back to camp." She waited, listening, peering into the gloom, loathe to leave the blue and moonlight. The trees rose higher, extending their arms out to her, and the sand under her boots stretched into a path, leading her away from the beach. The sound of surf retreated; the dark called.

She swung around at the sound of a trumpeting whinny behind her. Pawing in the shallows, Gwyndolyn glowed against the water. She wore no halter, and her mane and tail flowed in the wind that blew the water into shimmering foam. Beside her, a man stood, the hem of his long, loose garment sodden, his feet bare.

"Are you thirsty?" His voice was sonorous, carrying over the sea sounds that had filled her ears again when she turned. He held out a stone flask.

Tiann's throat prickled with a dry scratch from her run. Her lips gummed together. She approached, reaching to stroke Gwyndolyn's flank.

"Yes."

He passed the flask, and she put it to her lips, keeping her eyes on him as she drank. Gwyndolyn danced, splashing her, then nudged the man, blowing down the side of his head. He laughed, pushing her head aside. "Now, lovely beast, are you pleased? Were you worried about your friend? I told you she is drawn to the light."

Tiann handed the flask back, and as he reached to take it, she saw the markings on the inside of his wrist. Three interlocking spirals traced in his skin, then the marking continued up, disappearing beneath his loose sleeve. She lifted her eyes to meet his, and his face crinkled with a smile. His eyes were a deep gray like her father's, like her own reflection in the spring, but a gold band ringed the irises. The shimmering blue of the night lent an odd cast to skin and hair, but those eyes and the markings burned bright into Tiann's consciousness. Shivers shook her. She found her fingers tracing the shapes from the stone chamber on her thigh. "Are you one of the ancestors?"

He laughed again. "No. They had a name for me you no longer know. I guess you would say I am an Old One. You may call me Elior." He nodded toward her hand. "You have seen their signs."

"Yes. In the hidden chamber."

"Ah." His face grew sad, and the gold ring in his eyes dimmed. "Some things are not meant to be hidden. Hiding brings forgetting." His smile returned, and his eyes brightened again. "But now is a time of revealing and remembering."

The gold in his eyes gleamed and spread until they rivaled the moon's light. "Many who rule will be quieted. What was hidden will be seen. What was silenced will be heard. The arm that is reaching out—it is revealed! The royal hall grows, and the roof widens. Those who seek the light will find its glory and run to it." Elior took her hands in his.

Warmth flooded from her palms up her arms.

He turned her arm so that the scarred X showed clear in the moonlight. "Wounds from the dark transform to light. Remember this. The rising has come, and the shining from deep darkness. The gathering is here."

A thrill coursed through Tiann, setting her skin to tingling and her ears buzzing. "Sir, I don't understand. What is this light?"

"The light calls you. Sometimes it seems its glare will burn you away, but in its bathing is healing. Sometimes the light is faint as the winter sun, beckoning you."

Tiann remembered the way the forest had reached for her. "I

thought I heard Gwyndolyn in the dark. The path looked like I should take it."

Elior gripped her hands tighter. "No. The easy path, the wide path leading into the dark—this is not the way for you. In the light, even night is bright as day. The dark does not win. Remember the signs. Remember the wounds. When the time comes, look, listen, run to follow."

He dropped her hands, and the gold in his eyes retreated to ring the gray. "Now you must return to your companions. Your journey is just beginning. Come. Gwyndolyn will carry you back." Elior bent, interlacing his fingers and looking up at her expectantly.

Tiann moved to let him boost her up, but hesitated. "May I stay with you? To learn about the light?"

"No, child." He nodded to his hands.

She put her foot in them, grasping the mare's mane and swinging up.

Elior put his hand on her scarred arm. "The light will teach you. Do not fear, though the path will be grievous. The darkness does not overcome." His upturned face showed tracks of tears, and the gold ring was barely a thread. "Remember the signs. Remember the wounds." He gave Gwyndolyn a light slap on the rump.

The horse glided into a smooth gallop, sand and surf spraying under her pounding hooves. Tiann bent low over her neck, winding her fingers in the golden mane, gripping with her knees. They flew along the beach. Breath flooded into Tiann's lungs from the rushing air. She closed her eyes against the sting of salt, one with the rhythm of the gallop, faster and faster.

～

THE PACK under her cheek felt lumpy, and Tiann sat up, rubbing at the crease left on her skin. Goram poked the banked fire, bringing it back to life with bits of dry seagrass. Around the camp, people stirred and stretched, brushing sand off cloaks. The sun hung low and brilliant over the sea. Tiann blinked against the brightness, then scanned the sky, reveling in the bright blue overtaking the fading colors of sunrise. A pale sliver of moon hung above the dunes.

But the moon was full. Tiann's drowsiness fled. *Gwyndolyn!* She scrambled up, bolting for the picket lines. The horses raised their heads, ears turning, hooves stamping. Tiann forced herself to slow so as not to spook them, making her way through the group to where she had left the mare yesterday evening. There was Gwyndolyn, standing next to her picket, nickering a greeting. But her halter and line lay on the ground. When Tiann lifted a shaking hand to stroke the soft muzzle, there were strands from the horse's mane entwined in her fingers.

As the journey continued, puzzling thoughts of blue nights, stone flasks, and strangers faded, although Tiann still awoke from dreams with lingering images of eyes, gray ringed with gold. More often, she caught herself thinking about dancing brown eyes under wild curls. Somehow Devyn managed to always be at her elbow, helping her fill the horses' feed buckets with grain from the supply wagon or foraging for mushrooms, cress, or purslane to supplement their evening meals. Tiann also went in search of comfrey and mallow to replenish Shal's stores, a bag slung over her shoulder with skin pouches inside specially made for the purpose. Devyn offered to carry this for her, but she scoffed at him, and he backed away, grinning.

The party traveled northeast, relishing the warming weather. They followed the coast, moving from the wide marshlands and dunes to climb to rocky cliff paths above the surf. When they came to a village, they would stay overnight nearby. In the evening, they would join the villagers for a meal, songs, and exchange of news.

Tiann enjoyed seeing the respect Goram received, not just as a representative of Boudica and Prasudoc, but as the trainer of famous Iceni royal horses. The village children gathered near the picket line, begging to pet Gwyndolyn and the other mounts. Goram kept an eye out for any who showed particular aptitude and could one day come work at the royal stables. During the day Goram and the elders would conduct business: trading, collecting royal dues, checking on crops and livestock. Tiann grimaced when she noticed the dried cod being loaded on the wagons. So this was where it came from. The younger members of the traveling party rotated among these duties, watching and learning. In the afternoon, they moved on. Every few days they would make a more elaborate camp and stay while a few went inland to visit villages farther from the coast. Tiann suspected the route could be shorter, but Goram loved to stay near the sea where he spent his childhood.

One evening, they gathered with villagers around a leaping bonfire. Devyn's flute joined with drums and voices while children and dogs tumbled among dancers. Tiann laughed at the antics of a small boy who had escaped his mother and attempted to ride on a wolfhound. The dog sniffed at the impertinent thing struggling to climb on its back, then gave a great shrug and sent the child rolling. The mother hurried forward, scolding but laughing too, and scooped the boy into her arms and whirled him off.

Goram sat next to her and watched, silent, his face grave.

Tiann nudged him. "Why so sour? He will end up a fine rider, I'm sure. He just needs a mount the right size. Perhaps a lamb."

Goram smiled but grew serious again. "Tiann, I must tell you something. This village. This was your village. That is, your father's."

"No. No, I've never been here," Tiann answered, bewildered. "We lived on a farmholding. This place has a smith, and it is near the sea. I had never seen the sea until this journey."

"You wouldn't have, though, would you? Your da would not have brought his wee daughter about the countryside. The farm is half a day's journey inland from here. But this is where he came to trade. This is where I met him. This is where I told him that the queen and chief needed warriors for the uprising."

Tiann blew out a long breath and peered into the fire. "He went away for three days. I stayed with the women, and they made me keep in the enclosure in front of the roundhouse. I hated it, because Da always let me come with him into the fields or to see the cattle. When he came back, he told me he was going away for a long time and I was leaving to stay with the chief."

Goram nodded. "I can take you there tomorrow, if you like. To see your old home. It's not the same—no one lives there now. But maybe you'd like to see it."

"I don't know." Tiann stood. Moving blindly away from the festive atmosphere around the fire, she walked until she reached the enclosure barrier. In the deep shadow of an apple tree, she hoisted herself up to sit on the stone wall. The fragrance of the blossoms surrounded her, and she breathed in. There had been an apple tree at the farm too. *No, an orchard,* she corrected herself. *In the autumn, we harvested the fruit. I ate so many apples I had a stomachache, and my father laughed and told me I was greedy, but then he made me a hot drink with ginger root and told me stories until I felt better. When the days were sunny, we pulled out the wicker frames and everyone cut up baskets and baskets of apples and laid the pieces out to dry. When the air turned cold, he loaded sacks of them on the wagon.*

Tiann's eyes roamed, taking in the grouping of roundhouses, the stone smithy, light from the bonfire casting leaping shadows over the village. *He must have brought them here to trade.*

A figure detached itself from the mingling crowd and came

toward her. Tiann recognized Devyn's silhouette, lanky with flute in hand. She shifted, sitting up straighter and smoothing her braid.

His grin flashed in the night. "Here you are. Did you need a rest from that?" He jerked his head toward the bonfire, where uproarious laughter had broken out. "Me too. Do you mind if I sit with you?"

"Yes. I mean, no." Tiann gathered her scattered thoughts. "Yes, I wanted some quiet. No, I don't mind."

Devyn vaulted up to sit beside her. His head brushed a branch, releasing a shower of petals. Tiann picked a blossom off her tunic and held it to her nose. "I remember the scent from when I was a child."

They sat swinging their legs, not speaking. Tiann's shoulders loosened in the comfortable silence, and she was grateful Devyn had come to break her reverie. Guilt tinged her thoughts at how she had rushed away from Goram. She must go back and answer his offer, for they would need to leave at dawn if the farm was a half-day's journey. The problem was, she didn't know her own mind. Did she want to see her childhood home?

"The farmholding where I grew up is near here." The words slipped out before she even knew she was going to speak.

Devyn's eyes slid toward her. He didn't speak but reached over and unclenched one of her hands in her lap. He held it warmly in his own, offering silent comfort.

She let her palm rest in his, noticing that he had calluses in the same places as hers, from horse reins. "Goram asked if I wanted to go see it."

"Do you?" His question held no judgment, only a gentle curiosity.

"I don't know. Would I find traces of my old life there? Would it set my heart to grieving? But what if there is no trace? What if the echoes have gone? Would that be worse?"

Devyn opened her hand and placed a petal in it. "The season for flowers is beautiful, but the moon cycles, the flowers drop, and then the fruit grows. The tree changes again when winter comes. But the scent of the blossoms, the taste of the apples, these live inside us even when it is not their season. You carry the memory of your father and your childhood inside you. Maybe the scent and taste of your home will be gone, but you can still appreciate the tree for what it gave you in that season."

Tiann smiled. "You sound like Shal."

"No, no!" Devyn held his hand up in mock alarm. "Believe me, I am not drawn to that life. All that memorizing, and contemplating, and trying to counsel people not to be foolish. No, I think I sound more like . . . a farmholder."

"Is that what you want?"

"I think so. That life holds some of all the things I like. Some being alone, some working with others. Caring for horses, building and mending things. Music and stories in the evenings with a family."

"That sounds like a good life. But you don't want to be one of the chief's or queen's warriors? You are well trained."

Devyn picked up his flute and moved his fingers on the holes, as though playing a song only he could hear. After a moment, he said, "Well, we all need to be warriors now, don't we? These are troubled times. The clashes between tribes, even within tribes. The Romans building cities. They are not leaving. I heard there are more coming all the time. Not just soldiers or merchants, but people coming to live.

"But if I can choose, I will have a farmholding. Barley and horses. Wife and children." Lifting the flute to his mouth, he played a children's song, eyes smiling at her.

She smiled back, remembering the silly rhyming game they had played on rainy days.

Devyn ended with a flourish. "If you like, I could go with you to visit the old farm."

Tiann closed her eyes and took a deep breath, holding it for three heartbeats. Expelling it, she considered. She opened her eyes to find him watching her, his face kind. She put her hand in his. "Yes, I would like that."

Devyn jumped off the wall, pulling her along. Her face warmed as she stumbled into him. It seemed she was perpetually off balance around him.

THE DAY dawned gray and sullen, and the rest of the company was happy to delay their departure from the village. Tiann, Devyn, and Goram set off with their cloaks wrapped around them and hoods pulled up. The sun, hidden behind thick clouds, was too weak to burn off the fog. Water condensed on Tiann's cloak, making the wool sodden on her shoulders. The three rode through a perfumed fog as they approached the roundhouse. The familiar scent of apple blossoms hung in the mist, and the blossom-laden trees appeared as ghostly forms on either side of the overgrown trail. When they reached the enclosure wall, Tiann could see that sections had tumbled into disrepair. The courtyard looked overgrown and neglected as well, but the well still stood covered, and the half-walled shed for livestock was intact. Loom frames sat empty and broken in a heap. The cookhouse appeared to have burned down to its timber posts.

The roundhouse stood, overgrown with weeds but still sturdy. Tiann dismounted and looped Gwyndolyn's reins around a post. She held the post for a moment, shaking out and rotating her ankle. The old injury always ached in damp weather, and her limb had stiffened with the morning ride. Taking her pack from the horse, she moved toward her old home, bracing herself against a storm of memory. She ducked through the doorway, glancing back toward Devyn and Goram.

Devyn came at once, but Goram cleared his throat, "Mmh. I'll just take care of the mounts. Put them in the shed and wipe them down."

Tiann circled the room, touching the walls. She righted a stool, running her hands along the worn seat. She sat, watching Devyn clear debris from the center hearth. He left for a few minutes, and she kept quiet, listening, looking at the walls and thatched roof.

Devyn returned with an armful of kindling and a few logs. "I found quite a lot sheltered beneath the underbrush against the wall. It's only a little damp." He set about making a fire, and soon a fragrant smoke rose toward the thatch, filtering its way through. The scent did what sight had not, and the room came alive with memory.

"Applewood. When we needed to prune or cut down an apple tree, we were careful to season it and stack it under cover. We burned it on special days, like solstices. Also on the day of my mother's remembrance."

Devyn sat on another stool. "Do you remember her?"

"No. She died only a few days after I was born. The midwife had already left because all seemed well. But she grew hot with fever, and my father could not help."

"And he never had another wife?"

"He said he could never love like that again, and it would be an injustice to another woman. So it was the two of us. He even carried me about in a sling on his back when I was small. Sometimes I think I can remember how it felt to fall asleep with my head resting on the back of his neck, with his hair tickling my face."

Goram's form blocked the wan light in the doorway. He set down the packs and shrugged out of his cloak, scattering droplets that made the fire hiss. "The shed is sound enough on one side. I've wiped down the beasts and left them munching on their grain." He rustled in the largest pack and withdrew a small pot and bag of barley. "Not too exciting, but my belly could use something hot to fill it."

Tiann pulled her cloak up over her head, for the rain fell more steadily now, and went out to the well, brushing the cover free of dead leaves. The rotted wood crumbled in her hands as she shifted it. She tested the rope for soundness, then lowered a leather bag, drawing up water that was still clear. She cupped her hand and lifted a drink to her mouth, sucking up the cool mineral liquid. Careful to keep the water from sloshing out of its container, she turned back to the roundhouse. Behind her, footsteps sounded, and she whirled, clutching the water bag.

A stranger stepped into the enclosure, bow drawn.

CHAPTER

SIX

Tiann's ears pulsed with her heartbeat's acceleration, and the water gushed up from the mouth of the bag, soaking her front. The corner of the man's mouth lifted, and he relaxed his stance a fraction but did not lower his weapon. His gaze swiveled, taking in the horses in the shed and the smoke filtering from the roundhouse thatch.

Tiann took a slow step backward. The man's expression hardened, and his hand tightened on the bow. "Do not move." His words, though plain, came with an accent Tiann could not place. He jerked his head toward the roundhouse. "Call your companions."

Tiann kept her eyes on the stranger and shouted, "Goram! Devyn! Come out." She heard stirring behind her but did not turn around.

Devyn sputtered an exclamation, and his footsteps hastened toward her. The man swung his bow in the direction of Devyn's voice.

"Don't do anything rash, Devyn," Tiann warned. "I don't know if he is alone."

"Who is he?"

"I don't know." Tiann felt Devyn's presence at her shoulder, and she leaned into it, calmed by the arm that came around her shoulder.

Goram stood on her other side.

"Why are you here?" the stranger asked.

"We should be asking you," Goram shot back. "Coritani, aren't you? A bit far from home?"

Tiann's breath caught in her throat as she studied the man. His hair, though not long, flowed free rather than caught in a plait or tied back like Iceni men. Rain dripped from it over his shoulders. The pattern of his cloak differed from any she had seen before, but the colors of the dyes were familiar. A bronze torc circled his neck above a rather ragged and dirty tunic. He was short, and though his muscles had the wiry appearance of hard use, he had a gaunt and hungry look.

"Yes. I am on a journey. A—a merchant endeavor."

Goram snorted. "If you are a merchant, then trees grow down instead of up. Why don't you lower your bow, come share a meal, and you can tell us what you are really doing."

"Will you kill me?"

Devyn stiffened. "He has just invited you to our hearth. What kind of people do you take us for?"

The man's mouth quirked again. "No insult meant, lad." He lowered the bow. "I've not been around honest folk for some time. It would be fine to sit by a fire. I'd rather keep my bowstring dry anyway. And a meal would be most welcome."

Tiann refilled the water bag, since half its contents were now spilled down the front of her clothes. Once they were all inside, she poured the water into the copper kettle from Goram's bag, then removed her wet cloak and stretched it between two wall pegs to dry. She sat as close to the fire as she could while still keeping a wary distance from the stranger. Her wet tunic steamed in the warmth.

Goram waited to speak until their bowls of hot porridge were half-eaten. "Now, tell us who you are and what you are doing here, deep in Iceni territory, by yourself and on foot. And mind yourself—the rest of our company was only a half-day's ride behind us when we set out."

Tiann noted he didn't mention that their companions had no intention of coming to the farmholding.

The stranger scooped another mouthful of porridge and swallowed before answering. "You could say I lost my way."

Goram made a noise in his throat somewhere between menace and disbelief. The stranger sighed and set his bowl down. "I suppose that is not enough. My name is Shinoc. It is true I am Coritani. And it is true I lost my way. I am here in Iceni lands to— well, to gather information."

Devyn jumped up. "You are a Coritani spy? But there is peace between us."

Goram's hand shot out, and he tugged on Devyn's wrist. "You are not a naive child anymore. Sit. Listen and learn."

Devyn's face reddened, and he scowled, but he obeyed and sat fiddling with the remains of his porridge.

Goram patted his shoulder. "Finish eating it, boy. Everything is easier when the belly is satisfied."

Shinoc grinned.

The yellowed teeth interrupted by several gaps repelled Tiann.

"Too true," the man said, and picked up his own bowl. When he could scrape out no more, he set it aside. "Perhaps you will do me the honor of your names as well?"

Tiann drew breath to speak, but Goram silenced her with a look. "No, I don't think we will," he answered. "It is enough for you to know we are Iceni, on royal business, and part of a large, well-armed company."

Tiann felt her mouth hanging open and forced herself to put

another spoonful of porridge in it. She swallowed hard. Goram was always something of an oddity in the royal household—esteemed for his expertise and character but retaining the mannerisms and ways of his humble upbringing. But Tiann had never heard him make a blatant breach of courtesy. Glancing at Devyn, she guessed his wide eyes meant he felt the same astonishment that Goram would refuse their names to a guest at their hearth.

Shinoc, however, seemed to take no offense. "Ah. So then. Is there any more in the pot?"

"You are welcome to it," Goram said.

Tiann handed a leather pad to Shinoc so he could lift the hot kettle. As she did, her sleeve fell back, revealing her scars. The man's gaze sharpened on her arm, and he hesitated to take the pad, instead taking in every detail. Tiann thrust the pad into his hand. She withdrew her arm, tugging the sleeve down.

Goram did not raise his voice, but his tone was hard. "Eat your fill and then be on your way. You are under our peace as long as you head straight back to Coritani lands." He rose and stomped out of the roundhouse, taking Shinoc's bow with him.

The Coritani man turned an unpleasant yellow grin on Tiann, then ate the rest of the porridge directly from the pot. When he finished, he wiped his mouth with his sleeve and rose.

"Thank you for the hospitality of your hearth. I'll not forget it. Or you." He left the roundhouse.

Tiann gathered the dishes from their meal in silence. The bowls rattled in her hands. Devyn started to speak, but she shook her head and hurried outside. The drizzle had stopped, and a faint sunlight attempted to break through the clouds. She filled the stone trough and scrubbed at the dishes with unnecessary force. The memories had fled from the day. The stranger's visit filled the afternoon with unease. A vague sense of danger now tainted this place where she'd once felt loved and safe.

Devyn wandered out of the roundhouse and joined her at the trough. He ran his hand along the stone surface. "The holding is neglected, but it would only take some time and work to put it right. The well, this trough, even the roundhouse and the shed are all in good condition."

Tiann looked sideways at him, shaking the water off the bowls, but said nothing.

Goram joined them from where he had been standing post by the enclosure entrance. "I believe the man has taken himself off. Let's gather our things and be ready to do likewise at first light."

Tiann nodded, but Devyn spoke in surprise. "Why leave so early? Tiann will hardly have time to look around. I was hoping you could show me favorite childhood places." He took the bowls from her and set them on the trough, then held her hands. "We can check on the apple orchard. I know I said barley, but I wouldn't mind a farmholding with apples instead." His earnest eyes searched hers. "I thought we might do some dreaming together, Tiann."

Tiann flung his hands away from her. "Dream? I don't want to dream! Don't you understand? This farmholding is abandoned because my father was killed. This place is not safe. It is not some fantasy. There are enemies creeping around, looking for a chance to harm the chief, queen, and my sisters. We don't know where that man went next! We don't know what he intends or who sent him!" Fury and tears choked her, and she screamed through it. "There isn't going to be some magical future, Devyn. Are you blind or only stupid? The only things coming are more war and loss."

Devyn's face was white. He held his hands in front of him, as though he couldn't believe she had pushed him away. "Tiann, you don't know that. Shinoc didn't seem that dangerous. He surely wouldn't harm us if he shared our meal." He looked to Goram for help.

The horse trainer shook his head. "No, she is right. We cannot trust people to keep honorable ways. Times are shifting. We need to get back and report what happened here."

They spent a miserable evening. Devyn looked stricken and barely spoke. Tiann berated herself for her harsh words but didn't know how to repair the breach she had caused. When she suggested he play his flute for them, he shook his head, then sat poking at the fire.

They settled down early for sleep, but Tiann lay awake for a long time, aware of Devyn's restless shifting. She wished she could reach across the darkness and hold his hand, but shame held her back. He didn't deserve to be blamed for her fear. When she dozed off, she dreamed of a forest reaching for her and a yellow smile leering from its depths.

THE MORNING DAWNED bright and clear, the gloom from the day before as though it had never been. While Goram and Devyn readied the horses, Tiann wandered the enclosure. Part of her ached to stay and put things right. She could picture working with Devyn in the sunshine, scything the weeds, repairing the walls, rebuilding the cookhouse. But urgency bubbled in her belly. She wanted to vault onto Gwyndolyn's back and gallop all the way back to the royal village. She wanted to hold Mara in her arms and feel her whole and safe. She cupped the scar on her arm as though she could reach Mara through the blood they had mingled.

Pushing the horses and taking only brief rest breaks, by midday Tiann, Goram, and Devyn reached the village where the rest of the traveling party had stayed. Their companions, not expecting them until nightfall or the next day, gathered around them in a flurry of questions while they unloaded their packs and rubbed the horses down. Goram answered with short vagaries. As soon as they fed and watered the horses, he signaled to the other leaders, and they disappeared into the roundhouse of the village elder.

Tiann found minor tasks to keep herself busy — mending a worn strap on her pack, helping grind grain for bread. She avoided Devyn but was acutely aware of him. She watched him from under her lashes as she worked.

He seemed to have recovered his usual good humor, laughing and playing with the village children at a game that was part obstacle course, part mock battle. Two boys stood in a small handcart and Devyn pulled them around rocks and stumps, galloping and whinnying. From the opposite direction, another "horse and chariot" approached. All the young charioteers whooped, doing their fierce best to imitate a battle cry. They waved long reeds for spears and wore woven grass torcs around their necks. Rhythmically wielding the hand stone against the quern, Tiann smiled at their antics, while the nutty aroma of the ground grain rose with the fine dust.

Emerging from the elder's roundhouse, Goram was nearly run down, jumping back as the handcart rattled past him. He watched the game with narrowed eyes, and Tiann's amusement faded at his grim expression.

She scooped the ground grain into the storage jar, then stood and dusted off her hands. Joining Goram, she asked, "What have the leaders decided?"

"We are going to split up. You, Devyn, and I will head back to the royal village. The rest will finish the journey." Goram paused, eyes on the children, who had now jumped down from the "chariots" to thrust and parry with sticks. "I'm sorry you won't be able to go on, it being your first time and all. But the chief and queen will want to hear from all three of us about the stranger."

Fighting a pang of envy for the others who would get to see

the rest of Iceni territory, Tiann nodded. "I'll be ready at first light." All the children had now joined the mock battle behind their "chiefs" and were shouting threats and insults at the opposing tribe. For a moment, a red veil descended over Tiann's sight. "They shouldn't fight each other. The tribes shouldn't fight. The old enmity will bring us down." She blinked, and the red was gone. She turned to find Goram staring at her. Her words hovered in the air between them. *Why did I say that?* A deep sadness rose within her and she wished she could be slung tight against her father's back, his hair tickling her cheek. Safe.

Tiann, Goram, and Devyn kept a punishing pace back to the royal village. Divested of all excess weight in their packs, they pushed the horses, alternating between a trot and a fast walk. They cut away from the sea along the ancient path, not bothering to veer off to find comfortable lodgings in nearby villages. They slept rough by the path, taking turns keeping watch through the nights, weapons at the ready.

By the time they rode into the village paddock at noon on the third day, Tiann only wanted a meal and her bed. Her eyes were gritty from the dust of the ride and lack of rest. She slid off Gwyndolyn's back as people surrounded them with exclamations of surprise. She reached for the reins, preparing to lead Gwyndolyn into the stable and rub her down, water, and feed her.

But Goram took the leather straps and handed them to one of the horse trainers. "Take care of the mounts."

Tiann looked at him, astonished. Goram always insisted that the rider care for the horse, and that before doing anything else. He nodded sharply, took her elbow, and steered her toward the hall. "Special circumstances, Tiann. We didn't push them for no reason."

They found the queen and chief in the hall, conferring with the farmer in charge of the barley fields. Boudica caught sight of them first and held up her hand to halt the conversation. The others swiveled their heads, and Prasudoc strode toward the trio, putting out his arm to grip Goram's, then Devyn's. He gathered Tiann into an embrace, all the while shooting questions. "Goram! Why are you back so soon? Is everyone with you? What happened? Is there an injury? Was there trouble?"

Meanwhile, Boudica murmured a dismissal to the farmer, who nodded and left. She guided the group to a table, and they sat on the benches. "I've asked for some food for you and water to wash. Husband, let them talk." Boudica touched Prasudoc lightly on the mouth with an affectionate gesture.

Goram cleared his throat. "In truth, we don't know if our news is trouble or not. But it seemed important enough to tell you and let you decide for yourselves. No, Chief, the rest of the party did not come back with us. They are continuing the journey as planned. But something happened when Tiann, Devyn, and I went to visit the old farmstead of Tiann's father. Something unsettling enough that I felt it better to return and tell you at once."

The cook entered with two of her helpers, carrying a platter of food, a pitcher and cups, and a steaming washbowl. When they set them down, Boudica nodded her thanks and set about pouring water.

Goram seized a cup and drank it down in long gulps, and Tiann, vaguely comforted to see that she was not the only one who had found the ride home difficult, followed his example. They then joined Devyn, who was plying his hands and face with a warm, wet cloth from the washbowl.

Feeling a bit refreshed, Tiann sat back down, reaching for bread. Boudica refilled the cups, and between mouthfuls Tiann, Devyn, and Goram told the story of their visit to the farmholding.

When they recounted how Shinoc had held a bow on Tiann, Prasudoc pounded his fist on the table and Boudica cursed quietly. Their frowns deepened at the revelation that Shinoc was a Coritani spy.

"Perhaps I should have followed him," Goram said at the conclusion of the tale. "I keep asking myself that. But it seemed better at the time to remain together."

"Especially because of the way he kept looking at Tiann," Devyn burst out. "Like he was marking her down on a Roman accounting scroll."

"It was my fault," Goram said. "I told him we were on royal business. I wanted him to think we were not alone and there would be repercussions if any harm came to us. He may not know exactly who Tiann is, but he knows she's in the royal family. And he knows how to recognize her." He nodded toward her scarred arm. "That's why I thought it better to stay together, in case the scoundrel had fellows and they tried to abduct her for ransom."

Tiann choked on a sip of water. She had not considered that being a member of the royal family might cut two ways. Protection, yes. But also risk. No wonder Boudica and Prasudoc's children were not allowed to journey beyond the royal village until they had seen sixteen summers. A tinge of red blurred the edge of her vision. *This is Boudica's weakness. Her children. She is a wise and good ruler, shrewd and cautious, as well as powerful. But if we are harmed . . .* The tinge spread, then receded. Tiann set down her cup, seeing in a daze that it sloshed a little, as her hand shook.

"You were right to do so," Prasudoc assured Goram. "We will send out scouts to see if we can determine where he went. You three finish your meal, wash off your travel dust, and rest. We can talk more later."

∾

Tiann shifted the staff in her hand, seeking the balance point before her opponent reached her. *There.* It was farther down than she thought, one end weighted with a dense knot. She lifted and twirled the awkward weapon, parrying the blow from the enemy who charged her. She dropped the staff and moved on to the next, eyes on the opponent who had started running across the training field the moment the staff had hit the ground. The next weapon was light and slender, balanced but insubstantial. She had only a breath to decide how to wield it before he was upon her.

"Under the ribs!" The instructor bawled from across the field.

Tiann ducked the attacker's blow, came up under his arm, and disarmed him with a twist of her weapon.

"Follow up!" the instructor commanded.

Tiann swung her staff toward her fellow trainee's head, checking at the last moment.

Breathing heavily at the end of the exercise, she swiped her arm across her eyes and forehead, wiping back sweat and the wisps of damp hair that had escaped her braids. All across the field, young warriors were engaged in training, trampling the grass, coached by their elders. She swung her arms over her head, stretching her back and shoulders, glad she would not go back to the hall with new bruises today. When her heart slowed, she shook out her stiff ankle, preparing to complete the morning's training with a run around the village's perimeter. Removing her leather boot, she pulled a long strip of cloth from the pouch at her waist and wrapped her foot up to the shin. She pulled the boot back on, taking care to lace it firmly. She began with an easy jog, settling into a steady, if syncopated, gait as her tendons and muscles warmed. She had grown used to ignoring the slight anxiety that the old injury would betray her. Twice in the years since the initial healing, she had fallen in agony, having rolled the ankle over in a dip of the ground. The bones had not broken, but she'd lain for weeks each time, with a swollen and colored limb while the sprains healed.

As she approached the boundary stone near the barley field, a warbler sounded from the forest beyond. Tiann slowed, listening hard. The birdcall came again, and she glimpsed a flash of light. Smiling, she veered in that direction, maintaining her pace. With a glance behind her, she entered the cool green and slowed to a walk, waiting.

Mara landed with a thump in the path in front of her.

Tiann laughed and looked up to the branch where her friend had perched, now bouncing wildly. "You're not content to sing like a bird—now you must make nests in trees?" She flung her arm over Mara's slight shoulders.

The bronze pendant Mara had used to signal her hung from a strip of leather between her sharp collarbones. There was no answering smile on Mara's face. Rather, a crease settled between her eyebrows that Tiann only saw on rare occasions, like when visitors arrived.

"I needed to be high so I could hide but also see the training fields. I've been waiting all morning. I heard something last night, but I think Mother suspects. She will know I was listening if she saw me pull you aside to speak in private."

"What do you mean, 'she suspects'? You were there in the chamber with the ambassadors, weren't you?"

The night before, a ripple of astonishment had gone through the hall when the formal contingent of Coritani arrived. They had been ushered into a small chamber and served with a meal and water to wash. The royal family had gathered in the queen and chief's apartment, where they'd received the visitors.

Tiann had entered the hall late, after doctoring a gash in a horse's fetlock, with Goram. Devyn had told her the news in a whispered rush. Tiann had opted to stay away from the meeting, rather than interrupt. In any case, she'd needed to wash and change out of her bloodstained, horse-smudged clothes.

"Yes." Mara grabbed Tiann's hand and pulled her deeper into the woods. "Yes, I went in first. I sat on that little stool in the corner. You know the one."

Tiann nodded. The low seat was positioned out of the line of sight of people sitting in the visitors' chairs, in the shadow on the edge of the light cast by the central brazier. It was Mara's typical spot when circumstances required her to attend when strangers were present.

"So the queen knew you were there. Why would she be angry?"

"I didn't stay there. I lost my nerve. I hid behind that hanging loom Aife is using to weave Father's new cloak. It takes up practically the whole back wall."

Tiann pulled Mara to a stop. "She would understand. Besides, if you were meant to be there anyway, you could have heard nothing too secret."

"No. Listen to me, Tiann! Stop trying to reassure me. This isn't even the important part. I don't really care about Mother being angry. We need to make a plan to change her mind before we talk to her."

Tiann sat on a boulder. "I'm sorry. Tell me, then."

"I could see a little through the weave. Mother and Father came in, then Aife. They noticed I wasn't there, but Father said not to trouble about it. Then Shal came in, and Mother asked if he knew why the Coritani sent messengers. He said no but that he had heard rumors that the Coritani had lands and goods seized by the Romans on the pretext of keeping their allies secure. The guests entered with a handful of our warriors. Their druid and Shal knew each other and greeted each other. The room was crowded now, and one of the Coritani warriors stood with his back to me. I could have touched him through the weaving, and he blocked my view. I was afraid to breathe, in case he heard me.

"They are here to negotiate a new peace treaty. Their chief sent them because the Romans are using any unrest as an excuse to step in and take control. They call it Pax Romana. The tribes can't afford harrying raids or blood feuds."

Tiann moved over. "Mara, stop pacing and sit. The envoys are right. Every day the queen and chief play a dancing game with the Romans. One false step would spell disaster for the Iceni."

Mara ignored her plea to sit, twisting her fingers together. "I know. I know! We cannot continue on the present path. We would destroy our future. The Romans would not tolerate a disturbance of their peace."

"Then this is a good thing. Perhaps our tribes can make a lasting treaty."

"It is not a good thing." Mara's voice was a croak, and tears streamed down her face.

Tiann grabbed her hands and pulled her down on the boulder.

Mara laid her head on Tiann's shoulder, gulping back sobs. Raising her head, she looked into Tiann's face. "They said their chief would restrain his warriors on our borders. No, wait"—she put her hand over Tiann's mouth to stave off her interruption—"they dismissed everyone, even Aife, except the druids. Shal and Pleta, the Coritani advisor. The rest of the terms came out. The Coritani chief insists on an exchange of hostages. Royal hostages."

CHAPTER

SEVEN

Tiann's heart thudded. There were only a few members of the royal family—not like in other tribes. Neither Boudica nor Prasudoc came from large clans. Two cousins had been killed in the conflict with the Romans that had taken Tiann's father. Another had died in childbirth, along with the baby. The chief had a living uncle, but he was old and infirm. The journey itself might kill him.

Fresh tears flowed from Mara's eyes. "It has to be me. By Iceni law, the rulers and the heir cannot act as hostages. I'm the only one."

Tiann's throat closed. Wordless, she took Mara's hand and held the palm to her scarred arm. They were sisters, and more. What happened to one of them happened to the other. Tiann pictured their mingled blood in her body. She would find a way to protect Mara.

Tiann brought Mara to the stable. Prasudoc's prize hound had whelped, but one pup was sickly with a wheeze that could be felt with a finger laid to his chest. Tiann settled her friend in a corner cushioned with hay and gave her the tiny wriggling thing. She showed her how to dip a cloth in milk and drip it into the pup's mouth. By the time Tiann left, the pup was sucking at the cloth and Mara's body had relaxed into a contented concentration.

Searching for Shal, Tiann circled the problem with her thoughts. Sending Mara to the Coritani was out of the question. Even as an honored hostage, well treated and respected, Mara would wither among strangers, away from her family and village. Surely the queen and chief could see that! But Mara was right about the other side of the conundrum. There was no one else.

Walking through the village, Tiann absently returned greetings, keeping alert for a glimpse of Shal's tall figure. She rubbed at the scars on her arm, thinking back to the bonding ritual in the oak circle and how Shal had made her feel safe. She could trust his wisdom to find a way. *A blood bond means you are united,* he had said. *You agree to defend each other.* Tiann peered into the jeweler's workshop, where Shal often consulted with the craftsmen about designs. *United.* Tiann's feet skittered to a stop. For a moment, the memory of golden eyes filled her vision, overlaying the busy courtyard around her. *Remember the wounds,* Elior had told her that night by the sea. *United. That is the answer. Remember the wounds.* She turned back and hurried to the hall. *I can save her. I can be her protector. That must be it.*

Heedless of a stool she knocked over, Tiann wove through the main room and reached the royal apartment.

The warrior guarding the door raised his eyebrows. "Hello, Tiann. Do you need to speak to the queen? She is with the chief and Shal. I can ask if they will see you."

"Yes please." Tiann raised her hands to smooth her hair, suddenly aware she was still dressed for training.

The warrior grinned. "They are used to you by now." He opened the door and ducked through.

Tiann tried to gather her thoughts while waiting. When the guard came back out, he gestured for Tiann to enter. She took a deep breath and stepped through the doorway.

Boudica paced. Shal stood with his hand on Prasudoc's slumped shoulder.

"This is not the best time," the chief said.

Tiann's heart ached when he raised his face and she saw his red-rimmed eyes. "I know, my chief." Tiann moved toward him. "But I have the answer."

"My dear, I know you wish to help, but the problem is not what you think." Boudica's tone was hard.

Tiann winced but plowed on. "Forgive me, but I believe I understand. You think you must send Mara to be a hostage. There is another way."

Boudica stopped her pacing and faced Tiann. "How do you know this? We have told no one. Shal"—she swiveled her head slightly but kept her gaze on Tiann's face—"is this the sight? Can she listen in on us?"

Tiann sucked in her breath. *He told them. Do they think I can hear their private thoughts?*

But he was shaking his head. "No, Lady, I think not. She sometimes receives a gift of warning or knowledge, but not like this."

"Mara told me. She was here, behind the loom." Tiann's revelation startled Prasudoc into a chuckle, which collapsed into a sob.

"She has always been able to melt away, so no one notices her." He sank into a chair and put his head into his hands.

Tiann rushed to him, stumbling a little, until she knelt in front of him. "My chief—my father, do not trouble yourself. There is another way. That's why I'm here. It doesn't need to be Mara. I will go."

Prasudoc took her hands in his. "A blessing on your kind heart, daughter. I know you mean it. But the hostage must be from the royal family."

"I know. My parents were not royal. And I do not claim that

for myself. But Mara is, and she is part of me. We are united. She is my blood sister."

"Yes, and you could not be more our daughter if you had been born to us. But this is the Iceni practice—"

"Wait." Shal's command interrupted the chief. "Let me think a moment."

Boudica, Prasudoc, and Tiann watched him as he stood looking into the flame of the brazier, pushing his sleeve up and down. "I think . . . maybe . . ." He turned to Boudica. "We all took a vow and stood with her."

Boudica nodded, as though an idea was spreading to her from Shal. "Yes. Yes. And in the circle too. It was more."

Prasudoc looked hopefully back and forth between the two of them. "The Coritani would accept our adoption?"

Shal sat, his face thoughtful. "I'm not sure. Their ways of inheritance differ from ours. For them, an adopted child could never be an heir. But the druids would certainly accept it and uphold the claim that Tiann may act as a royal. And in Iceni law, an adopted child with a blood bond to royalty can act as proxy or even regent. You would do no wrong to send Tiann."

"But if the Coritani would not accept her?" Prasudoc objected. "They would not honor the treaty."

Boudica resumed her pacing. "They have not seen Mara nor Tiann. They might not even know their names."

"We cannot be dishonest!"

"But, my chief, it would not be dishonest." Tiann squeezed Prasudoc's hands. "In one way, Mara and I are two different people. It is true. But in another, we are one. United. And that is just as true."

Prasudoc looked down where she knelt in front of him. "Oh, child, do you know what you are asking? You would go to live among strangers, away from your tribe. For at least a turning of a year. You are so young, almost as young as Mara."

A tremor shook Tiann. *No, I haven't thought it through. I just know I must protect Mara. Would the Coritani let me continue training? Do they have horses? Gwyndolyn! How can I go a year without riding her? I wouldn't go to the sea on the next journey. And Devyn . . . but I can't think about him now.*

"Father, I am at least old enough that I have journeyed. Mara has not left the village. And even if I had not—Mara cannot go. You know she cannot."

Boudica stilled, as though she had lost all energy. Sitting next to her husband, she put her hand on Tiann's head. "How can I let any of my girls go? We have trained you for battle, for thinking, for running a household, for hunting, and a hundred other things. We never thought you would need to know how to live among strangers."

"But I do know that." Tiann's voice choked. "Life trained me. Was I not a stranger when I came to the royal village? Was I not alone when my father died? And yet I still found a good life, a new family. Sorrow did not kill me, nor being among people I did not know. But for Mara, how could she bear it?"

"Let me think on it." Shal's words drew Tiann's attention back to him, and she stood to face him. "I will go to the circle and consider the matter. Tomorrow I will advise you. For now, be at peace. Spend the evening with your family."

Shal left the room with a heavy tread, and Tiann hesitated, torn between hurrying after him and staying with the chief and queen, who looked undone. She murmured a parting and slipped out.

"Shal!" Tiann broke into a trot, trying to catch up to him.

He never looked like he was hurrying, gliding in the long garment that marked his vocation, but his long legs ate distances in gulps.

"Shal!"

He hesitated midstride, as though trying to decide whether to stop for her. He paused a moment as she reached him, then turned. He had dark smudges under his eyes, and the lines around his mouth seemed carved more deeply.

"It's right, isn't it? That I go? Why do you need to go to the circle? What will you learn there?"

Shal sighed, looking over her shoulder into the distance. "I don't know, child. I am unsettled. Everything seems as a dark cloud. For Mara to go is wrong. But when I consider you taking her place . . . the world feels out of joint, like what is supposed to hold us together is missing. But I cannot see what the missing piece is or where it fits."

"But the oak circle will make it all clear, won't it? Then you will see."

Shal closed his eyes on whatever invisible conflict he had been seeing. "Ahh, I hope so. Truly, I hope so." His lashes quivered, and he opened his eyes to gaze on Tiann's upturned face. Her breath hitched at the unshed tears and uncertainty in his expression. "Tell me, Tiann. Did you have a vision? Or did the golden-eyed man come to you?"

"N-No." The searching in Shal's voice made her ache to reassure him. "But I recalled what he said. 'Remember the wounds.' What else could he have meant? When you go to the circle, you will understand." *Won't you? Won't you? If we cannot trust the wisdom of the circle and the druid way, then what will become of us?* "Surely you will understand then."

Shal nodded, pressed a hand to her shoulder, and left her there. Tiann watched his tall figure moving swiftly away. Helplessness seeped into the crevices where certainty had leaked out with Shal's doubt. The buoyancy that had carried her into the hall to offer her plan to Boudica and Prasudoc vanished, replaced with a heavy dread. Clenching her fists, she expelled a forceful breath. There was no other choice. Shal would receive wisdom in the circle, and all would be well. She would spend a turning of the year as a hostage, Mara would be safe and unafraid, the tribes would be at peace, and the Romans would have no reason to intervene. Afterward, life would continue as it should.

THAT EVENING the hall buzzed with speculation regarding the visit from the Coritani contingent. Boudica, Prasudoc, and Shal did not make an appearance. Tiann wondered what she would hear if she crouched below the windows, as she and Mara used to do. Had Shal returned without her noticing, or was he still wrestling with questions in the darkening oak circle? She wanted to reassure Mara, but until the matter was settled, she didn't know how. She kept watch on the door, hoping Shal would come through, ducking his head slightly, serenity and confidence on his face.

Mara sat in her usual place beside her with the pup tucked into a looped fold in her cloak. "He breathes easier when he is close to me," she said in response to Tiann's raised brow.

Tiann's throat tightened. *So do I.* Feigning a stern expression, she said, "You had better check him all over for fleas before you bring him into our sleeping chamber. I'm not going to scratch for the next moon because you are smitten with a hound."

Mara smiled, but the crease between her eyebrows remained.

BOUDICA AND PRASUDOC reemerged the following morning, and the day proceeded like any other. Just before dusk, Shal walked into the village, looking every bit like a man who had spent a night sleepless in the wood. Tiann sat in the last of the sunshine with Boudica, listening to Aife talk about her plans to pair two of the three-year mares for chariot training. Seeing Shal, Tiann jumped up to intercept him. Boudica seized her arm and held her in place.

Shal disappeared into his roundhouse without a glance or word to anyone.

"Go ask one of the men to bring him water to wash."

"I can bring it to him." Tiann tugged her arm.

"No. Let him be until he is ready, Tiann." The queen held her a heartbeat more, then released her. "Do as I say."

"Yes, Lady." Tiann hoped the queen couldn't hear the frustration in her voice. She requested the washing water, then lingered about the courtyard, watching the man go in with a steaming pitcher and come out after a moment. What if Shal went to sleep? She couldn't bear it if she had to wait another night for his counsel. She performed useless chores, waiting for him, until full dark crept across the village and her stomach grumbled for its meal.

The hall glowed with extra torches, the light reaching to the far curves of the walls. A traveling bard, newly arrived and invited for the evening, had finished eating and was sitting in the center, tuning his harp. People crowded the tables, and Tiann sidled through to where the royal family sat. She grabbed bread and scooped some grain and meat from the broth pot into her bowl just as the platters were being cleared away to be redistributed at the laborers' tables. Dipping her bread, she glanced at Mara and saw that she still had a squirming, knotted bulge in her cloak, to which she was secreting bits of broth-soaked bread.

The bard thrummed a commanding chord, and a wave of stillness swept over the room.

"I bring you greetings!" His voice, though not loud, filled the space, rounding to reach the walls and seeming to make the light grow warmer. His words carried an accent Tiann had never heard. "I share with you a song from a far land and a far people."

"There will be silence and shouting
     And gathering.

104

Answers of deeds and wonder
And feasting.
All dusty edges of earth and trickling edges of sea
And high-girded mountains,
Still. Cease. Still.
The roar and tumult of the people,
Still.
There will be silence and shouting
And exulting.
Rising sun and setting sun
And overflow.
Stream full and grain prepared
Furrow watered.
Abundance and settling
And softening.
Blessed. Crowned. Blessed.
Paths dripping fatness.
Blessed.
Hills are girded and meadows clothed
And valleys covered.
There will be singing and shouting
And silence."

THE HALL RANG with the fading notes of the harp and the bard's voice. Tiann could not even blink as the moment shimmered in the air.

Boudica rose, the sound of her seat scraping back loud in the hush. She walked to the center of the room, unclasping a large golden brooch from her shoulder. The bard sat with his head bent over his harp, eyes closed, lips moving soundlessly. The queen pinned the brooch to his plain tunic. "Please come join us at our table before you sing again." She raised her hand toward the door and made a beckoning gesture.

Shal stood there against the far wall. The torchlight reflected off the tears on his cheeks.

As the bard followed Boudica back toward where the royal family sat, talk and laughter resumed in the hall. Platters and pitchers were fetched again, and conversations turned to everyday matters. Shal joined them at the table, and they all sat listening to the bard tell news he had gathered in Gaul and in other parts of Albion.

"Of course, many are following the Romans and calling your island Britannia now."

"Our island? Then you are not from here." Boudica refilled his cup. "I cannot place your speech."

"Ah, there is not a person who can, Lady. I spent many years in service to a chief in Gaul. But I was born in Anatolia and lived there with my family until my fourteenth winter. Brigands raided our village, and I found myself sold as a slave several times, always westward, until I ended in Gaul. The chief valued my skill as a bard and granted me my freedom in exchange for a vow to stay with him until his death. My obligation ended two years ago. So the many places where my tongue has spoken have colored my speech."

He told the story like a tale often recounted. Tiann stole glances at him, trying to imagine such a life. He was not old, maybe only twenty-five summers. He conversed with the queen and chief with an easy smile and untroubled expression. Although he was respectful, he did not seem overawed by the royal family. He had a tranquility about him that somehow fit well with his lively wit and genuine interest in the people around him.

The talk grew more animated as the evening went on, and under the cover of the raucous conversation, the bard pinned Shal with a piercing gaze. Tiann, sitting just to the left of them, sensed a change in the tone of their conversation, and her ears pricked up.

"The light you have been looking for has come, Seeker," the bard said.

Shal started with uncharacteristic clumsiness, spilling Prasudoc's mead.

The chief nudged Shal and roared with good-natured laughter. "Well, that's enough for you, my esteemed friend, but you didn't have to cut me off too!" He gestured down the table for the pitcher to refill his cup, chuckling at Shal's blunder.

Shal turned urgently back to the bard. "What, what . . ." he sputtered. "What do you mean, the light. . ."

The bard looked back at him steadily. "Meet me by the oak tomorrow at dawn and travel with me awhile."

Shal stared at him, then nodded once. The druid rose, dipped his head to Boudica and Prasudoc, and left the hall.

Tiann watched him go, baffled at what could have caused his strong reaction. She turned back to their guest, questions on her lips. Around the man a glow shimmered, gold and translucent, filled with peace and energy. Tiann stared, the questions dying. A deep longing, like grief, filled her. Tears blurred her vision, and she blinked hard.

When she looked back, the glow was gone. The bard sipped at his mead. He smiled at the lively commotion of people playing dice games, comparing the workmanship of their daggers, and in one area, demonstrating the tactics of a famous battle from a generation ago. Tiann wanted to demand that the bard explain what he had said to upset Shal. Was Shal going to leave the village with him? What could be so important? Her chest ached with tightness. She needed him. She needed him to reassure her that being the hostage for the peace treaty would be all right. That she could save Mara from the extreme distress it would have caused her and then come back to resume Tiann's life. She wanted Shal to help her break the news to Devyn, who was even now trying to catch her attention across the hall.

Tiann leaned forward to mouth a request for withdrawal. At the queen's nod of permission, she made her way through the throng to Devyn. He broke into a wide smile when he saw her coming, and looked around for a bench. Finding one only half-occupied near the wall, he grabbed her hand and led her to it. Seeing her settled, he took his cup to a nearby table for more mead, then rejoined her. Sitting with his legs stretched in front of him, he leaned back against the wall with a contented sigh. "Have you ever heard a song like that? Something about it . . ." He waved his hand, as though helpless to find the words.

"Yes, I know." Tiann wanted to tell Devyn about the bard inviting Shal to travel with him, how Shal had seemed shaken and cryptic ever since the Coritani embassy had come. But she couldn't share her concerns without also telling him that she had offered to leave for a year as a guarantor of the peace treaty. If the queen and chief had not told the tribe about the negotiations, she could not break the confidence. Devyn would not find it odd that Shal wanted to spend time with the bard. The druid often journeyed with no warning, coming back days or weeks later with news, or unfamiliar medicines, or even an occasional apprentice who would spend a season among them learning from Shal.

The wall felt cool and rough against her back, somehow comforting in the room filled with the heat of bodies and extra torches. She pressed into the texture of the daubed wall and took a long breath. She wouldn't worry about it now. Tomorrow she would remind Shal that he was needed here. He wouldn't just leave in the middle of the negotiations without speaking to Boudica and Prasudoc.

The bard returned to his harp. He filled the rest of the evening with songs and stories of heroes and lovers, both exciting and humorous. Tiann sat with her back against the cool wall, her hip and shoulder warm against Devyn's, enthralled or laughing with the rest of the company. Devyn reached over and took her hand, and when she looked at him, he smiled with a little pucker between his brows. Tiann pressed her palm against his. His forehead smoothed out, and he spread his fingers to entwine with hers. Their matching calluses scraped together, but the smooth parts of her skin tingled where it met his. She felt frightened of this new closeness and the sudden sharp longing to see where it would lead.

Will he be angry when he finds out what I've offered to do? Would he want to wait? Shal will help me. I'll ask him tomorrow what I should say to Devyn. But what if he really leaves with that man? Her focus returned to the bard, who was singing a ridiculous song about a sheep who went hunting with a fox. His audience roared with laughter. Was this the same man who had silenced them all with his song earlier in the evening? What was it that had cast the spell and moved even Shal to tears? What was Shal seeking that the bard claimed to know? Could it be more important than the peace treaty? *No. No. Surely not. Shal would never leave without advising the queen and chief. He would never leave me when I need him.*

CHAPTER

EIGHT

Tiann woke to a weight on her chest and something wet tickling her chin. She opened her eyes to Mara's pup, who wriggled and licked her entire face. Capturing the squirming creature, she planted a kiss on its soft head before calling out, "Mara, if you will not keep this little nuisance in your bed, I will put him in the chicken coop."

Mara's face emerged from its burrow in her bed, sleepy eyes crinkling with laughter.

"Give him here, then." Mara reached thin arms across the narrow space between their beds. Cradling the pup under her chin, she crooned, "You mustn't wake Tiann. You want to stay here with me and not with those nasty chickens, don't you? No licking that cranky girl when the sun is barely up."

The sun barely up? Alarmed, Tiann sat up, noticing the light filtering in the crack between the thatch ceiling and the walls. They had all gone to their bed late, listening to the bard into the night. Surely the bard himself was still resting. He couldn't have risen so early to meet Shal after entertaining them for so long. *And besides, Shal would have thought better of his agreement to leave with the bard.*

Tiann pulled on her tunic with panicked hands. She pushed aside the bedchamber curtain, hardly registering Mara's surprised questions, and raced through the hall. Many of last night's revelers lay here and there, stretched out on benches or the floor. Boudica and Prasudoc sat together at the head table, talking with their heads together and sharing bread. They looked up at her entrance. Seeing that Shal was not with them, Tiann called a good morning and hastened outside.

The village was just beginning to stir in the slight warming of dawn. She walked to Shal's roundhouse, hesitating a moment at the entrance. It was so early. Maybe he still slept. But her need to reassure herself he was still there overcame her courtesy. She rapped at the wicker-framed door. "Shal?" At the silence, she rapped and called again, louder. She pushed the door open and peered inside. Weak sunlight filtered in, revealing Shal's simple furnishings. His central fire was cold and his bed pallet neatly folded. The pegs where his clothes would hang were bare.

Heart pounding, she let the door clatter shut. She began to run. Her ankle felt stiff and sore. A light breeze whipped her unbraided hair into her eyes. As she passed the paddock, a nicker greeted her. Gwyndolyn pawed the earth near the fence. Tiann paused, considering her pace, hampered by the old injury. She had not taken the time to bind up her ankle or stretch it. She opened the gate and called for the horse. Gripping the mane, Tiann boosted herself with the fence post and sprang to the mare's back. Squeezing with her knees, she leaned forward and urged Gwyndolyn toward the forest.

Within the greenness, murky from the earliness of the day, the air was colder. Tiann bent low over Gwyndolyn's neck, slowing her to a walk, avoiding the branches that threatened to sweep her off the mare's bare back. They picked their way through to the concealed entrance to the oak circle. Tiann dismounted, loosely hobbling Gwyndolyn with her belt. She left the mare nosing at a patch of grass and slipped along the stone passage into the circle.

The clearing was still in deep shadow, and she walked the perimeter to be sure. Empty. She wandered to the spring, drew out the cup in its stone niche, and saw markings on the clay surface. She carried the cup to a brighter spot to scrutinize it. With a bit of charcoal, someone had drawn three symbols: a simple harp, a triple spiral like those in the tunnel cavern, and a six-armed star with the top point curled over in a hook.

Tiann understood the message. The harp belonged to the bard and the spiral to Shal. They were together. She didn't understand the third symbol. Was another traveling with them? A bleak numbness floated through her. She sat on the moss by the spring. The sun penetrated the thicket and made the dew sparkle. But now the beauty of the place meant nothing. She wanted to cry from frustration, from abandonment, from confusion. She rolled to her knees on the damp earth and cupped the icy water to her lips and drank. After a hesitation, she cupped her hands again and this time let the water spill from her fingers toward the oak. She closed her eyes and waited, but instead of the turmoil draining from her, she only felt it well up like the spring, then burst forth in a torrent. The wrenching sobs aching in her chest tore out of her with an ugly, agonizing force. She threw her head back and beat her fists on her knees.

The torrent retreated to a trickle, but she knew it was only the resignation of exhaustion. The pressure would soon rebuild. She lay down beside the spring, feeling the wetness seep through her clothing. She dabbled her hand in the water, letting it go numb from the cold. Shal had not found wisdom here but had gone searching. Perhaps there was not a way to wisdom. But even as she mulled over the thought, her heart thumped in painful beats of panic. She sat up, pulling her hand from the water. She rubbed the life back into her fingers fiercely. Then she stood and walked out of the circle.

Gwyndolyn pricked her ears forward when Tiann emerged from between the stones. Rubbing the mare's soft nose, Tiann whispered, "Where did he go? Why would he leave?" The horse lowered her head to nuzzle the front of Tiann's tunic. "Everything seemed so clear yesterday. They would all agree that I should go, and Mara would be safe, and Shal would make sure the path was smooth. Now what?" She put her arms around Gwyndolyn's neck, breathing in the warm, musky scent of her.

The horse shifted so that Tiann leaned into her. "Or maybe he would have come back from the circle with a brilliant idea, and then no one would need to go and we could still have peace." The horse snuffled into Tiann's unbound hair. "At the least, he needs to help tell people. Devyn will be disappointed, maybe even hurt. And Mara . . ." She pressed her face harder into Gwyndolyn's shoulder. The truth was, she had avoided thinking of how Mara would react. But she knew. "Mara will be furious. She will never agree." Boudica would hold her own emotions in check and resolutely proceed with the plan. Prasudoc would offer sincere but clumsy comfort and likely treat Mara as a child, infuriating her even more. Aife would bury herself in training and household management, trying to avoid the strife. Only Shal could be depended upon to look into the heart, to offer words both truthful and kind.

And yet even solid Shal seemed shaken these past days. Tiann heaved a breath, and another. She stroked Gwyndolyn's neck. "Thank you, my friend. Thank you for listening to me." Her legs felt leaden, so she retrieved her belt and led the mare to a stone to mount. They broke out of the forest into full sunlight and headed back to the village.

~

THE FULL MOON had waned to dark sleep and begun to wake again, and still Shal had not returned. The Coritani delegation was due to return any day, and the queen grew fretful. More than once Mara retreated, bewildered, from Boudica's temper. Tiann heard her sniffle sometimes in the night, and she longed to reassure her blood sister that she had nothing to fear. But until the queen and chief announced the terms of the treaty, Tiann was bound to silence.

Tiann perched on a stool with a wad of coarse grass, scrubbing at the mud caking her boots. After a week of wet feet, she'd given up trying to ignore that her boots needed care and had come in from the training field an hour before dusk to tend them. The deerskin softened under her ministrations, and she exchanged the grass for a sharpened stick. She used the point to pick the dirt out of each small lacing hole. When the leather was free of debris, she wiped the boots once more with clean grass, then picked up a pot of grease. Holding the pot in her palm and a boot between her knees, she rubbed the pungent stuff into the leather, careful to work it into each crevice. She was reaching to tend to the laces when she saw a figure in dark robes by the courtyard gate.

The man strolled into the courtyard, inspecting his surroundings. Tiann rose to greet him but stopped in consternation when he opened the door to Shal's dwelling and stepped inside. She froze, unsure if she was imagining things. Who would commit such a disrespect as to enter a dwelling without announcing himself and waiting for a reply? The stranger reemerged, wrinkling his nose with an expression of disgust.

Tiann's body sprang forward. "Greetings, visitor." She made the formal greeting, but even she could hear the outrage in her voice.

He looked her up and down, and an unfamiliar flush of shame swept through her. She was acutely aware of her training clothes, the smell of grease on her hands, and the laces trailing from her fingers. She tightened her lips and straightened her spine, refusing to let her gaze drop from his.

"Tell me where to find your chief." He held his voluminous robe closer, as though worried she would somehow sully it. Sniffing, he moved toward the hall. "Is he within?"

Tiann's breath froze inside her, and she opened her mouth but could think of no reply to his rudeness.

His glare returned to her. "Is. Your. Chief. In. The. Hall."

Exhaling in a whoosh, she glared back. "No, sir." The courtesy tasted sour on her lips. "He is yet on the training field. However, the queen is within."

"Very well."

Tiann stared after him as he glided away. When he disappeared into the hall, she shook herself and hurried to gather her boots and follow him. Her eyes took a few moments to adjust to the dimmer light in the hall. The stranger stood before the queen, where she sat with a sword and whetstone. He bowed, speaking too low for Tiann to hear. The queen inclined her head and handed the weapon and stone to one of her women. Rising, she gestured for the stranger to accompany her to the royal apartment.

Mara appeared by Tiann's side, her approach quiet as a wisp of fog. "That man. I remember him. He was here once before, when I was little."

"Well, he is the rudest man I ever saw. He didn't even exchange a greeting with me. He went into Shal's dwelling without announcing himself! Why is the queen speaking with him?" Tiann kept her voice to a whisper with some effort.

Mara took the boots out of Tiann's clenched fingers and headed to their chamber. Tiann followed, looking over her shoulder at the passage to the royal apartment, expecting to see the man expelled at any moment. Within the chamber, Mara set the boots down and put a finger to her lips. "Not here."

"But who is he?"

"Not here, Tiann. Come to the woods and I'll tell you. Let's bring a torch."

When they reached the point where the path plunged into thick trees, Tiann tried again to ask Mara about the stranger. She shook her head and kept walking. The green robe of the woods turned to silver, gold, and black in the rising moonlight, torch glow, and shadow. They walked in silence until they reached the entrance to the circle. Mara slid into the entrance. A chill coursed through Tiann, and her shoulders rose, as though a cold breeze had brushed wet skin. She wanted to turn, run back to the village, and burrow under her soft bed coverings. Splaying her hand against the stone, Tiann took two deep breaths, feet planted, as though she were about to face an opponent on the training field.

Mara stood by the spring, the torch casting a flickering light on her face. The light trembled and fell as Mara's arm dropped to her side. Hurrying to help before Mara set her tunic ablaze, Tiann looked to where Mara was staring. There on the ground was a dismembered hare. Next to the mess of blood and entrails lay the shattered pieces of the cup that always sat in the stone niche. Tiann wedged the torch into the ground with shaking hands.

Sinking to her knees, Mara said, "I can't believe he did this. Shal would never allow it, especially here."

"The stranger did this?" Tiann asked.

Mara nodded.

"Why? What does it mean? Who is he?"

"He is a druid, but not like Shal. Remember I told you he came here before? He met with Mother and Father and Shal in the royal apartment. I listened. You know." Tiann squeezed her hand. "I was little. I didn't really understand. But he talked about blood and the moon goddess and how the earth is angry with the Iceni because they have not fed her. It scared me, and I didn't stay to hear anymore. I went back to the hall to find Aife and ask her about it."

"Did she explain?"

"She only said he was one of the dark druids. She wouldn't say more. Then we could hear shouting from the apartment. The warriors all picked up their weapons, but no one went in. They just looked at each other like they didn't know what to do. Or like they were afraid."

Tiann tried to picture it. She could not remember a time the household warriors had been anything but bold. "Who was shouting?"

"First it was the stranger. It sounded like he was making accusations. Then Shal roared back. He said something about sorcery and serving the dark."

"Shal *yelled*?" Tiann could not imagine this either. Shal was almost invariably calm, good humored, although sometimes he might be sorrowful or thoughtful. *But Shal so angry his voice thundered through closed doors?* Tiann sat beside Mara and sifted through the shards of pottery. The sturdy cup, simply shaped and fired in its natural color, had been decorated with an uncomplicated but pleasing crosshatch design around its rim. With tears blurring her vision, Tiann thought back to the day she'd first met Shal. He had given her a drink from this very cup to ease her grief-tightened throat.

She arranged the pieces of the cup in order, laying them out like an unfurled scroll. In the middle, between the bard's harp symbol and Shal's triple spiral, a shard was missing. Tiann pulled the torch from the ground and looked for the missing piece. With sickness in her stomach, she found it—amongst the macabre remains of the hare. Tiann pulled it out with a thumb and forefinger.

Mara, watching in silence, went to the spring, dipped the hem of her tunic in the water, and wrung it out over the sticky fragment, then scrubbed the blood away. Tiann laid the piece in its place. Though still stained, the symbol marked on it showed again.

"What is it?" Mara asked.

"I don't know. It was on the cup with the others the morning Shal and the bard left."

Mara reached a finger toward the mark but didn't touch it. "He hated it. The dark druid. He hated that mark. He made the sacrifice to appease his gods. He smashed the cup to kill it. I wish I knew what it meant."

Tiann wasn't sure she wanted to know. What could be so threatening that a druid with dark power would seek to destroy it? "Let's go back. We'll tell the queen what we found. Maybe she has already had the warriors escort him away."

Mara looked down at the rabbit. "We should clean this away." Her voice shook.

"Don't worry about it now. I'll come back later. We should find out if there is a ritual cleansing for the circle and the spring."

Mara pulled off the cloth she had tied around her head for chores. She picked up the shard with the strange symbol, not touching it with her skin. She wrapped it carefully. "Come, then."

Boudica and Prasudoc remained closeted with the stranger late into the night. During the evening meal, an oppressive quiet pervaded the usually boisterous hall. No one lingered to talk or play dice games. Tiann and Mara ate and retreated to their chamber. A few minutes later Aife edged past the door hanging, arms full of bedding.

"Mother sent word I am to sleep here tonight. The visitor is to have my chamber." She dumped her load on the floor.

Mara jumped up. "Take my bed. I don't mind the floor."

Tiann grinned. The puppy had grown enough that Mara's narrow bed no longer held them both. He had been banished to the floor next to her. Many mornings Tiann almost tripped over the two of them tangled together, the bed empty.

Aife, who had been out on the training field all day under her father's demanding regimen, didn't hesitate. "Thank you, little hawk. I'm so sore and bruised, I don't know if I could rise from the floor in the morning."

Tiann sympathized. She knew from experience that the exercises she had seen Aife working on, while effective for building balance and agility, involved many falls and blows before mastery. She winced each time she saw Aife fall from a horse while attempting to stand on its back or get knocked over by a swinging log in the obstacle course.

Aife sank onto the bed with a sigh, shrugging and stretching her neck this way and that.

Tiann moved behind her, fingers kneading the muscles. "Why is he taking your chamber? Shal's roundhouse is empty. Wouldn't that be more appropriate for another druid?"

Aife snorted. "He says it is too plain. He practically called Shal a man of no consequence or power. Ayyee! Not so hard, Tiann."

"Sorry." Tiann softened her hands. "Why is he here?"

"I think he is talking to Mother and Father about the Coritani treaty." Aife rolled her head from side to side. "Thank you, Tiann—that feels better. I might be able to move tomorrow after all."

Tiann stepped over Mara, where she was curled in a burrow of bed coverings with her puppy. She crawled into bed, twining the covering between her fingers.

A shuddering, steadying breath came once, twice from her blood sister. It was the same sound Mara made when preparing to race a war chariot around the training course or make a running leap over a ditch. Mingled determination and fear. Tiann thought it was the bravest thing she ever heard.

A FINE MIST gave way to a dull, steady rain, turning the morning training exercises into a muddy endeavor. Tiann and Devyn sparred with dulled blades while one of the warriors called instruction. "Use the mud! You can move on wet ground in ways you cannot on dry!" Tiann ducked a blow, slid on her knees under Devyn's blade, spinning on the slippery surface to strike him on the back of the legs. Knocked off balance, he fell forward, feet sliding out from under him. Tiann was on him the moment he turned onto his back, pinning him down with her whole body, her blade at his throat.

"Yes! Good, Tiann," the warrior called.

Devyn grinned up at her. "You have overcome me yet again. Somehow, you always keep me off balance." He eased the blade away from his neck, brushed a tendril of her hair from his face, and tucked it behind her ear. Tiann's face grew hot, and she scrambled up with considerably less grace than the maneuver that had felled him. She wiped her blade with concentration. When she looked up, Devyn was working with their trainer, practicing sliding in the mud, first on his feet, then his knees. Her gaze wandered to the fence and sharpened on a hooded figure in a dark cloak, standing still in the rain. *The stranger.* The hood shrouded his face, but Tiann sensed his stare. She rubbed at the scar on her arm as though it itched. Shaking off her unease, she joined Devyn and the trainer.

When Tiann returned to the courtyard, she grabbed one of the pitch-lined baskets collecting rainwater from the eaves of the roundhouses. In the roofless enclosure used for bathing, she peeled off her mud-caked clothes, draping them to allow the rain to do the initial rinsing. She shivered as the heat from training dissipated from her body. Hurrying through scrubbing, she sluiced herself clean with water from the bucket. Opening a chest, she pulled out a length of coarse wool cloth, damp but clean. She wound it around herself, then walked across the courtyard with her head down, not making any eye contact, as was polite. She replaced the bucket under the eaves of the hall and entered. As she made her way to her chamber, the back of her neck prickled with awareness. Peeking up, she saw the stranger staring at her. Tiann fixed her eyes back on the floor and increased her pace. *How dare he! Who would look at a person coming from bathing? Did the man have no care for manners at all?* She whipped into the privacy of her chamber, breath heaving.

Tiann stayed behind the curtain, listening to the early evening sounds of the hall. She dressed in a clean tunic and breeches and unbraided her damp hair. Spreading it to dry, she laid back on her bed and tried to rest her weary body before the evening meal. But her mind jumped from place to place. She wondered where Shal and the bard were this day and what they talked of. Recollection of Devyn's grin and his touch on her hair brought a warmth to her face. But apprehension trickled through her as she remembered the dark figure watching her training and coming from bathing. She jumped up and paced the chamber, feeling caged in the small space.

The scent of bread and meat curled past the chamber curtain, making Tiann's mouth water. Tugging impatiently, she worked the tangles from her hair enough to rebraid it. She hesitated with her hand on the curtain. *Maybe I can get some food and eat in here. I could plead illness. I don't want to sit and try to eat with that man watching me.* She chewed on her lip, rankled by her own cowardice.

Retreating from the curtain, Tiann opened the chest that held her possessions. She rummaged through clothing, belts, and leather pouches containing an assortment of herbs for healing, dice for gaming, and small trinkets of rock or shell collected from the woods or seaside just because she liked them. From the bottom of the chest, she pulled a cloth-wrapped bundle, laid it on the bed, and undid the folds. On the intricately woven cloth lay a gold torc. The wrapping was made from the tunic, long since outgrown, that she had worn for the blood bonding ritual. She traced the embroidered symbols of spirals and her father's owl and caressed the royal Iceni moon crown.

She lifted the torc, a delicate thing compared to some of the thick, heavy ones worn by Prasudoc, Boudica, and Aife. When Tiann had come of age, before her first journey, she had chosen this slim design of twisted metal with triple spirals on the terminals. Unlike some in the royal household, who were never seen without ornamentation, Tiann had few brooches and bracelets and wore her torc only rarely. She put it on now, closing the terminals to sit over each of her collarbones. With a final smoothing of her tunic, she set her shoulders back, pulled the curtain aside, and strode into the hall.

As she feared, the dark druid sat at the royal table beside the queen and chief. Tiann ignored him, refusing to let her eyes meet his. Walking with deliberation to avoid any trace of her limp, she kept her gaze only on Mara. Without looking up, she sat down on Mara's right and answered the queen's greeting. She busied herself with filling her cup from a flagon of mead. The vessels used for the meal that night were not the usual decorated gray, but the smooth, glossy redware, a gift from a traveling prince from Gaul some seasons ago.

She sipped deeply of the fiery honey liquid, feeling it burn all the way to her empty stomach. Mara frowned and pointedly handed her a round of bread from the platter. Tiann only toyed with it. One more long sip and she felt the effect of the mead in her head. Her arms were loose and heavy as they rested on the table. She slid her gaze to the side and saw the stranger looking her way.

Blinking, she leaned close to Mara. "Does he have a name?" A kind of horror rushed through her. Perhaps he was nameless, like a wraith, or unnamable, like an evil spirit. Children's stories, whispered with giggles by the light of a dancing fire, flitted through her mind.

"He is Bultur." Mara hid her words behind a spoonful of stew. "He comes from the far West. An Ordowic. Eat. You've been training all day." Mara turned to Aife to ask after a pregnant mare her sister had been tending.

Tiann obeyed, putting a piece of bread in her mouth and dipping her spoon in the bowl of stew Mara had pushed toward her. The druid's silky voice carried to her ears.

"You must see it is essential the eastern tribes unite. The West is carrying on the fight. We will do whatever it takes. Some of my brothers in the druid council are ready to offer any means at their disposal. Any means."

"Why only some?" Prasudoc's question was laced with doubt. "What divides the council?"

"Some of the council are . . . reluctant to travel certain roads of power. They have not the stomach. But"—his voice lowered to a hiss—"some of us do. And we are not afraid to travel any road that leads to the extermination of these intruders who bring their abomination of an empire to our island."

A shiver shook Tiann, and her stomach rebelled against the stew. She pushed the bowl away, ready to excuse herself.

"You must make the treaty. Send the girl. It's not as though she is your true daughter."

Tiann clutched the edge of the table. *Had Mara heard?* But she and Aife remained in intent discussion of the mare.

Prasudoc made a protesting exclamation, and Boudica murmured, "Sir, to us she is as a true daughter."

Bultur lifted a placating hand. "Yes, yes. Of course. Commendable. Still, she will be well treated. You say the Coritani delegation is due. Your advisor is gone. It is fate that I am here. I will preside over the treaty. With your invitation, of course."

Tiann's stomach flipped again, and a small moan escaped her.

Mara turned to her, a concerned expression on her face. "Are you unwell?"

Tiann shook her head, but Mara's eyebrows drew together.

It is not right. How can that man want what I asked be done, when Shal was unsure? Something is wrong.

Boudica set down her cup. "It is essential the peace with the Coritani holds. The Roman beasts are straining at the end of their ropes, snapping at the opportunity to swallow us up like they have other tribes. I refuse to give them the excuse. Very well. We will move forward." "Do you agree, husband?"

Prasudoc frowned, crumbling a piece of bread into a pile on the table. At last he sighed. "Yes. I will agree. But I would rather Shal had been here to support the decision as well."

Boudica stood, drawing her dagger from its sheath on her hip. With the pommel, she pounded the table. A hush rippled through the hall as those nearer the royal table directed the attention of those farther from the queen.

"People of the Iceni. Your chief and your queen have decided to accept the offer of treaty with the Coritani. When their ambassadors arrive, we will greet them with honor. Our revered guest, Bultur, will oversee the negotiations." A buzz broke out as people absorbed the news.

Bultur rose to stand beside the queen. Tiann looked at his beaky profile and exultant smile, feeling queasy. *I must talk to Mara tonight. I can't wait for Shal to come back.* She focused her gaze on her own fingers, twisting her tunic into clenched fists.

"Do you make your promise, Boudica?" the dark druid asked. "You promise to make this treaty?"

"I have said so. Yes. I make my promise."

"Then all of Albion will thank the Iceni. And we also extend our thanks to your . . ."—Bultur waved his hands, as though searching for the phrase—"your esteemed ward, who has offered to serve as hostage."

CHAPTER

NINE

Tiann's head snapped up. The druid's eyes burned with a fanatic fervor as he held his hand out, gesturing for her to rise. Beside her, Mara made a strangled moan. Tiann rose in a daze, pulling away from Mara's hand clutching at her arm. The buzz in the hall increased to a rumble, but to Tiann it sounded like the roll of far-off thunder or the crashing of the sea. Behind Bultur, the light of a torch glared, outlining his dark figure with a red glow. She tore her gaze away from him. The scarlet haze spread over Tiann's sight until everywhere, it seemed, the hall and its occupants were bathed in a sheer red light.

Mouths moved in excited conversation, shouting questions, exclaiming. All she heard was the rushing in her head. Devyn's shocked face swam into focus. She thought he formed the words, "Tiann, no." She saw the talking cease and attention turn toward Bultur again. She, too, looked at him. He raised his arms, hands hooked like claws. He threw his head back, the tendons in his neck quivering with the force of his shout. The roar increased, and the haze darkened from the brightness of fire to the color of blood.

Tiann's stomach heaved, and all at once her legs carried her away from the table. She knocked over her seat and shoved her way through the red-soaked hall, her desperate goal the heavy doors on the far side. She took one look behind her as she crashed through them. Sprinting through the courtyard, she aimed for the back of the stable. Steadying herself with a hand on the rough-woven sapling wall, she bent over and retched. Her body heaved until nothing was left but empty spasms. She slid down with her back against the stable wall, eyes closed, throat burning with the expelled mead. She trembled with the aftereffects. Behind her eyelids, she could see her last glimpse of the hall before she'd run outside. Bultur, with his arms lifted, shouting his dark benediction. Mara's face, twisted with angry tears.

The scent of hay and horses drifted into her consciousness. Tiann breathed deep, trying to calm. The roaring in her head subsided, and she could make out the night sounds around her. Insects and the shuffling of hooves within the stable sang a song of peace. To the north, an owl sent out its call. *Da, I wish you were with me. I wish we could live among the apple trees, and go to trade in the village, and journey to the sea together.*

Footsteps approached. Tiann squeezed her eyes shut tighter, unwilling to surrender the comfort of the dark in case the world was still an unnatural red.

"Ah, Tiann, my girl." Goram's gruff voice fell gentle on her ears.

She peeked up at him, relieved to see that he stood over her in the shadowed blue and gray of night. He handed her a cup of water and she sipped some, swishing out her mouth and turning her head to spit. She took another sip and swallowed, glad for the cooling in her throat. Goram plunked down beside her and patted her knee. They sat silent as the stars brightened above them.

～

Since the announcement, Mara had vanished before dawn and crept into their chamber after Tiann was already in bed, turning her face toward the wall. She ignored Tiann's greetings with a stony silence, her back rigid. The three feet between their beds felt like a furlong.

The third day, Tiann left the hall with resolve. She had given Mara her space long enough. What could she say to smooth things over? She would probably botch it. But the rift between them was unbearable. Grabbing two flat loaves from the large clay bowl on the table in the hall, she set out. A quick look into the kitchens and outbuildings yielded no glimpse of her quarry. Nor did the stable or paddock. Tiann leaned against the wall of the paddock enclosure, closing her eyes to the misty morning, the damp gathering on her face and hair. The air carried a mineral tang that stirred an idea. She inhaled again, waiting for the thought to come clear. *Stone. And torch smoke.* She stretched her hand against the stone wall behind her, fingers searching for . . . *spirals. And links of three.*

She set off back toward the hall, blinking droplets from her lashes. Inside, the room was empty except for servers gathering the discards of the morning bread. Tiann made her way to the table at the far end, munching on one of the loaves she still carried, as though she had just come back from some chore and thought to rest a few minutes before going on with her day. After scanning the room to be sure no one was paying her any mind, she slipped down to the floor. When she heard the clatter of tables being pushed against the walls, she used the sound as cover, lifted the trapdoor, slid inside, and closed it shut. She wedged the bread into her belt.

Back to the wall, she edged down the pitch-black tunnel, reaching out with a hand and a foot before every step. When she reached the plunging gap in the floor, she held her breath, inching past it with feet sideways, the stone scraping her shoulders as she pressed hard into the wall. At last, she rounded a curve and saw a faint light. She had been right. Mara was there in the chamber. Peeling herself away from the wall, Tiann moved with soft footsteps.

Mara sat with her back to the tunnel. "I didn't think you'd come here to find me."

"Of course I would come. Once I realized this is where you would be." Tiann moved into the chamber, running her hands on the designs carved into stone.

Mara sniffed. "It's all wrong, you know. This treaty. You being the hostage. We can't trust that evil man to know what is right."

Tiann walked to the back of the chamber, warned by the steeliness in Mara's tone. No comforting platitudes. With one finger Tiann traced a carving over and over, an endless, interconnected design. She leaned her forehead against the wall. "But surely Shal would have done the same." Her voice bounced off the stone. The sound was hollow, like her confidence.

"Would he? Then why didn't he do it before he left?"

Tiann's composure crumbled. "I don't know. I don't know. I was so sure." She swiped the back of her hand across her wet cheek and turned to face Mara. "I wanted to save you. But with Shal gone and that man here instead . . . nothing is clear anymore." Her words finished on a sob.

Mara stood and crossed to her in one swift motion. She pulled Tiann tight against her, stretching to press Tiann's head down onto her slight shoulder. "Shh. I know. Oh, Tiann, you leap too soon. I don't always need you to save me. We are supposed to protect each other. It doesn't flow in only one direction. Why, why did you agree to do this? There has to be another way. We aren't meant to be separated."

And in that moment, Tiann knew it was true. Their wounds were for binding, not for parting. She had not remembered. She hugged Mara back, weeping for her own foolishness. "I should have waited. Your father would have waited if I asked him. What have I done?"

~

THE NEXT WEEKS passed in a flurry of activity. The Coritani ambassadors returned, and the treaty was ratified. Then began the tedious tasks of preparation to send the hostage off with dignity at the second full moon. Tiann chafed under the enforced inactivity of garment making and then in the new clothes themselves. She longed for her old, comfortable tunics and leggings, much mended and with incorrigible stains but worn to a softness brought about only by use. But the Royal Hostage must be properly attired to honor to tribe. She did, however, remain steadfast in her refusal to help with the tedious sewing on of the colorful bits of shell. Boudica, with an understanding twinkle in her eye, let the minor rebellion go unremarked.

Besides clothing, an amazing array of jewelry, cooking utensils, horses, dogs, bedding, wines imported from Gaul, grain, and an endless list of other supplies were gathered and marked off by Prasudoc's steward. Some of these would comprise a suitable household, as the Royal Hostage must have, but many of them were gifts for the Coritani chief.

Boudica's face grew more and more sour as she was clearly considering the price they were paying for the dubious honor of having Tiann taken away to their ancient enemy. Boudica was nothing if not a queen, however, and did not speak of her displeasure, determined to uphold Iceni honor with a display of both wealth and dignity. Tiann wondered at her foster mother's stony silences, bewildered by her cold demeanor. She felt exiled before ever having left.

As often as she could, Tiann slipped away. At the training field, she sparred with any willing opponent, wielding staff or sword until her arms and shoulders burned and her partner called quits. She bound up her ankle and ran the perimeter of the fields until she could run no more and flung herself on the grass, panting and wheezing. Sometimes she visited the stable, where Goram would nod a greeting and saddle Gwyndolyn for her. In the evenings, she and Mara spent every minute together but spoke little.

Devyn left, part of a small contingent of warriors visiting an Iceni stronghold to the south, charged with assessing its strength and maintenance. Tiann suspected Goram had suggested his inclusion to give him time to get over the shock of Tiann's impending departure. She was grateful to put off what would be a difficult conversation. A lump grew in her throat when she thought about leaving him behind. *Would he wait for me? Do I want him to?* The memory of his grin and his touch made her breathing quicken. *But that isn't enough to ask him to wait—to ask him to give up a year. What if he grows warm toward another while I am gone? He could not act on it, for his honor would bind him to me. I cannot do that to him.* She swallowed hard, forcing her thoughts to recite the instructions regarding her behavior among the Coritani. The Royal Hostage must always uphold Iceni honor.

The moon still hung low in the indigo sky when Tiann emerged from the hall. Restless turning had filled the sleeping hours. She had given up the attempt even before the morning scent of baking bread stirred the hounds. Rubbing at her gritty eyes, she headed toward the cistern to splash her face. Smoke from Shal's roundhouse curled across the face of the moon, arresting her. Heedless of the earliness of the day, she approached his door and rapped, the sound echoing in the still, empty courtyard. She heard movement within, and then the door opened and there was Shal, his beloved face tired but smiling.

Tiann threw herself into his arms, and he patted her back. "Tiann, my dear, I am so glad to see you. You have been ever in my thoughts. I know you have been worried and waiting, but everything will be all right now. The solution has presented itself."

She pulled back, searching his face. "The solution?"

"Yes. Yes. I have so much to tell you. But I must speak to all of you together, because the queen and chief need to hear as well. But I have traveled all night. Let me sleep a few hours. After the morning meal is cleared, send someone to wake me and we will gather then."

"But, Shal . . . there are things I have to tell you . . ." Tiann spluttered, feeling like all that had happened since he'd left would explode out of her. *He needs to know about Bultur!*

"Yes, there is much to discuss, but later, my dear. Send someone to wake me. I'm so glad to see you." He ushered her out and shut the door.

Tiann stood staring at the roundhouse. She raised her hand to knock again but thought better of it. *He's been gone all this time. A few more hours won't change anything.*

She returned to the hall, where some of the older children were setting out the tables with drowsy lethargy. Back in the sleeping chamber, she sat at the end of Mara's pallet and shook her foot. The hound lifted his head and rose, stretching his front paws and then rearing back with a great yawn. He ambled over to her and nosed her hand until she scratched him behind the ears. She shook Mara's foot harder. "Wake up. Mara, wake up. Shal has returned."

Mara sat up, and the hound left Tiann to greet her.

"What . . . Why are you . . . How do you know he is here? It is still night."

"It is morning. Early, but still. I *saw* him. He is here."

Mara swung her feet to the floor. "What did he say about the treaty? About Bultur? Does he agree? Did he advise you?"

"I could not tell him anything. He said he needed to sleep

because he'd traveled all night. He will talk to everyone after the morning meal is cleared."

Mara jumped up, and the hound whined, following her as she paced around the chamber, waving her hands with agitation. "So he doesn't even know that man is here? Sitting in his place in the hall, acting as advisor?" She sank back down on the bed, and the hound put his head on her knees. Leaning down to put her arms around him, she said, "I suppose he will find out soon enough." The pup's fur muffled her voice. "He might as well be rested when he does."

The morning passed with painful slowness. It seemed everything delayed the morning meal. A serving woman cut her thumb slicing a hard round of cheese, and preparations came to a stop while the gash was tended. A cow was giving birth, so the herders came one at a time at long intervals to eat. A handful of warriors went out on a patrol before breaking their fast and returned later than expected with a lamed horse. Tiann and Mara waited for Prasudoc and Boudica to come into the hall, but they spent the morning in the royal apartments, as they often did. Tiann couldn't blame them. From the moment they emerged to the moment they went to bed, people surrounded them, asking for decisions, judgments, favors, advice, or instruction.

At last, the hall emptied as the work of the day began in earnest. The tables and seats were pushed back to make room for household tasks like weaving, mending, and the sorting of herbs. Tiann settled to help with the latter task, which she found the least tedious while she waited. Her fingers moved over the aromatic leaves, picking out debris, swishing off dirt in a bucket, and spreading them on a clean board to dry. The rhythm and pungent scent soothed her edginess, though she still glanced toward the entrance to the royal apartment every few moments.

When Boudica and Prasudoc came through the door, they were laughing. The queen hooked her arm through her husband's, and their heads tipped toward each other in some private merriment. Tiann sprang up but then hesitated. Their intimacy made her smile, and she was loath to interrupt with news that would turn their attention away from each other for the rest of the day. Across the hall, Mara rose from behind a loom and rushed to her parents. They turned smiling faces to her but grew serious at her murmured words. The queen and chief separated, Boudica moving to send a boy out, presumably to fetch Shal.

Prasudoc strode to Tiann. "He is back? You have spoken with him?"

"Yes. But we only talked briefly. Not enough to share news. He was very tired."

The chief leaned against the table, the brush of his cloak scattering herbs. He crossed his arms, chin to his chest. "So, he has returned. Good. Good. I had feared . . . But it would have been better if he had come two moons ago. Nevertheless, it is good that he is back. That he is safe. But I am keen to hear what kept him from us for so long at such a time." Pushing off the table, he looked at the herbs in disarray on the floor and bent to gather them up.

"Leave it, my father. I will do it." Tiann took the leaves from his hands before he crushed them beyond usefulness. While she returned them to their piles, she looked toward the chamber that had been Aife's. The traditional curtain had been replaced with a door of newly-hewn wood. Bultur had complained the heavy drape did not afford him the security and seclusion he needed.

Tiann had waited an extra day for Gwyndolyn's bridle ring to be repaired because the smith had been charged with making the door hinges immediately. She wondered if Bultur still took his rest behind the closed door so late in the morning. Wherever he was, she hoped he would stay away long enough for her family to enjoy Shal's homecoming. She somehow doubted Bultur would have the delicacy to allow them privacy to talk. He considered himself an intimate and important personage to the queen in particular.

Shal entered the hall, with Aife at his side. As he made his greeting to the queen and chief, Aife rushed over to Tiann. "I was coming back from counting the stores of thatching. You know."

Tiann did. Aife talked endlessly about thatching since she had been put in charge of her first major stewardship project. The roofs of all the dwellings and other buildings in the royal village, including the hall, were due to have their roofs repaired, and in some cases, entirely rethatched. Aife was overseeing the project, from assessing the need for labor and materials, to gathering them from Iceni lands, to scheduling the work around weather and the necessary tasks of the village in a way that minimized disruption. Tiann admired Aife's dedication and attention to detail but did not mind if she never heard another word about the superiority of lowland water reeds over barley straw or the merits of one method of bundling thatching over another.

"Anyway, I saw Shal coming out of his roundhouse and ran to greet him. He says he returned a few hours before dawn. I'm so pleased he has come back." Aife lowered her voice. "Perhaps he will have communication from other tribes about renewing the war with the Romans. Maybe that's why he has been traveling."

Is that what Shal meant when he said a solution had presented itself? That the tribes were once again going to fight to reclaim Albion? Tiann's chest ached. *What would that mean for me? Would the hostage exchange still take place?* Shame flushed her face. She was petty to consider her own affairs in the grand scheme of events in Albion. But still, the ache of thinking that Shal had absented himself for political intrigue, while her life was in upheaval, remained.

"Tiann!" Mara beckoned her from beside the entrance to the royal apartments. Boudica, Prasudoc, Aife, and Shal headed inside, while Mara waited for Tiann to catch up. She cast one more look around to be sure Bultur was still not there and then hurried after them. The guard at the entrance gave her a nod and a smile. He'd shown special fondness for Tiann ever since he had carried her back from the bonding ritual years ago. The warrior, one of Prasudoc's men, had aged noticeably since receiving a wound to his thigh, and no longer rode out. He was a favorite instructor on the training field and also acted as a guard in the place of honor close to the royal couple.

The family settled in to talk, with Boudica in her customary seat and Prasudoc on a wide stool beside her, back against the wall and feet stretched in front of him. Shal sat near the brazier, although it was not lit. Mara, Aife, and Tiann made themselves comfortable on cushions on the floor. From where Tiann sat, she could see past the bed chamber curtain where it hung askew, to Prasudoc and Boudica's bed, still rumpled. Tiann averted her eyes respectfully but felt the smile again tug at her lips. Would her own marriage someday be as happy? She tamped down thoughts that drifted toward brown eyes and callused hands and forced herself to follow the conversation.

"You have been gone a long while, friend." Prasudoc's tone was neutral, his expression quizzical. "For us, it did not seem well timed. But I have never known you to be capricious. I am eager to hear the account of your journey."

"Such a journey. Such a journey, my chief! I hardly know how to begin." Shal's very being seemed to buzz with excitement. And yet his hands, loosely folded, spoke of serenity. There was no trace of the pushing and pulling of his sleeves, which had always accompanied agitation. He radiated a peace and energy in contrast to the last time Tiann had spoken with him, before he had disappeared. Then he had alarmed her with his look of weary uncertainty. Now he appeared settled, confident, unconcerned about trouble.

"Let me start with the lesser news, though I believe it will be welcome. You needn't send a hostage to the Coritani. I traveled for a time with one of the Cornovian princes. You know they inherit through the men? So he could be a choice for chief when his father lies with the ancestors. He is already much respected among the Cornovi, and a man of influence, even if he does not become chief."

Tiann controlled her urge to fidget or interrupt. *What does any of this have to do with anything?*

Shal looked over at her. "I promise I am getting to the point, my dear."

She shifted, embarrassed that her impatience had shown.

"The Cornovi lands border the Coritani on the west. They are allies and have been for many years."

Prasudoc, Boudica, and Aife nodded, knowing this already. Again, Tiann itched with embarrassment, wishing she had paid better attention when Boudica had tried to teach her about the convoluted tribal relationships in Albion. Those lessons had always seemed dull and unimportant compared to learning to fight, or drive a chariot, or take care of the horses.

"This prince and I became friends, as we were on similar journeys." Shal held up his hand. "I will explain about that later. But we talked at length about the Iceni troubles with the Coritani and the terms of the treaty. He has offered a solution." He beamed, leaning forward with his elbows on his knees. "The Cornovi will make their alliance with the Coritani dependent upon peace with us. In return, I have offered an alliance with the Cornovi." He sat back, smiling.

The queen and chief looked at each other, a silent, perturbed communication. Aife picked at a loose thread on her cushion, the line between her eyebrows so like Mara's when she was anxious. Tiann tried to glean understanding of the tension from her blood sister, but Mara gave a small, uncomprehending shrug to Tiann's questioning look.

Shal's smile faded at their lack of response. "Don't you see? It may take longer to become allies with the Coritani, but for now, there will be a truce. And alliance, when it comes, can be built on a friendship instead of a hostage exchange. We can take the time we need to forge a relationship. And no one"—he gestured toward Tiann and Mara—"must be separated or sent to strangers."

The sound of raised voices outside the chamber diverted their attention. Bultur thrust into the space, followed by the guard.

"I am sorry, Lady, Chief," the guard said. "He pushed his way past me, although I told him I thought you would prefer to be undisturbed."

"How dare you!" Bultur's face was red, and spittle flew from his mouth. "Whom do you think you are denying?"

Prasudoc scowled at the contention that burst into their company. "Here now. There is no need to shout nor to speak so to my man. He is only doing his duty."

Boudica rose, putting her hand on Bultur's arm. "I am sure he did not mean to be disrespectful. Now that you are here, let us get you a seat." She looked to the guard and to Prasudoc.

The chief still glowered but nodded, and the guard left to fetch a seat. Bultur huffed but allowed himself to be soothed by the queen's solicitous attention.

Once seated, he turned a venomous look upon Shal. "You were saying something about delaying the treaty, sir. There must be no delay. The treaty must be established now. There is no time to waste with softness." His voice thickened with scorn. "Hoping for friendship will not give the tribes the power they need to rise up against the intruders."

Shal opened his mouth to answer, but Bultur held up a hand. "Nothing you can say makes a difference. The gods have kept you away for a purpose. You cannot now offer a dulled blade for the sharp one they have decreed. The queen has made her promise."

Tiann watched Shal as the information sank in. She expected he might jump up and pace, pushing his sleeves up and down. But he only sat back, an expression of profound sadness accompanying his quiet words. "Is it true, Lady? You have pledged to this and to send your daughter to the Coritani?"

Bultur, looking triumphant, now tried for a hearty tone. "No, no, my colleague! Not the daughter—only the ward."

At this Shal rose from his chair. He drew himself to his full height and stood over Bultur. He enunciated each word with precision. "Tiann is a full daughter of the Iceni royal family. She was accepted by a sacred oath. She is not some animal to be sacrificed in one of your dark rites to gain power."

Bultur sputtered, leaning away from Shal, looking from Boudica to Prasudoc. The queen lowered her eyes to her hands, unwilling to placate him this time. The chief rose to stand beside Shal. Mara's hand slipped into Tiann's and gripped it hard. Aife shifted on her cushion and put an arm around Tiann's shoulder.

"Of course, of course. I am not used to how you view these things." Bultur turned an ingratiating smile toward the royal couple. "Excuse my blunder."

"Perhaps it would be best now to tell us your other news, Shal," Boudica said. "We can return to the matter of the treaty later."

"Are the tribes rising, Shal?" Aife asked. "Is that what you meant by greater news?"

"No. That is, I did hear some talk of that, but nothing imminent. But no, this news is much better."

"How could anything surpass the overthrow of the Romans?"

"Indeed," Bultur said. "That is the great hope for Albion. That is what we are all waiting for, seeking after."

"Not all." Shal's voice, though quiet, held complete conviction. "Some of us have been waiting and watching and hoping for something else, and from times before the Romans ever came to these shores."

"Those old stories?" Bultur said. "Are you still clinging to that nonsense? When have the legends ever brought power?"

"The old stories are not valuable because they are a source of power. That is not what we seek, at least not for ourselves. We seek to know the power that exists outside of the world."

"Shal, what does that mean?" Mara asked. "Don't you get power from the circle and the spring?"

Shal turned a kind gaze upon her puzzled face. "No, child. The circle and the spring point us to the One outside. The Maker. The One with strong life, like the oak. Ever-flowing, like the spring. A place of peace, separate from the world."

"And what about the powers of the earth you dismiss?" Bultur's face reddened again. "Do you dare anger them with your neglect and blasphemy, sir? Do you dare?"

"Yes, I dare. Because I have come to know at last that the Maker is the maker of all. Over all. And though the lesser powers still rage and bluster, they are defeated. That is the great good news." Shal turned a joyful face to each of them in turn. When Tiann looked into his eyes, she caught her breath. For there around the familiar warm brown shone a faint golden glow.

"Oh, my children, my friends, I have so much to tell you!" Shal returned to his seat. "When I left with the bard, I could not have imagined what I would learn. It is beyond human imagination!"

"Are you telling us that some traveling singer has imparted wisdom beyond the druid masters? Yes, I can believe that this former slave is the wisest man on earth." Bultur's sarcasm drenched the heat of Shal's enthusiasm. "And what momentous event brought about the defeat of the powers of earth and heavens, sir? The stars continue to shine as they always have. The moon waxes and wanes. The sun rises and sets. What story has this singer sung to turn your head?"

"It is the story of a Man hung on a Roman cross to die."

Bultur snarled, the sound rising from his chest. Boudica sprang from her chair. "No. No! I will not listen to another tale about those beasts. You call this good?"

"It is not a tale about the Romans, Lady. It is about the Man."

"A man foolish or unlucky enough to be executed! A man without even enough power to save himself from these Romans!" She paced, then hit the wall with the flat of her hand, hard enough to crack the plaster daub.

"Lady, Chief, this Man gave Himself up willingly. But His power overcame His death, and He lives."

"So he did not die from his crucifixion?" Prasudoc asked.

"He died. He was buried, but . . ."

"Willingly?" Boudica interrupted. "Willingly? What kind of man gives himself up? What kind of honor is that? Shal, have you lost your senses?"

"That is no kind of honor, Lady," Bultur said. "No warrior would behave in such a way. So how could he defeat any kind of power? And no wise man would put himself in the hands of uncouth ruffians. This is nonsense. Shal needs to rest and recover and have some time to think."

"I am more well than I have ever been," Shal said. "And my head is more clear. And my soul is awake for the first time. Please, listen to what I have to say."

"No. Bultur is right. You need more rest and time to consider what you are saying. I will not listen while you debase yourself with strange new ideas. I will not. We are done here." Boudica stalked from the room.

Tiann gaped after her. She had never seen the queen so discomfited as to lose control. Bultur swept after her, reeking of self-satisfaction. Shal lowered his chin to his chest, interlacing his fingers, hands resting in his lap. Prasudoc rose and patted his shoulder with helpless air and followed his wife out of the room.

"We should go too," Aife whispered.

Shal looked up. "Yes, go, children. All is well." He did seem well. His face was sad but still peaceful.

The young women scrambled up from their cushions. Mara turned back. "Shal, will you tell me more about the man?"

"Yes, daughter." Shal offered the words like he was holding out a treasure richer than the finest gold torc. "I'll tell you all I know."

TEN

In the warmth of midday, Tiann stood balanced on a stool in the paddock, trying to loosen a bit of bramble caught in Gwyndolyn's mane. At the sound of horses approaching at a trot, Gwyndolyn whinnied and shuffled. Tiann circled her arms, trying not to fall. She looked over her shoulder. The party had returned from the southern stronghold. She caught sight of Devyn and froze on her perch.

"Trying to make sure he sees you?" Goram said, chuckling as he went to greet the returnees.

Tiann scrambled down, narrowly missing a pile of dung. She went into the stable to retrieve the materials to rub the horses down. She sent girls to fetch buckets of water in case the warriors had not stopped to water the horses at the stream before coming to the village. Hesitating in the darkened doorway, she watched the party dismount, exchanging slaps on the back and jests with a gathering crowd. Devyn held his mount's bridle, grinning at whatever Goram had said. He unhitched his saddlebags, slinging them over his shoulders. He looked relaxed and happy, and Tiann was glad Goram had sent him away from the stresses of the royal village. Would he still smile when he saw her?

Stepping out of the stable into the sunlight, Tiann started distributing the rub-down cloths to the warriors, who were unsaddling their mounts. The joking conversation faltered, and there was more than one glance thrown Devyn's way. They had talked about her on their journey, that was clear. *What had Devyn confided? What had they advised him?* She drew a quick, steadying breath and went to where he still held the bridle.

"To rub him down." Tiann held out the cloth, but instead of taking it, Devyn caught her hand and held it.

"It's good to see you." His smile was warm, and his brown eyes locked on hers. His thumb moved across her hand holding the crumpled cloth.

"You as well."

He slid the cloth from her fingers and removed the saddle from his horse. He applied himself to drying off the damp flanks. "Would you mind taking the saddle in?" he asked over his shoulder.

"No. No, of course not. Perhaps . . . perhaps we will talk later?"

Devyn's grin flashed at her. "Be sure of it."

THAT EVENING TIANN took extra care with her braids. She considered wearing her torc again but scolded herself for foolishness. She might need extra courage to face Bultur, but this was Devyn. Devyn, who had known her since childhood. He had seen her sweaty and bloody and filthy. Devyn, who knew she preferred a simple tunic and braccae with little jewelry. She contented herself with fastening the open neck of her tunic with a small enameled brooch. He had once remarked that the polished stone in the middle matched the gray of her eyes.

At the table, she ate and drank without tasting a thing. She tried and failed to keep her gaze from wandering to where Devyn laughed and exchanged tales with his companions. When the food was cleared away, she expected him to make his way toward her. Instead, he remained clumped together with the warriors who had returned that day. Prasudoc and Aife joined their conversation, and the merriment increased as each vied to entertain the chief and his daughter with his own exploits or the blunders of the others. Aife glittered with gold at her neck and wrists, smiling, the firelight glinting off the red in her hair.

Tiann slipped outside, relishing a deep breath of clean air after the smoky hall. The quiet of the night wrapped her in a comforting, dark embrace. She sat on the edge of the cistern, tipping her head back to look at the stars, brilliant in the moonless sky.

I don't mind. I'm glad he is happy without me. I would worry and fret if I thought he was missing me while I am gone. It is good to know that his care for me is not all consuming. She told herself the lies, willing her sore heart to believe them.

A glow from the opening hall door caught her attention. The exiting figure, silhouetted against the light from within, made her straighten. *When did his shoulders get broader?* The lanky form strolled into the courtyard. He peered around, eyes not yet adjusted to the dark. *Should I call out?* But Tiann waited, watching him. The lift in her heart told her the truth. *I do care for him. And I want him to miss me. Maybe even wait for me.*

Devyn's head turned toward her as though he could hear her thoughts. She shifted to make room for him next to her, and he came and sat.

"When the moon is fully awake again, you will be leaving."

"Yes."

"I have asked Prasudoc something. But I won't do it if you would rather I didn't."

Tiann kept her eyes fixed on the stars until they seemed to pulse in rhythm. What could this be? *Was he asking the chief for permission to become betrothed to someone, but doesn't want to hurt my feelings? Or perhaps it is about my father's farmholding. It is probably that. He wants to leave the royal village and start a new kind of life.* She was both anxious and let down. "All right."

"I asked him . . . and he said yes . . . but I won't if you . . ."

Tiann looked at him then, his face so full of hope and discomfort. "You can say it. You know I want you to be happy."

"I asked if I could be a member of your guard. Your household when you go to the Coritani. To go with you for your year there."

Tiann's breath hitched, as though it had forgotten how to reach her lungs. "Go with me?"

"Yes. I want to go with you. To see if . . . but only if you want to. I am not asking anything from you, Tiann. Now is not the time for talking about promises. Just tell me if you want me there, as your friend and guard. There will be time for anything else later."

He would give up a whole year. Just to be there with me. "But you would miss your warrior ceremony. It will be this harvest."

"It doesn't matter. I can do it the next harvest." He stood, stepping away from her, looking up at the sky. "You don't have to find an excuse or objection if you don't want this. Just say. I will understand."

She leaned forward, catching his hand in both of hers and pulling him back to sit with her. "I do want it. To have you there with me. To help me be away from home. To see if we . . . To be my friend."

"And your guard."

A smile stretched Tiann's mouth. She put her head down to hide the foolish giddiness inside her. But when she cast her glance sideways at Devyn, he was watching her with a matching grin. "Do you want to go back inside? They asked me to play my flute."

"Yes. Just don't let the chief sing. Last time he didn't stop until dawn."

Boudica watched from the paddock fence while Tiann led horses hitched to a wicker chariot out the gate. "Is that the new pair Aife is training?"

"Yes. She asked me to take them through some paces today, since she has to meet with the thatchers."

Boudica's eyes gleamed. "What if I drive them instead?"

"Please, my mother!" Tiann swept her arm in a grand gesture.

Boudica laughed and stepped onto the chariot platform, spreading her feet wide, one ahead of the other. Tiann handed her the reins, admiring the bold picture.

"Aren't you coming, Tiann? Bring a spear. One for me too."

Hurrying to oblige, Tiann ran to the edge of the training ground to retrieve two spears from the equipment pile. When she returned, Boudica was testing the horses, taking them in a tight turn, then having them back up. It had been a long time since she had seen the queen with reins in hand, balancing deftly in a chariot. Boudica pulled the horses up. Tiann stepped up beside her, their feet forming an X on the platform, for stability. She held the rounded edge of the side wall, made from a steamed and shaped sapling and covered with roughened leather for grip.

The horses leapt forward at the queen's "Ha!" Tiann absorbed the jolt with her legs, keeping her body fluid. She and the queen swayed in unison, hip to hip. The horses, obedient to the strong hands holding the reins, turned toward a distant open field. When they reached the edge, Boudica pulled up, squinting in concentration. "You see the tree on the right, about halfway? That's your target. We'll turn at the end, and I'll take that boulder. There." She pointed to the middle of the field. "Then we'll swing across. You will retrieve your spear, and I will come back for you. We will switch positions and do the same maneuver on the other side. Are you agreed?"

"Yes, my queen." Tiann's heart thumped with excitement.

Boudica bared her teeth in a fierce smile. "Ha!" The horses broke forward at the slap of the reins, racing down the field.

Tiann crouched, hefting her spear, finding its balance point. She fastened her gaze on a knot in the tree trunk, ignoring the strands of hair escaping her braid to whip across her face. The horses settled into a flat-out gallop, and the tree seemed to rush toward her. Lifting the staff to her shoulder, Tiann braced herself against Boudica's hip and thigh. Just before the chariot sped by, Tiann launched the spear, all her weight behind the throw. She didn't hear the thwack she hoped for and whipped her head around to glimpse the spear lying just beyond the tree.

"Very close," Boudica shouted. "You waited just a bit too long. Here's the turn. Get ready to take the reins." Tiann turned her concentration back to the course ahead of them, bending deeply at the knees to keep the weight of the platform balanced through the sharp curve. Once they were pointed toward the boulder, she planted her feet and put her hands on the reins. Boudica let go and hefted her spear in her left hand. She had mastered the art of throwing from either side, and Tiann envied her skill.

As they approached the boulder, Tiann pulled on the reins to direct the horses to the right of it. The pair resisted, veering left as they thundered closer. *Never approach a foe on the driver's side.* She pulled harder. *The driver has no defense.* They defied her. *If she is speared, both warriors are at risk.* Leaning back, she shrieked commands, hauling with all her strength on the reins. At last the horses obeyed, swinging wide to the right. Boudica leaned on her hard, pivoting and making her throw as the boulder flashed by. A satisfying crack told Tiann the spear had hit its target.

"Battling with you, are they?" Boudica put her hands on the reins. "That's what training is for. Catch your breath and get ready."

Tiann followed her instruction and took deep, steadying

breaths. She visualized her next maneuver. She remembered a patch of grass just beyond the roots of the tree. Another hard turn and the chariot headed back toward where her spear lay. Turning to face the back of the platform, she crouched again. She could feel the horses slow as Boudica applied subtle but steady pressure to the reins. In the corner of her eye, the tree drew closer. When the chariot wheel was even with it, she sprang, rolling to the ground with her arms around her head. She somersaulted again, and once more, hearing the queen's "Ha!" urging the horses back to speed. Dizzy, Tiann scrambled to her feet, looking for the spear. *There.* She snatched it up, then ran toward the middle of the field, eyes on the chariot making its turn. The horses raced back toward her, and she ran in the same direction, hearing the galloping hooves gaining on her. She forced herself to keep looking ahead, to not look over her shoulder to check that the horses obeyed Boudica's hands. Just when it sounded like she would be trampled, the horses shot past her.

"Now!" Boudica called.

Tiann hurled herself, reaching her hand. Her mother's iron grip hauled to the platform. She clutched the side, panting.

Boudica laughed exultantly. "Yes! Oh, you are becoming a fine warrior, my daughter!"

Tiann moved to take the reins, catching her mother's high spirits. They performed the maneuver in reverse, with Boudica retrieving her spear and making the running leap back onto the chariot platform.

When they pulled up at the end of the field, both women and horses were panting and sweating freely. Boudica put her arm around Tiann's waist as they headed back to the paddock, horses at a walk. "It has been too long. Thank you for riding with me, daughter."

Tiann dipped her head to rest on Boudica's shoulder. "It's a privilege, my mother."

Boudica squeezed her waist, then let go to take the reins with both hands again. She turned the horses into the paddock, pulled them up, and dismounted the chariot.

Tiann began to unhitch the team, but Boudica interrupted her.

"I'll do it, Tiann. I like this pair. Maybe I will take over their training. I will need something to occupy my mind when you . . . and they will remind me of today while you are gone."

Emotion tightened Tiann's throat, and she nodded, moving aside for the queen. She left Boudica crooning to the horses while she finished unhitching them.

In the courtyard she spotted Mara sitting with Shal on a bench outside his roundhouse. The two were in deep conversation. When Mara looked up and saw her, she called and waved Tiann to join them.

Shal made room for her on the bench. "Did I see the queen driving a chariot out?"

"She and I took the new pair for a training exercise." Tiann sat, wincing from a bruise on her hip.

Mara laughed. "No wonder you look like you've been rolling on the ground and running through an autumn storm." She plucked a leaf out of Tiann's hair. "There's no gentle ride when Mother is at the reins."

"Perhaps you could use something to drink." Shal withdrew into his roundhouse and emerged with a flagon and three cups. He poured them each a measure of goat's milk.

Tiann took a long swallow of the creamy drink, realizing how thirsty she was. "Thank you. That is good." She turned the cup in her hands. It was a plain thing, gray and rough, practical. *Unlike the redware that has been on the dining table in the hall.* She had overheard the cooks talking about how Bultur disdained their local pottery. Boudica had ordered the fine imported dishes to be used every night. Tiann thought the smooth red glaze was not as beautiful as the intricate designs on their own wares. But Bultur prided himself on having developed his tastes during a season he had spent among tribes in Gaul. He had come back to Albion with a preference for wine and Gaulish housewares—and a honed hatred of Romans and their governance.

Pondering the difference in the cups, Tiann remembered the broken and defiled cup in the circle. "Shal, the morning you left, I went to the circle. I saw the cup by the spring, with your mark, and the bard's, and another. What was the third mark?"

"Ah. I asked him the same question. Who was this unseen person traveling with us? For I saw no one else. But indeed there was another, and the bard introduced me to Him. He traveled with us, and He is still here with me, and with the bard."

Tiann squirmed, uncomfortable with the hard bench on her bruise and with the conversation. *Was there another person or not? How can a person be both here and there?*

Shal patted her knee. "You think I am speaking in riddles. I assure you, I am not. I am talking about the Man who brings the light. It is His mark, the first letters of His name in the Greek language."

"The one who died? Is he a ghost, then?"

Mara leaned forward. "No, not a ghost. Tell her, Shal."

"He came back to life. He died and came back."

Tiann couldn't look at him. His voice was so confident, so full of happiness. How could he believe such a tale? "I'm sorry, Shal, but that doesn't sound different from the stories of ghosts."

"Does a ghost eat with his friends? Can a person touch a ghost and feel his flesh and his wounds? Does a tomb lie empty because of a ghost? And yet these are the reports of Christos."

"He broke it," Tiann said. She did not want to tell Shal, and the words spilling out surprised her. "Bultur smashed the cup. He sacrificed a hare and put the piece with the mark in the blood. If this man is powerful, will he come to destroy Bultur?"

"Bultur has been using the circle?" Shal stood and paced, pushing his sleeves up and down.

Tiann had not seen him perturbed since his return.

He stopped, hands on his hips, head bowed. "I am going there. I need to see for myself."

"I cleared it away . . ." Tiann said, but Shal was already striding out of the courtyard.

"Have you been back since then?" Mara asked.

"No. I didn't want to see if he had done it again."

"We should go with Shal."

Tiann looked at his retreating back. "Is it our place?"

"I don't know. I just know he is upset, and he is our friend. If what he finds is distressing, maybe our presence will comfort him. I don't care if it is my place." She started after Shal. "Come on."

By the time they reached the green cool of the wood, Shal was out of sight. While they walked in silence, Tiann considered what Shal had said about the man. Of course, she had heard accounts of ghosts but had never given them much credence. Those tales belonged to firelight storytelling and song. And she knew there were legends of the gods in other lands who'd died and then lived again. Shal himself had told her a story like that once when showing her a rare parchment filled with pictures in rows from a place called Egypt. But a man who lived as other men, dying and returning to life? What kind of man was that?

Tiann and Mara slipped between the stones of the passage into the circle. Shal faced the spring, still, head bowed. He held the cup he had filled for himself from the flagon of goat's milk. Wiping out the inside with the hem of his robe, he knelt, then filled the cup from the spring. He hesitated, even in the familiar motion of spilling out the ritual libation. Instead, he laid the cup down, unspilled. Then he stood and lifted his hands.

"Light of light. Living Water. Root of creation. I know You

know my name, but I am only learning Yours. I have lived so long in the darkness that it hurts the eyes of my heart to look at You. Will You accept the petition of a man who thought he was wise, but lacks all true knowledge? Will You listen to one whose heart has longed for You without even knowing it?"

Tiann and Mara waited by the passage stone. Shal continued to speak, his voice rising and falling, so Tiann only heard snatches. It sounded unlike any ritual she had ever heard, more like one person talking to another. At times he paused and stood quiet for a space of time, then spoke again. Tiann looked around the circle while she waited for him to finish and noticed changes. The smell of old smoke and burnt flesh scented the air. Strips of cloth, some threaded with beads, were tied in the thicket. On the oak, something hung from several branches, swaying in the breeze. She peered more intently and realized they were bones. In the niche by the spring, a new cup sat, glossy red against the green and gray of moss and stone.

Shal lowered his arms and stopped speaking. Turning, he caught sight of Tiann and Mara and lifted his hand in greeting. They moved to join him, and together, they walked the perimeter, looking at the strips of cloth and the bones. They paused in front of the cup. For Tiann, the place had always breathed a gentle peace, a gift of quiet separation. Now it spoke to her of the quest for power, of transaction.

"Will you take these things away from your circle?"

Shal sighed. "No. The circle is not mine. It belongs to the Maker, to be used by any druid. That has always been my belief. Besides, these things"—he gestured around them—"they only hold power for those who already keep them in their hearts. Those who walk the dark path."

Gwyndolyn's whinny echoed in Tiann's memory, and she remembered how the path away from the beach had reached for her. "The night I met Elior, I saw it. The dark path. I thought . . . it wanted me. But Elior said there is another way."

"There is. And it is my great hope that both of you—that all the Iceni—will become followers of the Way." Shal looked grave. "Tiann, you must heed what Elior told you. I believe he is a servant of the Maker. Do you still remember all of it?"

"No, only pieces and images."

"No matter. I remember. I will teach it to you again."

"But it was ages ago, and you only had me repeat it once."

Shal's eyebrow rose. "What do you think all that druidic training is for? We keep the stories and the wisdom. We just don't always show it off."

Mara laughed. "Not everything is as plain to see as skills on the training field. Shal, will you teach me too?"

"Yes. You both need to know. I will give you as much as I can before I leave."

"Leave! You only just returned. Why must you go again?"

Shal took Tiann's hand and shepherded them toward the passage back to the forest. "Ah, daughter, I must go to the holy isle, Mona. I must tell my brothers that the Light has come."

Tiann bit the inside of her lip, willing herself not to react like a child. Somehow she had assumed everything in the village would remain the same while she was away. That she could come back and find everyone just as they had always been.

Shal squeezed her hand. "I don't know how long I will be gone, but when I return, I will take the route through Coritani lands and visit you there. And then, Mara, I will come here to you and let you know how she fares."

They slipped through the stone passage. The air outside the circle expanded Tiann's lungs, and her heart lifted.

~

As the moon waxed fuller in the sky every night, activity increased during the day. Tiann ricocheted between exercises on the training field, etiquette and diplomacy lessons from both Boudica and Aife, and Shal's tales about the Maker and His Son. She collapsed into bed at night, body sore and mind reeling from all the things she was supposed to remember. When she woke, dreams of gold eyes and swaying bones floated away with the dawn. Devyn, equally busy, grinned at her when their paths crossed, but they did not have time to do more than exchange a few words in the hall after the evening meal.

A day before the full moon, the Coritani delegation arrived. Boudica and Prasudoc met them in the courtyard. The royal couple dressed in their most elaborate garments and jewelry. The visitors also wore fine cloaks and gold torcs, brooches, and bracelets, but they somehow lacked the splendor of the queen and chief. They appeared awkward in their finery as they exchanged formal greetings.

"Do you recognize any of them?" Mara asked as they watched from an inconspicuous spot near the forge. "I thought the same ambassadors would come to escort you."

"No, they are not the same." One of the Coritani stepped out from the group to offer a gift to Boudica, and Tiann gasped and clutched Mara's arm. "It's that man from the farmholding! The one who was spying in Iceni territory."

"The man who held a bow on you?"

"Yes." Tiann could see his yellow smile as he spoke to the queen. "He is better dressed, but it is him. Shinoc, his name was. He must have served his chief well to have been appointed to this delegation."

The line appeared between Mara's brows. "I don't like what you told me about him. And Goram didn't trust him."

Prasudoc swept his arm toward the hall, ushering the visitors toward the great doors standing open to welcome them. Boudica hung back, her eyes sweeping the courtyard. When her gaze lit on Tiann and Mara, she beckoned them with tip of her head and motioned to her own clothing.

"I guess I am done with wearing what I want. Come on—help me choose what scratchy new things to wear."

Mara laughed. "You would just wear an old tunic and training braccae for the rest of your life if you could. I like seeing you cleaned up and looking magnificent once in a while. Let me do your braids too."

Tiann grumbled, but she let Mara have her way. When they exited the sleeping chamber, Tiann wore a deep-green tunic over long, loose brown braccae. A cloak of complex weave hung down her back to her knees, pinned at each shoulder with gold and enameled brooches. Her hair was braided in an intricate style, with another brooch woven in. Her own torc adorned her neck, and Mara made up for its slender size by lending two wide gold bracelets, one for each wrist.

"I hardly feel like myself," Tiann said as they made their way through the crowded hall toward the royal table. She glanced at Mara. The line between her brows was back, and her color was high. She slowed to a stop, her gaze fixed on the strangers. Tiann stopped too and planted herself between Mara and the Coritani. "Don't come to the table. Go sit where I can see you."

"No! Tiann, you need me."

"Yes, but I have you." Tiann put Mara's palm to her scar. "This is where my journey begins. I will serve our people by learning to be a royal representative. And you will serve our people here and lend me strength from afar. Just sit where I can see you."

Mara nodded and straightened Tiann's torc. Tiann watched her find a place on a bench along the wall diagonal from her own seat at the royal table. Drawing a deep breath, she strode toward the front of the hall. Taking on the persona lent by her appearance, she lifted her chin and held her shoulders back, careful not to limp.

"Ah. Here is our daughter, Tiann, who will accompany you back to your royal village." Prasudoc rose, coming around the table to present her to the Coritani delegates. They each bowed as formal greetings ran over another.

"I greet you and welcome you to Iceni lands," Tiann said, as she had been taught. Her gaze caught on Shinoc, who offered his yellow smile.

"Thank you for your greeting. It is a pleasure to see you again. And to be made free of your name." His eyes gleamed with a malicious amusement.

"Yes, it is good to meet without threat," Tiann snapped back.

His eyes narrowed, and Tiann regretted her sharp words. It would not do to show her dislike.

Boudica rescued her. "Come. Let us share a meal."

Prasudoc escorted Tiann to her seat, and the Coritani were shown to a table laid with an impressive array of delicacies. They ate and drank heartily, but to Tiann, the special foods tasted like sand. Down the table, Boudica also ate little. The hall doors opened to admit a latecomer, and a familiar shape slipped through the opening just before the door swung shut again. A laugh bubbled up in Tiann's throat as she watched Mara's dog make his unerring way to Mara. He slipped under her bench, and Mara's food disappeared under the table at a steady pace. Grateful for the distraction, Tiann watched the little drama play out for the rest of the meal.

That night, Aife, Mara, and Tiann sat up late, playing with the dog until he fell asleep in Mara's nest of blankets on the floor. They talked of inconsequential things, of the horses, and thatching, and training. None mentioned the future or Tiann's departure. At last, they curled up in their coverings, and their murmurs faded to silence. When Mara and Aife stopped rustling and breathed the even rhythm of sleep, Tiann still lay awake. Rubbing the comforting fabric of her bed coverings between her fingers, she recounted to herself Shal's lessons. She recited Elior's message, stored in Shal's memory and relearned over the last days.

"Now is a time of revealing and remembering . . . The arm that is reaching out—it is revealed . . . Wounds from the dark transform to light . . . The darkness does not overcome. Remember the signs. Remember the wounds . . ."

She recited it three times, but still sleep eluded her. She thought through the stories about the man who'd died and then lived. How he'd healed a man who could not walk. She stretched out her stiff ankle. *I would like the man to touch my bones so I can run like I used to.* He'd fed a multitude, as many as three tribes, from the meal of one boy. He'd traveled with women, healed them, and treated them with respect. Tiann remembered how the Iceni queen, her daughters, and all her women had to pretend subservience before the Romans. Shal told them the customs where the man had lived were even stranger than those of the Romans. *This man did not pay attention to those rules.* Most of all, Shal had told her about the man's death and coming back to life. He said because of this, anyone's spirit could enter into life. *The dark does not win . . . the darkness does not overcome.* Tiann puzzled it over. *Shal says the man is the Light. Perhaps because his light was strong, stronger than anyone, because he was from the Maker. If Shal is right, then while he lived, he did not take any darkness into himself. So when the darkness of death tried to cover him, the light burst out.* Every time understanding seemed within her grasp, it slipped away, like dipping her hands into a pool and trying to hold the water.

PART THREE

CHAPTER

ELEVEN

Mara's fingers curled around hers, gentle and cool. Tiann resisted the urge to grip that calm hand. The harsh grief threatened to bubble up into tears. She focused on the water falling from the eaves. If she allowed herself to look into any of the beloved faces gathered in the courtyard, she would weep. She longed to mount up and leave the royal village behind, to skip this parting hour. How could she say farewell?

It is only for one year's turning. Tiann stared hard at the drips coming from the thatch. *I told them I can do it, and I will. The sun will rise and set, rise and set. When that has happened enough times, I will come home.*

Two wagons sat just outside the courtyard gate, each hitched to a team of two Iceni horses. Six more horses waited for their riders, shifting and blowing in the damp morning air. Deep in the wagon beds lay Tiann's household goods and gifts for the Coritani royal family and nobles. Necessities for the journey were bundled on top, covered with waxed woolen cloth and fastened down with rope. Goram moved among the ten Iceni horses he

161

was sending. He made a show of checking their hooves and tack, but he gave each a whisper and caress. A handsome gelding named Stadder had been chosen to serve as Tiann's mount. She had ridden him several times over the last days. He was friendly and obedient, with a solid pace and comfortable ride. Still, she would miss flying over the land, laid out over Gwyndolyn's neck. Stadder did not have Gwyndolyn's understanding eye or mysterious attunement to Tiann's feelings.

The six riding horses were for Tiann and the five warriors who would accompany her, including Devyn. The Coritani had sent ten men to be part of the escort. They milled around the courtyard, impatient to be on their way.

Boudica had gathered her daughters in the royal apartment the previous night for a private evening meal. They'd washed Tiann's hair. The queen had produced a slender golden cord made from several of Gwyndolyn's tail hairs, which she wove into Tiann's own braids. The hands of her mother and sisters combing, sectioning, and weaving her hair conferred their own kind of benediction.

Now she reached under her cloak's hood to the traditional Iceni braids, feeling for the bright streak of coarser hair, so different from her dark wild strands. She was glad for the reminder of the mare's spirit.

Badgered by Tiann and Mara, Goram had told and retold the story of Gwyndolyn's namesake queen. When he'd deemed them old enough, he had filled in the details of the woman's tragic marriage, battle to overthrow her faithless husband, and wise reign. As Goram explained it, Queen Gwyndolyn's decision to execute her husband's foreign lover and child kept Albion from invasion and fracture. "She kept our land for the tribes until her own son was old enough to rule." He would sigh and add, "Still, the child had done her no wrong."

Bultur, overhearing, had sniffed and said, "What is one puny child compared to the good of the land?"

Tiann looked for the dark druid now, but he had not joined the gathering to honor their departure. *He is probably in Aife's chamber behind his door, staying close to his brazier.* Bultur was well known for his distaste of damp or chill. Tiann didn't see how anyone could stand being indoors as much as he was. Conversely, his constant presence in the hall made her spend as much time as possible in the open air.

Shal stood by his roundhouse, uncaring of the drizzle. His eyes met hers, and he strode to her, his long legs crossing the courtyard with unhurried swiftness. "The day is here, child." He smiled down at her. "I must break the habit of calling you that. You are a woman with a woman's task."

"I feel like a child today."

"That is a promising sign. I would be far more concerned if you told me you felt fully capable." He placed his hand on her head. "The great good God watch over you and light your way." The droplets on his shoulders shimmered. He reached for Tiann's and Mara's clasped hands, pulling them apart. Placing Mara's palm over Tiann's scar, he said, "Your bond is true, no matter where you are. The same is true of the Maker's bond with the children." Shal's gaze sharpened on something over Tiann's shoulder, and he frowned. "Prasudoc, are you unwell?"

Tiann spun to where the chief stood hunched over, clutching the frame of the massive hall doors. His face was red, and his hand fluttered to his chest. Shal hurried to him, putting a supporting arm around him. He ushered him into the hall. Tiann flew after them, pulling over a stool. Aife ran to the cistern for a cup of water. Prasudoc sat breathing heavily while Shal held his wrist with his fingers, murmuring questions. The queen stood behind her husband, hands on his shoulders, and he leaned against her.

Shal looked to Mara. "Go to my roundhouse and get my chest of medicines. Be careful with it, child." He nodded to the cup in Aife's hand. "Warm that, but not too hot. Blood temperature."

Tiann pulled her sleeve down over her hand and wiped the sweat from her father's forehead and cheeks. When Mara returned with the chest, Shal set it on a table and rummaged through it. He selected a box containing what looked like thin, round slices of wood. Crumbling one of these into a mortar, he ground it into a fine powder. This he shook into the cup of warm water, stirring.

"Drink, my chief."

Prasudoc sipped the liquid and grimaced. "I already had a pain in my stomach, man, and you give me this bitter brew? What is this?" He swirled the gritty liquid.

"Finish it. Your pain is not from what is in your stomach, but from your heart. This is a medicine from the bulb of a plant that grows by the middle sea." Shal guided the cup back to Prasudoc's lips.

The chief scowled but gulped the medicine. Tiann watched with relief as Prasudoc's panting slowed and his face returned to a more natural shade.

Costri, the leader of the Coritani delegation, appeared at the threshold of the hall entrance. "Every pardon. The morning escapes us, and we have no wish to delay. With your permission, we will take our leave."

Boudica's knuckles whitened where her hands held her husband's shoulders. "Of course. We are saying a few private farewells. Tiann will be ready in a moment." Her expression warned her family to make no mention of Prasudoc's episode.

The Coritani inclined his head and went back outside.

Tiann waited until he had gone. "My mother, I cannot leave! Surely we can wait until my father recovers."

The queen's lips tightened. She drew a sharp breath. "Tiann, you will obey me. I know you are concerned, but you will hide it. This peace is new and untried. We will not give any reason for the Coritani to doubt our strength. We will not let on that the chief felt unwell. It would only make them speculate. You will carry on as planned. Do you understand?"

"Yes, my queen."

Prasudoc grasped Tiann's hand. "I'm sorry to cause you worry on your leaving day. I will be fine." He tugged her closer, and she knelt beside him. He put his arms around her, his beard rough against her face. "Have a peaceful heart, my daughter. We will all be together again soon. Go now. Go with my blessing and my love."

Tiann hugged him back, careful not to clutch him too fiercely. She then stood, straightened her clothing, and smoothed her hair.

Aife fussed over her, settling Tiann's cloak on her shoulders so the three-spiraled clasps hung straight. She stepped back, her face a stern imitation of her mother's, although tears wet her lashes. "I am proud to be your sister." Aife's voice quivered, and she cleared her throat.

Mara rushed forward and squeezed Tiann hard for three heartbeats. "Come back. Do not be late. I'll be watching for you." She whirled around and ran to her bedchamber.

The hound whined, pacing after Mara, and coming back to nose Tiann's hand.

"It's all right." Tiann scratched him around his soft ears. "We're all right. Go to her. She needs you." She pushed the hound toward the bedchamber. He whined again, then trotted after Mara.

"To serve one's people is a great calling, my daughter," Boudica said. "I know you will acquit yourself well. I look forward to meeting with you on a chariot platform again." A hint of a smile crinkled around her eyes.

Shal held out his hand. "Come, child. I will escort you to those who await you."

Tiann clasped his hand and looked around the circle of her family. A lump in her throat stole her voice. She nodded to each one, trying to convey her heart.

Outside, Shal led her to where Goram held Stadder's reins. She embraced the horse trainer, who gruffly wiped his eyes on his sleeves. Lacing his hands, he boosted Tiann into the saddle.

Shal looked up at her. "Remember what I have taught you. When the dark confuses you, look to the Maker for the light. Seek the risen one, whose name is the Light."

With a creaking of wagon wheels and stamping of impatient hooves, the party moved through the gates and soon left the main village behind. Tiann allowed herself one long look over her shoulder. Smoke curled from roundhouses and the hall. The paddock stood quiet and the training field empty, all morning activity paused to see her off. From the gate, a stream of people followed them, waving and calling farewells. Shal stood by the gateposts, head bowed and hands raised in blessing.

Tiann huddled under the damp wool blanket draped over her head and shoulders. The first two days of their journey had been long and muddy. Bogged down by inclement weather and the difficulties of moving a large train of people and goods, they had not yet left Iceni territory. She looked forward to stopping in a Coritani village instead of spending the night in a makeshift camp. If the weather had been fine, they would have reached the edge of Coritani land that afternoon. Her hosts would not stay in any Iceni villages. Devyn had questioned this, and Shinoc, bowing, had said, "We would not want to strain the hospitality of your people. We wish only to be considerate guests."

To Tiann it seemed they were going out of their way to avoid interacting with anyone outside their company. When she mentioned this to Devyn, he frowned. "He is hard to trust, I'll grant you. But we shouldn't look for ill intent just because he is unlikeable. There is no set protocol for a journey like this."

She saw him confer with the four Iceni warriors who were part of her escort until she reached her destination. They had been chosen not primarily for their ability as warriors but because they were schooled in etiquette, having grown up in the royal village. The four of them would escort the nephew of the Coritani chief back to Boudica and Prasudoc. They spoke quietly, shrugging their shoulders, not looking concerned. Shinoc sauntered to the group, inserting himself into the conversation. He made some jest and waved a hand toward the fire. The group laughed and headed to where the evening meal awaited, with plain food and plentiful mead.

They sat on stumps and rocks around a sullen, smoking fire. Tiann ate, not in the mood to share in the banter of the men. If her men had been chosen for their manners, it did not seem the Coritani group had the same qualifications. Only Costri appeared to be of a noble class, but he held himself aloof from the rest. When Tiann rose, he approached her.

"I know you had a wet night last night. We will try sheltering you under one of the wagons." He beckoned one of his men and gave him instructions. They rolled the wagon so that its side nestled in a yew hedge, then draped the other sides with blankets. Rocks weighted down the edges. A waxed-wool blanket was laid on the ground to combat the moisture soaking the earth.

"Thank you," Tiann said. "What about the rest of you?"

"Ach, we'll make a shelter under the other wagon. We can fit three or four. We'll take it in turns with the changing of the watch."

Tiann nodded and crouched to enter the shelter. It wasn't

much, but it was a vast improvement over the previous night. She had hardly slept between the rain and the grief over leaving her family and home. The day's hard slog after the restless night left her body leaden and her head aching. The sounds of the men at the fire and the horses faded, and she slept heavily.

The next day dawned gray, but the rain had stopped. They continued to steer clear of any villages or farmholdings. The noon meal was meager, and Tiann thought they would surely need to reprovision if they did not reach Coritani territory soon. Drops spattered on the leaves overhead when they reached a boundary stone some hours later. But the village where they stopped for the night left much to be desired in terms of hospitality and comfort. After a look at the offered bedding in the small roundhouse that served as both inn and stable, Tiann wished that her own blankets were not so deeply packed in the wagon.

More uncomfortable than the accommodations was their reception. The people of the village scattered at their approach, perhaps a wise reaction when a large band with armed warriors comes to town. It was the way they stayed hidden, peering out from behind doors or reluctantly coming to perform services that was disconcerting. *Why are these Coritani villagers nervous around their own warriors, to the point of rudeness? Don't they even want to profit from our visit? Why aren't they enticed to offer trade by the sight of obvious wealth?*

Shouting, followed by a cry of pain, drew Tiann's attention. One of the Coritani warriors loomed over a village girl, who held her cheek. Leaving the meager shelter at the side of the wagon, Tiann bolted, mud squelching underfoot, to where the girl bent, shaking, trying to gather the scattered firewood at her feet.

"Trying to sneak past and see to your own comfort while we stay here cold and soaked," the warrior said. He drew his foot back to kick her.

Tiann grabbed his arm and yanked, pulling him off balance. He slipped, falling on his backside into the mud.

"What is going on here? Why did you strike this girl?"

The warrior scrambled up. His face was deep scarlet, and his fists clenched. His glare made her want to flinch. She stood her ground as he stepped toward her, and Tiann heard the girl gasp. Readying herself for defense, Tiann glanced down to check his feet for clues to his next move, then watched his face. His gaze slid beyond her, and he stepped back.

"Do you need assistance?" asked an Iceni warrior behind her.

Devyn also appeared at her side.

"Thank you," Tiann said, neither denying nor acknowledging the threat from the Coritani man before her. "I was inquiring as to the reason for this girl's punishment."

The Coritani man spoke through gritted teeth. "She was bringing a load of firewood to her own roundhouse while we are still waiting for fire and food."

"I am sorry, sir," the girl said. She still trembled, and a welt rose on her cheek. "Please, I only just returned from the field. I did not know you needed firewood."

An old man hobbled to them, the drizzling rain plastering his thin hair to his head so that the pink scalp showed through. "Please forgive my granddaughter for her error. She will bring the wood to your accommodations at once."

Tiann put a hand on his arm. "Do not trouble yourself, sir. She has done nothing wrong." She turned to the girl. "Take the wood home and care for your family. We ask pardon for your mistreatment. When we reach the royal village, this man's behavior will be reported and your chief will deal with him."

The girl began to cry. She scooped up the rest of the wood and fled toward a small dwelling. The old man bowed. "Thank you, Lady." He hurried after his granddaughter.

Tiann eyed the Coritani warrior. Although he had regained

control of himself, his face glowed with scarlet rage. "Go search out some dry clothes. I'm sure we can find someone to clean the mud off those. And remember, we are guests of the people in this village, even if they are your tribe. We will show them courtesy."

His eyes narrowed. "Yes, *Lady*," he said, sarcasm tinging his tone. He stalked off toward the wagons.

The Iceni warrior at her back laid a heavy hand on her shoulder. "You haven't made a friend there, Tiann."

"Thank you for coming to my aid."

Devyn laughed. "You were doing very well. He has no idea how good you are at fighting in the mud."

The warrior did not join in the laughter. He looked after the Coritani man. "Still, we will keep closer to you. I don't like the temper on that one."

They settled at last in the guest roundhouse. Although a meager fire smoked in the center, Tiann shivered with damp and chill. There was not enough room for all in the roundhouse. Half of their party sheltered in a large three-sided outbuilding. Even with a wagon drawn in front, the rain would still find its way in. Still, they shared the outbuilding with the horses, which would keep them warmer.

Two older women ducked through the entrance, carrying baskets and a clay vessel that steamed. One woman had a clouded eye, the color and pupil merged into a fixed pale gray. They were skittish, passing out bread and ladling broth into cups with shaking hands. Neither raised her head when Tiann thanked them.

One of the Coritani men waved his empty cup as the last of them were being served. "This wasn't enough for a child. Bring more, and put some meat in it this time. Actually, don't bring it. Send it in with some pretty ones."

Tiann bristled and saw an echoing flash of anger from one of the village women. Her companion quelled her with a hard look from her good eye. "Yes, sir."

Tiann's heartbeat accelerated, and she felt choked. *I am a representative of the Iceni royal family. I am Boudica's daughter.* It had been easier to prepare to fight in the mud than to defend with words. *What do I say that will not anger the Coritani warriors?* She had already seen the man she'd confronted earlier speaking hot words with his companions, and all of them casting baleful looks her way.

She cleared her throat. "Of course he jests. Surely you have already shared the main portion of your village's evening meal with us. Thank you for your hospitality. I am certain your warriors are proud to fight for you."

One woman bit her lip, blinking, then nodded a quick bow and rushed from the roundhouse. The one with the clouded eye turned her face to Tiann. "Thank you, Lady. Yes, I know they are." She hesitated, lips parted as if she would like to say something else. Instead, she shook her head and shifted her basket to her other hip. "A blessing on your journey, Lady," she said, and then she too ducked out.

The exchange made Tiann uncomfortable. The warrior had been rude and coarse, but those women had seemed afraid even before his discourtesy. Did the Coritani disrespect their women like the Romans did? Tiann was sure Boudica would have known and warned her if this were so. And it was not fear she saw in their faces when they looked at her. She could have sworn she saw sadness or even pity. Did they think being a hostage in their chief's household would be so terrible?

Tiann shrugged off her unease and lay down to sleep her first night away from her ancestral land. Her stomach rumbled, far from satisfied with small portions of bread and broth. She rasped a breath over the lump in her throat and squeezed her eyes tight shut. She longed for Mara's steady presence. Finally, she fell into a fitful doze.

She found herself wandering through a dream version of the familiar forest path to the circle. Although she knew it was nearby, dense brush blocked her at every turn. She knew her father waited for her there by the spring. She was desperate to reach him, to have him hold her and reassure her, as he had done when she was small. Her frantic hands ripped at the vines and branches, but they only grew thicker and thornier under her fingers. A voice in the distance called her, but she could not locate the source. Suddenly, light infused her dream, and Elior was beside her, laying his hands over hers and stilling them from their panicked effort.

"Not that way, child."

"But I'm lost, so lost! Why can't I find my way? My father is there! I hear him!" A wail rose in her throat.

"Yes, your father waits for you by the living spring. You hear his voice. But you cannot get to him on this path. Remember what I told you. Look for the Light. Remember the signs. Remember the wounds."

Tiann awoke, heart thumping. Her hands were balled tight with the residual sensation of the dream brush in them. Echoing through her mind, Elior's voice repeated, "Remember, remember." She clenched her fists tighter until her nails cut into her palms. She didn't want to remember.

BLEARY EYED, Tiann rolled the camp blankets and carried them to the wagon. The Coritani warriors insisted on an early start, saying they would eat the morning meal on the road. The small courtyard remained bare of villagers, except for a handful pressed into service to fill waterskins and baskets of bread. As she tucked the bedroll in and cinched the cords fastening it in its place, a small voice whispered behind her.

"Iceni lady." The young girl from the day before, her cheek dark with an ugly bruise, made a show of helping her with the blankets. "Don't show that I'm talking to you. I'm not supposed to tell anything. They would burn our village, maybe kill us. But you have been kind to us. You behave with honor. We wish to do the same."

"Who?" Tiann whispered back, pretending to struggle with a knot. "Who is threatening you?"

"Your captors. They are not Coritani, at least not most of them. And the ones that are have been outcast for many years." The girl's words streamed out, the sound just above a breath. "The escort party from our chief was waylaid when they went to get you. Five killed, two wounded. The other two rode back to the chief. He has search parties out, but they thought you would be taking the inland route. We sent a runner when you arrived here, but it may take time to find the chief."

"Who are they? Where are they taking me?"

The girl slipped away from Tiann, her wary eyes on a warrior who was striding toward them. She breathed a reply as she went.

"They are Brigantes. They're taking you to Cartimandua."

Tiann turned her back to the approaching warrior, sure her shock must be evident in her face. She tugged at the knots, pretending to test their security while she struggled to school her expression.

"Are you having trouble?" The warrior leaned on the wagon, peering at the ropes holding the load in place.

"Ah. No, I have fixed it now. It . . . it was a bit of a tangle." To her relief, her voice sounded normal, even though she felt breathless. *I have to get to Devyn and the others and tell them what the girl said. Can it be true?* Moments of unease flickered through her memory. None of the original Coritani diplomats arriving to accompany Tiann.

The discord between the warriors and the villagers, supposedly from the same tribe. The way the Iceni party never found themselves together without one of the supposed Coritani escorts. The avoidance of villages along the journey. "I'll go gather the rest of my things." She stepped briskly toward the guest roundhouse, hoping to get to Devyn or one of her other warriors.

"I'll help you." The man fell into step with her.

Tiann opened her mouth to protest but thought better of it, fearing to give the girl away. She wished she knew her name.

As the morning wore on, they headed north at a steady pace. Tiann watched for any opportunity to speak privately with one of her men but never found one. An escort was always at her side. She couldn't decide if they had been so careful for the entire journey and she was only now noticing or if they had tightened their watch because they had seen her talking to the village girl. She hoped the village would not suffer for their bravery in warning her. Her stomach felt sick from the tension as the sun rose higher. The rain of the previous days had given way to a hot haze, steaming the dampness of the earth into a sticky humidity.

They stopped at midday to rest the horses in a clearing and take a meal. Tiann tried to be casual as she took her bread and cheese over to where Devyn stood, stretching his back and talking to one of the Iceni warriors. Just as she reached them, Shinoc materialized.

He slapped the backs of the Iceni men. "Finish up your food. There is a brook just over the rise and a pool to cool off. Most of us are there now." He steered them away from Tiann. Looking over his shoulder, he said, "I am sorry, Lady, but it is not a place that affords privacy. I am certain you would not wish to bathe in the presence of us men." His leering yellow grin suggested he could imagine her doing just that.

Frustrated and disgusted, she watched them head over the

rise. She could hear splashing and shouts from others of their party who'd already enjoyed the cool water. She did a quick scan. All the Iceni men had gone to the brook. Two of the "Coritani" warriors remained. One stretched out in the shade of a wagon. He looked relaxed, but Tiann noted his sword was close by. The other, the man who had struck the young village girl, sat leaning against a tree. He whistled tunelessly through his teeth, sharpening his dagger.

Strolling around the small clearing, Tiann forced herself to nibble at her food while she assessed the situation. Would this be a good place to catch their captors by surprise, attack, and escape? Her own sword was with her baggage, so she had only her dagger. She swept the area with her gaze and located a couple of stout-looking fallen branches that could work as fighting staves. The horses were either still harnessed to the wagons or loosely hobbled. She chose one that grazed a little way beyond the wagons, a smaller, fleet mare. Tiann thought she could get to her, release the hobble, and mount before being stopped. If only there was a way to strategize with her men, or at least warn them in advance, so they would be ready to arms.

She halted at the sound of laughter drifting from over the rise where the men were bathing. *They are not just unready to fight— they are unarmed.* Tiann's stomach lurched. She had been so preoccupied trying to plan an ambush that she'd never considered maybe one had already been planned.

A shout of alarm sounded from the brook. Tiann dropped her bread and cheese and sprinted toward the rise. A rock underfoot twisted her bad ankle, and pain jolted through her. Falling to her hands and knees, she cried out, scrambling to regain her feet. Brutish hands lifted her from behind, pulling her arms to her back in an iron grip. Kicking and thrashing, Tiann fought to break free. She threw her head back and was rewarded by a crunch and grunt of pain. Her assailant dropped her to the ground, and her ankle collapsed under her.

The warrior advanced. Blood streamed from his nose. A dagger flashed in his hand. *Roll away.* Tiann screamed a warning. "Iceni! Iceni! To arms!" *Draw my dagger. No. His reach is longer than mine.* One of the fallen branches she had noted earlier lay near her hand. She snatched it. *Under the ribs.* She drove it upward. His breath whooshed out, and his mouth opened and closed as he struggled to capture air. *Follow up.* She clubbed the side of his head. Using the makeshift staff for balance, she regained her feet in time to see the other warrior edging toward her, sword in hand. She crouched, finding the balance point of her staff.

"Now, we don't want to hurt you, girl." The man glanced at his compatriot on the ground. "Just put your stick down. And give me that dagger too."

Tiann bared her teeth. "Maybe it is you who will be hurt." She listened for conflict from the brook. Cries and sounds of deadly combat drifted to her. At last she heard the sound of sword clash, indicating that at least one of her men had reached a weapon. The warrior coming toward her flicked his eyes in that direction, and she knew he heard it too. "The surprise is over. Put your sword down." Tiann circled, pulling her dagger from its sheath. She entwined her fingers around the slim handle so she could still wield the staff. She visualized how to disarm him. Her reach with the staff was longer than his with the sword. It was not the longer sword carried by the Iceni. She narrowed her eyes, paying atten-tion to his feet but studying the sword. She had seen one like it. She shifted her grip on the staff while her mind sorted through images. A ripple of memory floated through her. *Pain and terror. Romans. My hand on the stone. A gladius.*

Crashing steps through the brush drew her awareness. Devyn's voice called her name with desperation. He burst over the ridge, wet hair streaming behind him, clothed only in braccae. His eyes fixed on her. Mud and blood streaked his torso, and he held his arm to his chest. A gaping gash in his shoulder dripped a red trail behind him.

Tiann watched the Coritani warrior's feet turn away from her, his knees bend, his body twist. She blinked, confused by the withdrawal of his threatening stance. Then he sprang—not toward her but toward Devyn.

TWELVE

A scream ripped out of her. Devyn redirected his gaze to the warrior and raised a bloody hand, staggering. The warrior plunged the gladius into Devyn's belly, angling it upward with a grunt. Devyn's gaze came back to Tiann as he sank to his knees. Blood bubbled from his lips. The gladius pulled free from his falling body with a sucking sound.

Tiann's mind was a white fog. Another scream reverberated on and on somewhere in the burning sunlight. Her staff whirled, thumping flesh and cracking bone. Her dagger grew wet and slippery. She cast it down, scattering red enemy gore. Panting and pulse throbbed in her ears.

Her vision cleared, and she was kneeling over the warrior's body. She crawled away. Devyn lay with his hand out to the side. She put it on his chest. Closed his eyelids. Scooped up leaves, trying to cover the obscene wound in his belly. When she kissed his mouth, the taste of salt mingled with the iron tang of blood.

A kick sent the dagger spinning away from where she had dropped it. Two sets of hands dragged her away from Devyn. She went limp, and they dumped her in a heap by the wagon. She curled up, dully watching them wiping off swords. One of her enemies inspected the bodies. He called that she had killed one but the other was unconscious. "Lump the size of a horse turd on his head," he said, beckoning for someone to help him get the man on the wagon.

"Not too bad." Shinoc unstrung his bow. "We took out all of them. For us, only one dead, two wounded. Not bad at all."

They dumped out some of the Iceni baggage to make room for their own wounded. "Don't leave the girl's things behind. Don't let him bleed on them either. The queen will want all that."

"She can't have my bedcover," Tiann whispered. A longing rose in her to snatch the comforting fabric from the wagon. To burrow under it, shut her eyes, and pretend she was home. Mara breathing serenely nearby while the hound sighed in his sleep. The predawn scent of baking bread. The last dreamy moments of night clutched close, like the silken cocoon wrapped around her.

Shinoc squatted in front of her. "Come on now, girl. I'll bring you to the brook so you can wash before we move on. Just don't you look downstream."

Tiann kicked his kneecap, and he landed on his rump. The smirk disappeared from his face. He jumped up and hauled her to her feet. "Trying to treat you fine. You can get in that water right next to those bodies now." He dragged her toward the rise.

"Shinoc." Costri spoke with sharp authority. "Don't be a fool. The girl's already taken down two of our men. Leave her here and go fetch her a bucket of water. Clean water."

Shinoc glowered but dropped her arm. Tiann returned to sit, leaning against the wagon wheel. She tucked her knees to her chest. The spokes dug into her back. She welcomed the discomfort, concentrating on it to keep from remembering the sound of the gladius in Devyn's body. She closed her eyes to shut out the sight of the bodies being moved into the underbrush. The scavengers would find them soon enough. There would be no tomb and bonfire for Devyn and the others. They would not even have their swords, which were being loaded into the other wagon. *Will the queen and chief learn what happened to them? Will they be able to have a season of mourning, or will they always wonder if we are dead or alive?*

When Shinoc set the bucket down next to her, the water sloshing onto her braccae, she opened her eyes. Her lashes felt sticky. Using the cloth he tossed to her, she did her best to scrub away the blood drying on her hands and arms. Her tunic was spattered, but she could do nothing about that. The water turned deep red, and still she had blood under her nails and in the creases of her knuckles. Costri took the bucket away without a word, dumped it, and went to the brook to get her fresh water.

"Your face, girl." He handed her a clean cloth. She dipped it in the water and swiped it over her cheeks and mouth. It came away red. She stared at it. Devyn's blood. Their only kiss. She carefully wiped the rest of her face, then folded the stained cloth and tucked it into her empty dagger sheath. Dipping her hands in the bucket, she threw the water over her face and head again and again. When she could no longer fill her hands, she tipped the rest of the water over her head. The water streamed over her hair, met the ground, and soaked into the earth.

Tiann sat, mind numb, until Costri came and nudged her with his foot. "We're moving on. Are you going to cause difficulties, or can I leave you unbound on your own horse?"

Tiann wanted to cause difficulties. She wanted to spit and kick, whirl through them with a sword like the hero of a song, run all the way back to the royal village. Her arms weighed her down, as heavy as when she'd drunk too much mead. Her thoughts refused to come together. She dragged her stiffened body up. All her energy had melted into the ground like the bloody wash water. She wondered if she would even have enough strength to sit her horse.

"I can ride." Her voice croaked. The ache of her screams lingered in her throat.

The leader nodded. "Mount up then." He hesitated, looking at the treetops. "We will be guarding you. But if you behave, I'll make sure no one ill-treats you."

Tiann shuffled to Stadder, noticing that her saddlebags hung askew. Peering inside, she could see someone had tossed the contents about, likely searched for weapons. She straightened the bags and adjusted the girth. The placid creature gazed at her with soft eyes. Tiann stroked his neck and nose. "I'm glad for an Iceni friend." The horse stood shorter than Gwyndolyn, but hauling herself up to mount still made her arms shake. A Coritani warrior drew up on each side of her, staying half a length back. *Not Coritani. Brigantian.* She nudged Stadder with her heels, steering him to continue from the clearing in the direction they had been traveling.

"Not that way. Back the way we came." The party retraced their route from the morning. Sickened, Tiann realized they had taken a turning off the main track for the specific purpose of the ambush. The place had been scouted and chosen. *How could we have all been so unaware, so trusting? Especially me, when I was warned?* The shame burned in her chest. When they reached the crossroads where they had turned, instead of rejoining the main track, they crossed and continued along a wilder way.

Costri called a halt when there was barely enough daylight to see. Dismounting, Tiann nearly tumbled to the ground on nerveless legs. Bruises and muscle strains made themselves felt. She looked after Stadder, forcing her tired limbs to the work of unsaddling him and rubbing him down. Grateful for his companionship, she took her time. She brought him water and left him loosely hobbled to graze in a patch of grass.

By the time she finished, the men had made a crude and hasty camp in the growing dusk. They bickered over who had to care for the riderless Iceni horses. The day's heat dissipated with the twilight, and Tiann wrapped herself in one of the camp blankets. She ate when someone handed her a bit of cheese and some parched grain. She drank when a waterskin was passed. No one addressed her. Pillowing her head on a saddlebag, she watched a star wink into view. It pulsed and swelled, gold against the night.

The light will teach you.

The path will be grievous, but do not fear.

The darkness does not overcome.

Tiann shut her eyes tight. *But it does. It does! The darkness won today. Where was the light today when Iceni were murdered over the rise? Where was Shal's great god when the gladius plunged?*

Somewhere in the night, an owl sounded its call.

Remember the wounds.

Tiann clamped her hands over her ears. She wished for a draught of the medicine Shal had given her when he'd set her ankle. She wanted to sleep and sleep, and wake to find the day had never happened.

IN THE MORNING, they continued away from the rising sun, following a faint track through ever thicker forest. Tiann fought to keep from succumbing to the dull haze that crept into her mind. She let Stadder pick his way through, ducking when he brushed under low-hanging branches. Forcing her senses to alertness, she watched for landmarks that might assist her if she could devise a way of escape. Eventually, the sameness of the landscape and her deep weariness overtook her. Her eyelids grew heavy, and she dozed in her saddle.

Voices calling a halt jerked her awake. They had emerged from the forest to a wide swath extending to the left and right, cleared of trees. Tiann blinked, eyes adjusting to the brighter light. She leaned, peering around the captors in front of her. They were dismounting and leading their horses down a ditch and up the opposite side. Hooves rang against stone. Before her lay the stuff of scout reports brought to the queen and chief from other regions of Albion. A *via*, built by the Romans to speed their armies and supplies the length and breadth of Albion.

This route stretched north and south as far as Tiann could see. She dismounted and traversed the ditch, holding the reins and clucking to her horse. Behind her, a squabble broke out about how to maneuver the wagons across. Tiann ignored the argument, examining the unnatural land beneath her feet. The road lay smooth and slightly curved, higher in the center. It was wide enough for two carts side by side. Anxious to be back in the familiar shade of the forest with earth under her feet, Tiann searched the opposite side for the continuation of the track they had just left. But the men were not leading their mounts across the road. They left them milling there while they struggled to put shoulders to the wagons, lifting them up onto the stone surface.

When they accomplished the task, they passed around water-skins and parched grain. Costri handed a portion to Tiann without comment.

She grabbed his sleeve. "Why are we stopping here? Surely there is a more suitable spot along the trail after we cross." Tiann looked up and down the uninterrupted enemy construction. Still empty. "They send patrols along their roads."

"We have safe passage." The leader pulled his arm away and turned, but not before Tiann saw his mouth twist into a frown. She stayed close to Stadder, stroking his nose. His placid eyes followed the movements of the group forming up to ride again. His hooves lifted and stepped on the hard surface, the ring making his ears twitch quizzically. Still, he did not shy.

Tiann smoothed his forelock. "You are not worried, are you?

Give me some of your calm, friend." She mounted, holding the reins in one hand while she munched on her handful of grain.

Hoofbeats and wagon wheels on stone made an unfamiliar racket. The scent of dust and men replaced that of earth and undergrowth. They tramped north, a party of eleven, with two wagons and six riderless Iceni horses led by reins attached to the saddle of the mount in front of them. The sun dropped to the west. Shadows from the forest running alongside the road reached fingers toward them. At regular intervals, they passed a dressed stone with carved markings. Tiann recognized these patterns from the accounting scrolls the stewards used when recording the taxes levied by the Romans every harvest time. She supposed they marked off bits of the road in the same way they counted bushels of grain or numbers of livestock. Certainly, they had to make their own landmarks, since the road ran straight on and on, with no way of telling one portion from another. They had passed two handfuls of marked stones, when a cluster of buildings became visible in deep afternoon light.

A sturdy bridge crossed the roadside ditch toward the settlement, and they turned onto it, coming to a halt in a gravel courtyard. The buildings stood in rows with narrow lanes between them, also paved with gravel. Walls constructed of stone and timber rose straight from ground to roof, with walls meeting at corners. People crowded the courtyard, talking in small groups, hurrying to and fro. Their party drew glances but little curiosity. Some of the people milling about wore familiar dress of tunic, braccae, and cloak, but more wore the uniforms of Roman soldiers.

A shudder passed through Tiann. This place screamed *enemy*. The buildings forced their way onto the landscape with neither natural shapes nor care for the surroundings. The air sounded of voices, the clang of an unseen blacksmith, and feet on stone and gravel. There was no song or children's play. And at every Roman waist, a gladius hung in a sheath from a studded leather belt. Tiann's stomach heaved, and she leaned over Stadder's neck. She squeezed her eyes shut and willed herself not to be sick. Not here. Not in front of them. Her head swirled with dizziness. She pressed her cheek into the live, warm horseflesh, clinging to wiry strands of his mane.

"We will spend the night here." Costri's voice spoke low next to her. "Are you able to dismount?"

Tiann opened her eyes. He stood holding her bridle. Straightening her back, she swallowed. "Yes. Of course I can dismount." She swung her leg over, but when her feet reached the ground, her legs threatened to buckle.

The leader put a hand under her elbow. "Just stand here and breathe for a moment. Perhaps you can look for something in your saddlebag."

Tiann shook off his treasonous hand. Still, she took the suggestion. Her fingers shook as she undid the opening of the bag. With one hand, she rummaged inside while she clung white-knuckled to the saddle with the other. She brushed a familiar small bundle, and the fragrance of healing herbs met her nose. Drawing the sachet to her chest, she lightly crushed it to release the scent. She schooled herself to breathe slow inhales and long exhales, grateful to her fighting instructors. Every spear-hurling and archery lesson had included exercises to steady the heart and hands.

Feeling less wobbly, she replaced the herbs and unfastened the saddlebag. She slung it over her shoulder and unsaddled her horse. Every muscle ached. Pain and grief had weakened her, but she would never give them the satisfaction of seeing it. The saddlebag bounced against a bruise on her back. She hauled her spine straight, holding the saddle with both arms and the reins wrapped around her hand. She led Stadder to the trough where the rest of the party—the murderers—watered their horses.

A Roman approached them. "I am Amlethius, the castra commander. Permits." His speech, though serviceable Celtic, was not that of a cultured man.

Costri opened the pouch hanging from his belt and drew out a small scroll. The Roman unrolled it, squinting at the contents. His eyebrows lifted. "From Cerialis himself. What does the Ninth have to do with your lot?"

"I believe the legate and the Brigantian queen feel that the young woman we are escorting will be valuable as a negotiating tool."

"Brigantes—aren't they the pack north of where the Ninth is stationed at Lindum? Yes, I can see why Cerialis would want friends up there." Amlethius tapped his thigh with the scroll, scanning the party. "So there's a woman with you. Is that her?" He pointed the scroll toward Tiann. "She doesn't look like much."

"We have been traveling, and there was some . . . trouble. She is the daughter of the Iceni chief and queen."

"Ah yes. To the east, isn't it? And the king's name is Persagus or some such." Amlethius seemed pleased with his knowledge. "So, barbarian royalty. Well, well. Have her dress in something decent and join me for dinner." He wrinkled his nose. "To the baths first, of course. I'll send a slave to help her."

"Sir," the leader said stiffly.

Amlethius turned back.

"May I have the safe passage back?"

"Ah. Of course." Amlethius tossed him the scroll.

"Also, the young woman. She is my charge, and I am under orders to watch over her. I must insist on being permitted to accompany her to your quarters. Only as a guard, you understand."

Amlethius looked him up and down. "Very well. But be sure you get to the baths as well."

Tiann listened to this exchange with growing horror. Cartimandua was in league with the Romans. They had conspired together to abduct her. And now she was expected to attend one of them at dinner. Would she have to serve this Amlethius as Boudica had done when the Romans had come to the royal village? Heat washed through her body, chased by ice. Why did he want her to bathe? Two kinds of women at their feasts, Aife had told her.

Costri swung around to look at her. "Don't be afraid. He just wants to boast he had dinner with the daughter of a king. I'll make sure no harm comes to you."

A stout woman carrying a bundle of clothes bustled up to Tiann. She wore a tunic that was too long for her, hitched up with a rope belt. Her hair was coiled in an untidy knot. Though she was not smiling, the lines around her eyes and mouth suggested that she did often. Her gaze lit on Tiann, and she gave a brisk nod. "Come along then, dear."

"My horse . . ." Tiann protested.

"I'll care for him," the leader said. "I'll see that he is fed, wiped down, and bedded."

Tiann nodded, suddenly wanting nothing more than to lie down for a moment. She gritted her teeth, hitched her saddlebag more securely on her shoulder, and followed the round woman. They walked down the gravel lanes between identical structures, turning twice. If not for the position of the sun and angle of the shadows, Tiann would have been completely disoriented. The uniformity unsettled her. Among the Iceni, every dwelling bore the marks of its makers, from size, to the carvings on the doorframes and lintels, to the weave of the walls.

The woman stopped at a larger rectangular structure at the end of a lane. "Here we are. Fortunate you came when you did— the women only get two days a week because it's the only one and there are so many more men."

Tiann stepped into the building after her, blinking in the dimness. "Only one what?"

"Only one bath. It's not exactly the middle of civilization here, is it? Here it's all about the army. A decent bathhouse rates below the armory. Not even a tepidarium. Straight from the hot to the cold." Pulling back a curtain to a small side room, she gestured Tiann inside. She laid her bundle on a bench, pulled Tiann's saddlebag from her shoulder, and set it down. She gestured toward the hooks on the wall. "You can hang your clothes here. I'll come back and get them for cleaning in a moment."

"You want me to undress? But I have not fetched a bucket."

The woman stared at her. "Bucket? Dear, this is a bath. Just come through once you're undressed." She made a shooing motion toward the hooks and disappeared through a door deeper within the building.

Tiann drew the curtain closed, sat on the bench, and drew off her boots. She lifted her feet in alarm as they contacted the floor. Where she had expected cool tile, her feet met warmth. Uneasy, she tested the unnatural heat with her bare toes. When she was sure she would not be burned, she stood and pulled off her outer garments, hanging them on hooks. The garments hung stiffly, dried mud and blood crusting the surface. She looked for a length of cloth to wrap around herself, but finding none, she kept her inner tunic on. She poked her head out from the curtained alcove. Seeing no one, she opened the door the woman had gone through.

A wave of steam assaulted her. She stepped back. The smell was not like cooking. Nor did it smell like the huge boiling pots of dye she had so hated to labor over, swirling cloth through using wooden paddles. It reminded her of the ointments Shal used on wounds, made of oil and herbs. From within the cloud of steam, voices protested in Latin.

The round woman materialized and pulled Tiann within,

shutting the door. "It takes some doing here to build up the furnace. You mustn't let all the warmth out."

Through the haze, Tiann could make out a large rectangular cistern in the floor, filled with water, which was the source of the moisture wisping through the space. A handful of women occupied the room, immersed in the water or sitting on the edge, talking. One lay prone on a bench while a girl appeared to be applying an ointment to her back. None wore a garment or a drape.

Embarrassed, Tiann averted her eyes. "Surely I can wait until this family finishes, Lady," she whispered to the woman still tugging her arm.

"Oh no, there is plenty of room. They don't know each other either, most of them. And what—you call slaves 'Lady' in your tribe? Just call me Clothilde, dear." With a swift motion, she grabbed the hem of Tiann's tunic and yanked it up over her head and off. "Now get in the caldarium, and I'll be back soon."

Tiann wrapped her arms around her body and scurried toward the water, sliding in to sit on a built-in ledge and trying to ignore the frank assessment of the other women. After a moment, they lost interest and went back to their conversations.

Tiann swirled the warm water with her hands. What made it this temperature? She knew there were sacred springs in the West but had heard of none North. A furnace, Clothilde had said. Like a fire at the smith. Was this furnace also why the floor was strangely hot? Maybe it was lit in a space under the floor. The idea made her uncomfortable, like the earth had transformed into a beast from a story. If the floor gave way, she would drop into its fiery breath. None of the other women seemed concerned. In fact, they seemed to be here more for relaxing and enjoying themselves than for cleansing their bodies.

Tiann lifted her hands from the water. Her nails and the grooves of her knuckles still held dirt and blood. She rubbed them together, scratching to loosen the grime. Sinking down, she submerged her head. She massaged her scalp with her fingers. The braids were loosened and knotted. If she didn't release them and comb out her hair, it would be hopelessly tangled. A broken fingernail caught on the plait of Gwyndolyn's mane hair. With the pain of the nail, torn below the quick, came memory. Boudica, Aife, Mara combing out her hair. Their tender touch as they prepared her to leave. Their teasing and laughter, snatches of song. A bubble of grief rose in Tiann's chest and burst from her mouth in a sob. Tears, hotter than the surrounding water, flowed from her eyes. She surfaced with a heaving gasp.

The other women paused in their conversations to look at her. Tiann was helpless to stop the tears or the ugly sounds coming from her throat with every breath. She felt nothing, no shame, no dignity, nothing but the agony of the last days. The two women in the pool with her and the two sitting on the edge dropped their eyes, murmuring to each other. With haste, they rose and grabbed bath sheets from a folded stack. Wrapping themselves in the cloths, they hurried to a door on the far side of the steamy room.

The woman on the bench propped herself up on one elbow to observe Tiann. She gave an instruction in Latin to the girl who attended her. The girl withdrew to the antechamber where Clothilde had disappeared.

"You are the Iceni hostage." The Celtic words were those of a native speaker, though her accent was Gaulish. Tiann nodded, still sobbing. The woman lifted herself from the bench and gathered two bath sheets from the pile. She wound one around her body, then slid into the pool beside Tiann. Draping and tucking wet cloth around Tiann, she covered her nakedness, then drew her into her arms.

"There." The woman held her firmly, pressing Tiann's head to her shoulder. "There. The story is already flying about the castra. I don't wonder you are undone. It doesn't matter here, with me."

Somehow, Tiann believed her. She sagged into the woman's

embrace, shaking and weeping. The woman rocked her, crooning soft words of comfort. Tiann's sobs became ragged sighs, and the tears trickled to an end. She sat up a bit, and the woman released her hold. Tiann expected to feel self-conscious, but she was only aware of a great hollow exhaustion.

"I am Tiann. Will you give me your name?" Tiann's voice came out with a croak through her aching throat.

"I am called Cattia."

"You are not Roman."

"No. But I have lived among them for many years. They took me from my tribe when I had fourteen summers. I am used to their ways. Some I have come to quite enjoy." She waved her hand to indicate their surroundings. "But I have not forgotten."

"They killed my father." Tiann lifted her arm out of the water. "They did this to me."

Cattia traced the scars with dripping fingers. "Mine are on my back, but they have faded. The girl says she can feel them when she oils my skin, but they are not visible anymore. It is to my advantage. He . . . Well, let's just say that kind of mark would not be well regarded. No one wants to be reminded of the cruelty of one's people." She dropped her hand from Tiann's arm. "But these scars are old. This is not why you are here now. The story is, you are a hostage guaranteeing the submission of the Iceni. But I sense a greater grief than homesickness."

Tiann choked at the half-truth. "I was supposed to be a peace-keeping hostage. But it was a treaty between the Coritani and Iceni. The Brigantes laid a trap—they have killed my kinsmen. Killed my—They are taking me north. And they are cooperating with the Romans. I don't know if my family even knows yet."

A cool wash of air blew behind them. Clothilde came into the room, puffing the hair out of her face. "Oh, she's in here with you, then. Hello, Cattia. I wasn't sure what the girl meant, that I should give it a few minutes before I came in. I guess you two needed time to talk. Well, I can see why you might have things in common, but there is doing to be done, and she needs to get ready now. The commander ordered her to attend dinner."

Tiann felt Cattia stiffen beside her. "She is to attend him at dinner?"

Clothilde came up behind her and began to undo Tiann's braids with brisk hands.

"Wait. Wait!" Tiann protested. "Make sure you save the special weaving."

"What? Do you mean this?" Clothilde pulled free the strand of Gwendolyn's mane hair and examined it. "What is this, some sort of tribal marking?"

Cattia stood with an abrupt motion, streaming water from the wet sheet wrapping her body. "Get her washed and bring her to my chamber. I will see that her hair is redone." She held out her hand for the decorative braid. Exiting the room through the same door the other women had taken, she shed the wet cloth in a sopping heap on the floor.

Clothilde clucked her tongue over the tangled state of Tiann's hair. Her fingers were firm but gentle as she scrubbed the scalp. "Close your eyes, dear. I'm going to rub a little soap in. It may make the tangles worse, but it's clear you've been sleeping rough. We need to get the dirt out."

There was more blood than dirt in her hair, but Tiann did not mention that to the kind woman. The hollow feeling stayed with her, and she submitted to Clothilde's ministrations, obediently presenting arms, legs, and back to be washed. When Clothilde was satisfied she had conquered every speck of dirt in Tiann's hair, from underneath her fingernails, and from between her toes, she helped her out of the water and over to the bench that Cattia had left unoccupied. In the open air, Tiann's embarrassment returned. "May I have a dry sheet?"

"My dear, why do you need a sheet? I'm going to rub unguents into your hair and your back. It will feel lovely. Now just don't you worry."

Into the hollow spaces inside her, courage flowed from the pride of her heritage. Tiann drew herself up and dropped her hands from trying to cover herself. She spoke imperiously, trying to embody Boudica's persona. "It is not our custom to be unclothed in front of others. I would like a sheet. You are welcome to undrape the areas where you administer the ointments, but for the rest of me, I would like to be covered."

CHAPTER

THIRTEEN

Tiann emerged from Cattia's living quarters to find Costri waiting for her. His eyebrows rose and then lowered at the sight of her, the frown lines on either side of his mouth deepening. Lifting her chin, she met his eyes. She was determined not to show her discomfort with the long Roman dress and soft shoes that made her steps trip, or the kohl Cattia had painted around her eyes. Tiann had refused to allow the skin of her face to be whitened with chalk. Though Cattia had sighed, she acquiesced, remarking that although Tiann's skin was golden from too much sun, it was yet free of wrinkles and age spots.

"I do not like this." Costri took her arm and steered her toward one of the larger sharp-angled buildings on the same straight lane as Cattia's quarters. "I will be just outside while you dine."

Tiann resisted his pull on her arm, unable to keep up with his stride with the unfamiliar restriction of the dress. What worried him so? Did he think she could escape from this compound? She had lost all sense of distance and landscape as they had traveled on the road. She only knew they had been heading steadily north. But if she were to try to return home, she could not take the road. And the sameness of the hours of traveling had not left her with a clear impression of how to get back without it. She'd never make it on her own. Would Cattia help her? A faint hope rose in her.

A guard stood at the door. He looked them up and down with a sardonic slowness. Costri's hand tightened on her arm, and she felt rather than saw his anger.

"Is this the royal girl? Well, go in. He is expecting you." He opened the door, angling his body so Costri could not accompany her.

Entering, Tiann found herself in a large rectangular room lit with candles and the remains of the day's sunlight slanting in through windows covered with pale wax-coated cloth. The floor was hard-packed earth, as it had been in Cattia's quarters, but instead of reed mats, it was strewn with colorful rugs. The plaster and timber walls were more ornate as well, the whitewash painted with designs in red, green, and brown. Along three walls couches lined up, with low tables set within easy reach alongside. These held cups and flagons as well as dishes with sliced apples, bread, and cheese.

The commander lounged on the couch at the far end of the room. To Tiann's left, a woman whom she recognized from the bathhouse and another officer shared a couch. The third couch sat empty. She hesitated, not sure what etiquette demanded of her, wishing for her own clothes. Perhaps with her torc.

"Ah, here she is. The royal Briton." The commander waved his cup, sloshing some of the wine onto the floor. "Join us." He wriggled as though to make room for her beside him. Horrified, Tiann hastily sat on the unoccupied couch. The commander hmphed but did not object, slurping a long drink from his cup. "Exotic, isn't she? Look at that hairstyle. That fashion never came from Rome. Nor even the civilized tribes in Gaul, I'd wager."

The woman laughed and shared the commander's words in

Latin with her companion. He smiled and looked at Tiann, whose face became hot under their scrutiny.

"I thought you'd prefer her to keep her own look." Cattia swept into the room, resplendent in a shimmering yellow gown. Her curled hair coiled around her head, held up with delicate enameled combs. Round gold earrings swung halfway to her shoulder. A wave of perfume met Tiann's nose as the older woman passed her. "We wouldn't want to civilize her too much, would we? She is so interesting as she is." Cattia gracefully lowered herself to the other end of the commander's couch. She tilted her head and scanned Tiann. "No, a thorough bath and a few touches were all she needed."

The commander took Cattia's hand and kissed it, apprising Tiann at the same time. "Of course you are right, my dear. She is actually quite a beauty in a way, isn't she?"

Cattia's eyes narrowed, but she laughed lightly and reached for an apple slice, popping it into his mouth. "Yes. You have always had a weakness for a bit of wildness."

Tiann squirmed under the attention. Was Cattia this man's wife? Why did she not mention this during all the time she had readied Tiann, combing out and rebraiding her hair? She seemed like a different person from the one who had wrapped a weeping girl in a sheet and held her while she cried. How rude they were to speak as though she were not here. And not one introduction had been performed. They just lounged there looking at her and talking about her. She was reminded of the time one of the other children in the royal village had found a dead bat. They had all gathered around while Shal spread the creature's wings out to show them the bone structure.

The door opened to admit servants with platters of grilled meats and vegetables. To Tiann's relief, everyone applied themselves to the food for a while. She felt queasy at the thought of eating in this alien room among enemies, but still, after days of dried meat and parched grain, her mouth watered at the scent of well-prepared food. Amlethius filled a cup with a deep-red wine and had the server bring it to Tiann. She took a cautious sip of the strong liquid.

Cattia rose and handed her a dish. "Here is bread for enjoying the sauce with the meat." With her back to the others, she met Tiann's gaze and made a subtle motion toward the cup. She shook her head almost imperceptibly.

Startled, Tiann accepted the dish. She searched Cattia's bland expression. Perhaps the woman was a friend after all. "Thank you. I will follow your advice." The meal was reassuringly familiar, made of fowl, parsnips, and herbs. Tiann ate, pushing aside her disturbed state of mind, concentrating on nourishing her body. She needed to heal and get strong if she was to be ready when an opportunity for escape came.

When the dishes only held scraps and bones, conversation resumed. Tiann found she could follow the general flow as it shifted between Celtic and Latin, filling in her scant knowledge of the Romans' language with context and some translation help from Cattia. The commander and the woman the others called Vidia became louder and more boisterous with every cup of the free-flowing wine. The other man, addressed as Servius, appeared to be listening intently, but said little. His cup also required refilling much less often than the others. Vidia cooed and touched his arm, and though he smiled at her, he did not respond in kind. Tiann had the impression they had not known each other long, and the man was taking her measure.

"So, Vidia, you and our guest here are both Britons. And yet your Latin is almost as good as mine, and you could probably pass for a citizen in Gaul, if not Rome itself. Tell us, what must we do to civilize the rest of your people?" The commander thrust his cup in Tiann's direction, spilling his wine again. "How could she, for instance, become a good Roman?"

Indignation burned in Tiann. "Sir, I would not want to become Roman. I am Iceni, and that is how I wish to remain." She looked at Vidia. A red haze surrounded her pretty face. Tiann's stomach lurched, but she could not stop the words from pouring out of her. "True daughters of Albion do not live in these cities and adopt these foreign ways. Where did you say you grew up? Londinium? Do you even know which tribe the Romans stole that land from? They are invaders, and they will pay for their theft."

Cattia sighed, and Tiann looked at her. The red extended and shadowed the room. Cattia put her head in her hand and closed her eyes. The commander spluttered over his cup, his face flushing. "Now see here!" He lapsed into heated Latin. The other man sat up straight and made a sound of protest.

Cattia took the commander's cup and refilled it. "She is young and has seen little of the world. Why, she didn't even know what to do in the bathhouse. We must give her youth some allowance. She will learn."

The commander slumped back, drinking his wine. "Humph." He eyed Tiann, who fought to not to flinch before him. The redness receded, leaving her shaken and nauseated. After a moment, he nodded. "Yes, she is young. An education is what she needs." He leered a sloppy grin. "Perhaps we can make a beginning for her. A first lesson for the wild little barbarian Briton." He laughed, and Vidia's titter joined in.

"Well, we cannot blame her for being wary." Cattia's voice was calm. "Tiann, come here and show the commander your arm."

Tiann froze to her spot. Why would she suggest this? Was there to be no end to her humiliation?

Cattia's gaze bore into her, compelling her to obey. "Come. It's all right."

Tiann rose and approached their couch. She held out her arm.

Cattia took the cup from the commander's hand. "See the scars? She had a run-in with one of the more . . . strict Roman officers."

The commander grasped Tiann's arm, turning it this way and that. Out of the corner of her eye, Tiann saw Cattia reach into an inner fold of her gown. Quick as a brook trout, she tipped a small vial over the commander's cup.

The other man spoke, his words halting. "You . . . a child. Old marks."

"Yes." Tiann shut her lips tight, determined to say no more. She would not display her inner self to these people.

"Here, sit with us so I can begin your lesson." The commander pulled her off balance.

She sat down hard on the edge of the couch. She could smell his sweat and the wine on his breath.

Pulling Tiann toward her own end, Cattia handed the cup back to the commander. "Let's drink to the virtues of Roman education." She lifted her own cup to her lips.

Vidia laughed and drank, though her companion just looked on.

"Hear, hear!" The commander quaffed the contents of his cup. Cattia continued a stream of lively chatter, springing up to refill Vidia's cup. When she sat again, she placed herself between the commander and Tiann. For his part, the commander's responses became slower and more slurred. Eventually his loud snore interrupted a rambling tale Vidia was telling in an incoherent mixture of Celtic and Latin.

"Ah, perhaps one cup too many for my dear commander," Cattia said. "Time to end the party, I'm afraid. It has been such a delightful evening. I'm sorry to see it over." She gripped Tiann's elbow and made for the door, dragging her along.

Once outside, she gave Tiann's arm a shake. "What were you thinking?" Turning to Costri, who hurried from his post to meet them, she gave orders in sharp succession. "Bring her back to my quarters. You don't need a guard once she is inside. Clothilde is waiting for her there. If you value her safety, leave with her at first light. No, before light."

"I'm sorry. I know I irritated him. Did you . . . What was . . ." Tiann struggled to reconcile this Cattia with the frivolous woman from a moment ago.

"Irritated! Would that you had only irritated him. You might as well have drawn a dagger. Go now. No questions. When I have gotten rid of them, I will come."

Costri put his hand on the small of Tiann's back and pushed her away from the commander's dwelling. "I knew this would be trouble." They strode in silence to Cattia's quarters, where he rapped on the door.

Clothilde opened it and pulled her into the room, which glowed with the light of two large candles. "Ah, the dinner is over. Don't you look pretty! Did Cattia lend you that dress? But you must be tired, poor thing. I'm glad Cattia befriended you. So much better for you to rest here than in the guest barracks." She shooed Costri away. "No, no, off you go now to your own meal and bed. She is in good hands."

"I will come for you before dawn." Costri hesitated by the door. "Sleep well."

Clothilde shut the door and began to divest Tiann of her borrowed dress. "So early! Men. They never understand the niceties of a leisurely breakfast and chat. Always must be rushing to the next thing." She dropped a linen shift over Tiann's head and sat her on a stool. "Close your eyes, dear." She applied something oily to Tiann's eyelids, then wiped it away with a soft cloth. "Now open and look up." She did the same below her eyes, the cloth coming away blackened from the kohl. She was just wiping away the last traces when the door opened and Cattia came in. She shut the door and stood leaning against it for a moment.

"Thank you, Clothilde." She pushed herself off the door and removed her earrings.

Clothilde laid aside the cloth and held out her hand for the jewelry.

"Tiann, would you mind sitting on the bed? Undoing all this takes a bit of time." Cattia sank down on the stool once Tiann had moved.

Clothilde turned her attention to Cattia, uncoiling the elaborate hairstyle and laying the combs on the table next to the earrings. Once Cattia's hair hung loose, she wrapped it in a cloth away from her face and began removing cosmetics.

Tiann watched the lengthy process from her perch on the large bed, itching to ask Cattia to explain all that had happened at the dinner. But she kept quiet, determined not to let her impulse to speak cause any more trouble. She would wait until the other woman indicated it was the time to talk. When all vestiges of her finery had been removed, Cattia sighed and stretched her arms up, then rolled her head from side to side. She smiled, and Tiann thought Cattia, dressed in a plain shift with no ornamentation and looking weary, was far more lovely than she had been at the dinner party. It was the difference between a warm summer day and an icy winter morning. Both beautiful in their own way, but the summer felt friendly and welcoming, and the winter, brittle and distant.

Clothilde opened a large chest, releasing the scent of herbs and a vaguely familiar wood. Tiann sniffed, trying to place it.

"Cedar," Cattia told her. "It grows in eastern lands and is good for keeping insects away."

Tiann recalled the gift chest the Romans had brought, from which the cloth of her bed coverings had come. The cloth had retained a hint of that scent for a long time.

Clothilde laid the dresses inside, smoothing them. The jewelry she placed in a smaller box with compartments, which she then also placed inside the chest. Gathering the soiled cosmetic cloths, she took a brisk look around. "There, I think that is everything. Can I do anything else for you tonight? Some warmed wine, perhaps?"

"No, thank you, Clothilde. I am tired, and I'm sure Tiann is even more so. We will be asleep in moments."

Clothilde nodded, bid them good night, and left. Cattia waited a moment with her head cocked, listening. Then she spoke in a low voice. "I can see the questions about to burst out of you. I'm glad you had the sense to keep quiet while Clothilde was here. She is kind, but she has been a servant of the Romans her whole life. She does not understand."

"I don't understand either. Are you the commander's wife? Why did you make me show him my arm? Was there something in my wine?"

Cattia rose and stood with her back to Tiann, fidgeting with the cosmetic accoutrements on the table. "No, I am not his wife. His wife and children are on his estate in Gaul. It pleases him to have my company, especially when posted away from his home." She glanced sideways at Tiann. "I was younger than you when they took me from my tribe. To pay a debt, they said. Within a week I found myself at a dinner much like this one tonight. I drank only a portion of the wine in my cup. Yet my head became dizzy, and I fell asleep. When I woke, I was in the commander's bed."

"Oh! How terrible. I'm so sorry." Tiann rushed to her, reaching to put a comforting hand on her shoulder.

Cattia shook her off. "Do not be sorry for me. Learn from me. I have made a life for myself by keeping my eyes open and knowing when to speak and when to keep silent. Tonight you were foolish. The commander has the power here, and you spoke to him as though he could do you no harm." Cattia paced the length of the small room. "Vidia, for all her silliness, can be vindictive, and you insulted her as well. I have no idea about that other man—I don't know if he is a nobody or the son of some high official. The way Vidia was hanging on him, I would guess he is important."

Tiann sat back down. "Yes. I am always being told that my words run before my wisdom. I am sorry. Thank you for warning me about the wine."

"I thought if I kept the conversation and wine flowing for long enough, he would naturally pass out. But then you antagonized him and sharpened his attention."

"Did you add something to his cup?"

Cattia raised an eyebrow. "You saw that? I hope you were the only one. Yes. That's why I had you show him your arm, to distract him. The way he was talking, I didn't dare leave it to chance." She sat on the stool.

Coming to kneel in front of her, Tiann took Cattia's hands in hers. "Thank you. Thank you for rescuing me. You have been so kind. But I am still a captive. Will you help me escape? Surely you know a route I can take back to my people. You understand what is like to be taken from your tribe. Please."

Cattia thrust her away. "No. I admit I feel a softness for you, but do not mistake that for foolishness. I have a life. A position, such as it is. Rescuing you from an unwanted 'education' preserved my place. If he cast me off, I would have nothing. I will not risk this for you. I have done all I can. My advice? Give up the idea of escape and consider how you can make the best of your situation. Start by not making enemies of those in a position to harm you."

"Please, please, Cattia. You said you remember what it's like—to have a tribe and then be taken away." Tiann's voice choked on a sob. "Please, I have a blood sister—she may think I am dead. They killed the boy I might have married. Please help me get away."

Cattia rose, leaving Tiann kneeling before the empty stool. "No. Compose yourself. You think you are the only who has ever had a family? The only one who lost a love?" Her voice was hard. "You do not have the luxury of continuing to dwell on it. You endanger yourself. And you will endanger anyone who befriends you. I have risked enough." She sat on the bed and turned the bed covering back. "I am tired. And you must journey tomorrow. Get in bed. You will be safe here with me. I keep a knife under the pillow, and I have not forgotten how to use it."

Tiann put her hands on the stool, leveraging herself up, weary to the core. She shuffled over to the bed and climbed in, settling on the far side. After blowing out the candles, Cattia lay down next to her. "Sleep, young Tiann. Tonight, you feel you can't possibly accept your situation. But tomorrow the sun will rise, and you will discover you can."

TRUE TO HIS WORD, Costri rapped on the door while the sky was still gray and the stars just beginning to fade. Clothilde had left Tiann's travel clothes, washed and folded, the night before. Tiann dressed, glad to be in her own garments again. She buckled the belt at her waist and put her fingers in the dagger sheath. The cloth with Devyn's blood was still there. She closed her eyes for a moment, picturing his laughing face, remembering the feel of his hand in hers. With a deep breath, she dragged herself back to the present.

Cattia draped her cloak over her shoulders. Opening her hand, she showed Tiann a tiny leather bag dyed almost black. "I don't have much. But there are a few coins in here. No one should be completely without resources." Her deft fingers wove the drawstring of the bag into the underside of Tiann's braids. "The darkness of your hair will hide it."

Tiann's throat tightened. "Thank you." With an impulse she

did not understand, she laid her hand on Cattia's head. "The Maker watch over you and bless you for your kindness."

Costri's voice sounded low outside the door. "Are you ready?"

"You must go." Cattia's eyes shone with tears. "Hurry on your way. Be safe, Tiann."

Tiann stepped outside into the cool predawn. Costri held up a hand when she would have walked past him. "I am going to check you for weapons."

She backed away. "You will not."

"Would you prefer to be bound? Or for me to have one of the other men do it? I think you will find I am more respectful."

Tiann gritted her teeth. "I do not have a weapon." In truth, she had considered asking Cattia for a knife but had not wanted to press the other woman's kindness.

"Then I will not find one." He spun her around and lifted her braid, patting along her back and sides, down each arm and leg. He felt through the soft leather of her boots. He turned her to face him. "Pull the front of your tunic against you."

Face hot, Tiann complied.

Finally, he reached into the dagger sheath at her waist, pulling out the stained cloth. He looked at it for a long moment, then returned it to its place. "Good. Now we will go."

At the stables, the rest of the Brigantian escort waited, bleary eyed and grumbling. The wagons and horses stood ready to depart.

Shinoc sneered at Tiann. "All clean and well fed, I see. Did you enjoy your introduction to the delights of Roman life?" His tone insinuated more than a bath and a dinner.

Tiann stiffened but ignored him, greeting Stadder with soft endearments as she checked his tack.

"Mount up. And do your best to be quiet. We don't want to wake the whole place." Costri led the way through the deserted lane along the back of the paddock, heading toward the side gate instead of the main entrance. Although Cattia had indicated that the commander would not be in a position this morning to obstruct their departure, Tiann was glad of Costri's caution. She had no doubt the Roman could make her captivity even more cruel.

The heady smell of new bread wafted from the bakehouse as they passed it, and Tiann turned to look. A figure lounged against the whitewashed building, smoke from the oven swirling past him. The man straightened to watch them as they passed. Tiann recognized him as Servius, the mysterious guest from the dinner, whom Cattia had not known. He had witnessed her insult to the commander. Would he inform the commander of her departure in this predawn hour? The man met her eye. He gave a slight bow, then returned to his relaxed posture. When Tiann looked over her shoulder, he was still there, tearing a piece of bread from a loaf that steamed from the oven. He raised a hand of farewell, then popped the bite into his mouth.

Traveling ever northward, the party made steady progress. The weather remained clear and mild. Tiann counted two handfuls of stone markers the first two days. The next day they passed two more than that and did not make camp until deep twilight. Costri did not stop overnight again in a village or Roman castra, although he sent two men off the road to buy supplies.

Tiann noted landmarks, tapping her fingers and reciting them silently to commit them to memory. A village near the marker stone that went with her left thumb. A stream that needed fording, along with a fort under construction, between the markers corresponding to her middle and fourth fingers.

In the evenings, when her back ached to be stretched and her eyelids grew heavy, she sometimes dismounted and led Stadder.

She missed challenging her mind and body with training. The plodding monotony of traveling at wagon pace made it too easy for memories to rise and overtake her. She pictured the dusty stillness of the stable, sitting with Mara and the puppy. The laughter and good-natured one-upmanship of the hall when the hunters came back from a successful expedition. The images of her home and her tribe ran in her mind, still peopled with those who lay dead and unmarked beside a stream in the land of another tribe.

When she could not bear it, she expanded her inner recitation to anything she could think of: the landmarks, stories of ancient heroes, and the teachings Shal had impressed on her of Elior's words and about the Man who'd died and then lived again. When the words ran dry, she drew up the carvings in the tunnel chamber from the well of her memory and traced the designs in rhythm with her steps.

On the fourth day, they approached a settlement larger than any Tiann had ever seen. Costri drew up alongside her. "That is Lindum, one of the cities the Romans have built. It is the largest one in this region of Albion. The Ninth Legion is stationed there."

Tiann stared, fascinated and repelled. Stone walls circled the city, and a steady flow of people came and went on the road leading to the large main gate. Romans of every class mingled with Celts as well as merchants from other parts of the empire. The road led to the gate straight into the city. They stayed on course until they reached the crush of people waiting to navigate the bottleneck through the gate. Then at Costri's command, they swung off onto a rough dirt trail that circumvented he city.

As they passed, Tiann marveled at the sprawl outside the city itself. A host of small dwellings huddled against the outside of the walls, and she could make out various trades and crafts as well as pens for animals and small vegetable gardens. It was as if a huge hand had gathered a whole village and swept it into a heap against the stone wall. When they got to the far side, she realized the road did not continue out of the city. Looking back, she could see that construction was beginning from the northward gate but had only progressed a few paces. The trail wound into distant hills, looking like a natural part of the landscape after the uniform straightness they had just left.

What had the commander said about this place? The legate of the Ninth Legion—Ceri something—was here. He had issued the safe passage to the Brigantian party. Because he had arranged it with Cartimandua. Tiann stopped turning her head to look at the walled city and whipped her gaze north. They must be close. Soon she would be there, with the queen who made friends with Romans. Who engaged in warfare with her own tribe, even her own husband. Who practiced dark sacrifices. Who wanted a hold over the Iceni queen and chief and was willing to murder and kidnap to achieve it.

Tiann was nearly there.

CHAPTER

FOURTEEN

The day after they passed Lindum, Costri gave the order to stop and make camp early. He led them to a small clearing that held evidence of previous use. The afternoon sun filtered through the leaves. Nearby, a rushing sound signaled water.

Tiann took her time unsaddling Stadder. She scratched and kneaded his coat where it was becoming matted, promising him she would comb and brush him when they reached a stable. She had taken to only conversing with Costri, and she looked for him now to ask about bringing Stadder to water. To her surprise, he was at the wagon, lifting off the box with her formal clothes.

"What are you doing with that? Those are my goods."

He set the box down, wincing, as though his back hurt. "Really? I thought it was full of stones."

Tiann's words fled. Was Costri making a joke? Surely not. She gathered herself. "What do you want with my box? Those garments were sent for me to use as a representative of the Iceni royal family."

"Yes, I know." If he had been teasing, all trace of it was gone. "Tomorrow midmorning we will arrive at Cartimandua's stronghold. I thought you would like to dress in something other than your traveling clothes."

Tiann clenched her hands behind her back to hide her trembling. "Those garments were intended to honor a peace treaty. I do not intend to wear them as a show of a respect I do not have, for a queen who has kidnapped me and murdered my kinsmen."

Costri frowned. "No. I would not expect you to. I thought perhaps . . ." He cleared his throat, looking up at the sky. "I thought wearing them might make you feel . . . that is, might give you a confidence to face the day. It is your decision, of course." He pointed past the clearing. "The stream forms a small pool just past that yew. You can water your horse there." He strode away.

A pile of rocks diverted some of the current to quieter water. While Stadder drank, Tiann removed her boots and waded. The coolness bathed her hot feet with a healing current. Upstream the water flowed over a series of flat ledges, forming inviting shelves where the sunlight sparkled on the spray. The brightness of the reflection dazzled her eyes, and she blinked against the glare. When she opened her eyes again, the sparkle had coalesced into a figure seated on one of the rock ledges.

Stadder lifted his head, his nostrils flaring and his ears tipped forward. He gave a soft snort and shook droplets from his muzzle.

Elior laughed. "Ah, you have been a comforting companion to our girl. Go ahead and enjoy your drink, friend."

"You are here. I am not dreaming."

"No, not a dream. But it is a moment out of time. We will be uninterrupted for now."

Tiann moved upstream, the water cooling her ankles and calves as she waded deeper toward the ledges. Elior waited for her with a serious expression on his face, although the crinkles around his eyes spoke of an easy smile and kindness. He held out a hand to help her up the slick stone steps to where he sat. The sunlight cast a glow over the markings on his arm.

When she settled beside him, he removed a cup from his inner cloak. "Drink deep, beloved. The water is healing for your body and your soul." He held the cup under the cascade and handed it to her.

Tiann drank, and the liquid spread a refreshing balm down her throat and through her body. When the cup was empty, she held it, looking at its wet sheen dripping into her lap. "Shal says you are a messenger from the Maker."

"Ah, dear Shal! He is a very great favorite. How we sang when the light filled him!" Elior tipped his head back and closed his eyes, as though listening. The sunlight intensified, and the air thrummed with energy. The scent of green and growing things floated like a heady incense.

Tiann longed to sink into the sensation of vitality, but anger crashed through. She set the cup down sharply. "You told me the dark does not win. You told me to remember the wounds. I tried! When Mara was to be sent away, I thought about the wounds that bound me to her. I tried to do the right thing. But it has all turned out wrong." Tiann heard the ugliness in her words but could not hold them back. "You were wrong. If we had just waited, we needn't have sent anyone. And then Devyn . . . and the others . . . You were wrong. The dark did win that day. The message wasn't true, so how can the Maker be trusted? If the darkness wins, then why follow the Light?"

A tear trickled down Elior's face. "Child, we wept with you. You are right—the darkness of this world won a battle that day."

"But why? Why?" Tiann's cry echoed off the rocks and the water, her anguish reverberating in the peaceful place.

"We do not interfere with your decisions, child. We try to guide you and protect you, but we cannot turn your feet away from a path you are determined to take. You decided to go. Boudica decided to follow the words of dark power."

"Bultur."

"Yes. He has followed the path into deep darkness. He believes this will give him the power he craves. And the more he believes, the more the darkness persuades him."

Tiann cupped the scar on her arm. The skin rose in a smooth lump where the Roman dagger had marked her. "You said to remember the wounds. That's why I offered to take Mara's place. Wasn't that part of the Light?"

"Was it?"

The question stung. "Of course it was. Or it should have been. I was trying to do as you said. I was trying to save my sister."

"Were you asked to save your sister? Were you told to remember your own wounds? Were you following the Light or trying to be the light yourself?"

Words dried up in Tiann's mouth. The ring of gold in Elior's eyes widened, and she felt laid bare before his sight. She dropped her gaze. It was true. She had taken the words he had given her that night by the sea and bent them into something she could do. She had longed to be the answer, the hero. She had not waited for guidance or wisdom. And Bultur had taken her reckless solution and added his own desire for influence, pushing the queen into a hasty vow. No wonder Mara had been so angry and hurt. No wonder Shal had been distressed and sorrowful.

She raised her eyes to meet his. "What would have happened if I had waited? Held my tongue? Would Devyn still be alive? Have I ruined everything?"

"There is no 'would have been' that I can tell you. Once the threads of decisions—yours, Boudica's and Prasudoc's, Devyn's, Bultur's—once all these fibers were twisted together and woven in, all other fibers flew away. Only the All-Wise can see all the possibilities. But do not fear. This thread has its place in the Great Making. This thread, too, will bring beauty to the pattern."

"I don't understand—the pattern?"

"Listen. Listen and you will hear it."

Elior closed his eyes, and Tiann followed his example. Around her, the rush of stream over stone and the sigh of wind intensified. She sensed the heartbeats of nearby birds and Stadder. The hum of insects brushed the upper edges of her hearing. The sounds swirled and melded into a song, sung with heartbreaking beauty, grief and joy mingled. Tiann perceived the voice of the bard surrounding her but just beyond her understanding.

"Have you not heard?" Elior's words wove into the harmony of the music. "The Maker has no beginning or end. The mystery of the ancients belongs to the Maker."

The song formed itself into pictures from her memory, and Tiann's fingers reached into it to trace the shapes of spirals.

"The marks. On the walls and on your arm. Is that the pattern?" Tiann opened her eyes to find Elior looking at her like a father observing his child's first steps.

"The marks are like a taste of the feast. Like going into the kitchens, where the cook breaks off a bit of the bread for you. What do the marks taste like to you?" Elior dipped his hand in the water and drew three interlocking spirals on the rock ledge with a wet finger.

"They . . . do not end."

"Yes. What else do you see?"

Tiann ran her finger around a spiral. "If I follow the path, I come back, but not to exactly the same spot." Her fingertip traced the fading mark to the next spiral. "It is one design, but also three." Understanding hovered at the edges of her consciousness, like when she considered Shal's stories of the man whose light overcame death. "Tell me what it means please, Elior."

"The Maker does not have a beginning or an end." The gold in Elior's eyes warmed with the conviction of his words. "The Maker is always steadfast, always the same, yet ever new. And the great mystery of the Maker is the three in one—the God who is in heaven, the Spirit who moves like the wind, and the Man who is light to this world."

Tiann struggled, scraping her finger on the stone, where the mark had disappeared in the drying sun. "I can't understand. I can't see it. I am no druid."

Elior put his hand over hers, stilling the motion. "It's all right, child. Would you want to follow if the Maker could fit inside your understanding? The bit of bread in the kitchen does not give you the experience of the feast. But its presence on your tongue, the scent of the food and spices, the preparation for the celebration— these lead you to anticipate. Will you love the pattern the Maker is weaving? Will you long for it? Believe what you know. This is more valuable to the Maker than any druid's great wisdom."

Downstream, Stadder gave a soft whinny. Elior raised a hand. "Yes, friend. She will return to you now."

The gravity of her situation crashed down on Tiann. "Must I go back? Please, they are keeping me captive. Help me escape, Elior. I must get back to my family. They will be wild with worry about me. Please help me!"

"Oh, child, that is not my mission. You must follow this thread you have chosen. There is more to the pattern, but you must go north among your enemies to find it. It is not time yet for you to return to your loved ones. But I can tell you Mara draws close to the Maker. Your sister has her own part in the pattern. Only follow the light, child. It still shines in the darkness. Remember the signs. Remember the wounds."

The lowering sun found a gap in the trees. The brilliance of the ray's reflection on the water blinded Tiann for a moment. When she looked again, Elior was gone.

∼

IN THE MORNING, Tiann returned to the pool carrying a bundle from her box. She laid out the garments she had chosen on the rock ledge. Undoing her braids, she set aside the golden cord of Gwyndolyn's hair and the hidden pouch of coins Cattia had given her. Ducking her head under the icy cascade, she scrubbed at her scalp with a handful of fine-grained clay from the bank. She rinsed until her head ached with cold and she was sure every bit of the clay had washed out. Taking her time, she washed her shivering body with a clean cloth, then dried with another. Donning a finely woven, long green tunic, she sat on the rock ledge, blotting the water from her hair and working her fingers through the tangles.

The sun warmed her, promising a fine day. At least she wouldn't have to ride into the Brigantian village muddy and bedraggled. She grinned, hearing Mara's scolding voice in her head, telling her not to disgrace the Iceni with her training clothes smelling of horse and physical exertion. Tiann's amusement faded, and her throat felt tight as she wished for Mara's teasing and her nimble fingers making the traditional braids. *I will do my best to honor you.* Tiann wove the promise in with the golden cord. Her hands felt clumsy, and the braids were not as elaborate as her sisters or Cattia could fashion, but she felt presentable when she was done. She fastened the coin pouch into the hollow at the base of her skull, pulling the braid around it.

If only she could stay sitting in the sunshine with the stream sparkling beside her. She longed for the shadows to remain in place, for the moment to still and stretch. Every step north brought her closer to the queen who had devised the plan to capture her and kill Devyn and the others. And yet Elior had said she would find more of the Maker's pattern there. But did the Maker care about her? Or was this God so far off that the people who walked the world were beneath the Maker's notice?

A breeze brushed her cheek. *Remember the wounds.*

Just beyond the yew, someone cleared his throat. Costri

stepped into view, his gaze directed at the treetops. "Are you ready? We must be going."

A grudging gratitude for his tact made Tiann answer with courtesy. "Nearly. Please give me a moment." Costri left and Tiann pulled on soft brown braccae, belt, and boots. She secured her torc at her throat, then swung the elaborately colored cloak to her back, fastening it at the shoulders with gold and enamel brooches. She adjusted the tunic under her belt so that the side slits were placed to make riding easy. Sliding her fingers into her dagger sheath, she touched the bloodied cloth. With a deep breath, Tiann left the peace of the stream to face the day.

Timber gates, flanked by two warriors, barred the entrance to the Brigantian village courtyard. Costri halted the party a hundred paces back and rode forward to speak to the guards. Within the ring of defensive ditches and earthen mounds, cleared land surrounded the village enclosure. The layout resembled the Iceni royal village, but there were no signs of grain fields. The sun, just past its zenith, shone on stumps and scythed grasses and two large areas of trampled bare ground. Tiann guessed these were training grounds, for they had the look of hard use by many feet. The two guards hailed others on the inside, and the gates swung open. Costri dismounted, handing his reins to a guard, and strode back to where Tiann and the others waited.

"Make yourselves ready. The queen will receive us in the hall shortly. Take what you need from the saddlebags, but leave the rest." Costri beckoned a handful of men emerging from the gate. "Unload the horses and get them to water and pasture. Don't unhitch the wagon with the Iceni goods yet. It will come into the enclosure with us."

Tiann dismounted, keeping her hand on Stadder's neck a few moments. "We are here, friend. I don't know what is coming next." She murmured the words only loud enough for his ears, which twitched back to listen. He turned his head, and she stroked his soft nose. "But thank you for being with me."

A scrawny boy of eight or nine summers approached her, holding out a hand for the reins.

Tiann hesitated. "Do you know how to care for horses?"

The boy nodded. "I will take good care of him. The horses are my responsibility." He spoke as though his mouth hurt him, and a bruise reddened his cheekbone. He reached to stroke Stadder's nose.

"His name is Stadder. He is good-tempered but will overeat if you let him. Please rub him down well and check his hooves. Thank you . . ." Tiann's tone asked for his name, but the boy merely ducked his head in agreement and led the horse after the others.

Tiann walked through the courtyard half a pace behind Costri. Curious eyes rose from tasks to follow her, and the reassuring scent of cooking hung in the air. She concentrated on keeping her posture from showing her weariness and her steps from revealing the stiffness in her ankle. She had seen visitors arrive to visit Boudica and Prasudoc a hundred times. Now she was the visitor. Of course, she was an unwilling guest. And there were no children peeking out from doorways or from behind the cistern, whispering and giggling. Tiann swept her gaze over the courtyard to be sure. No children, and only one woman, an elder dozing on a stool.

At the entrance to the hall, a guard stopped them again. He banged on the door with a staff. The doorposts were imposing, made of stout tree trunks, but they were not carved or decorated. When the doors swung open, the inside hall continued the atmosphere of stark utilitarianism. A dozen men milled about the space, including a few Romans. Only the figure standing on a dais past the banked central hearth was out of keeping with the serviceable plainness of the village.

Cartimandua wore a silver filigree band on an elaborate mound of curls piled above her round face. Earrings reaching almost to her shoulders dragged her earlobes downward next to rouged round cheeks. A rose-colored gown billowed around her, cinched between her breasts and at her middle with a criss-crossing sash. From where Tiann stood, the queen looked like her eyes were two black hollows in a face as white as the full moon.

Costri led them forward, dipping his head to the queen when they reached the dais. Tiann had to look up, but not much. On the same level, she would stand a head taller than Cartimandua. Up close Tiann could see the paste of white makeup and scarlet lip coloring painted larger than the natural shape of the woman's mouth. The black hollows resolved themselves into brown eyes ringed with heavy kohl.

"So you have arrived. You are Boudica's daughter?"

Tiann stared at the Brigantian queen. How should she address her? All the formal protocols she had learned said nothing of this situation. Shinoc stepped out from behind Tiann, grabbing her right arm and pulling it forward. She stumbled a bit, and Costri steadied her with a hand under her other elbow. He growled a rebuke, but Shinoc ignored him.

"It is the daughter, Lady. See, here are the markings I told you about. It is the same girl."

"Hmm. Well, that is one obstacle overcome. I confess I thought Boudica might be canny enough to send a decoy."

Words spilled from Tiann's mouth before she even knew she was thinking them. "On the contrary, my queen deals honorably, even with adversaries. The Iceni do not pretend to be what they are not. Although, apparently, that is a Brigantian practice."

Costri stiffened beside her and dropped his hand from her elbow. She could have sworn his face reddened.

Behind her the doors swung open with a decisive bang. "Costri, you have returned! It has been too long. What is your news?" Attention shifted from Tiann to a hearty, full-bearded warrior striding through the hall. "The information on where you were traveling was a bit vague." The man waved his hand in the queen's direction before stopping to pound Costri on the back and then grip his wrist in greeting. His gaze sharpened on the group, lingered on Shinoc, and came to rest on Tiann. "And who is this?"

Costri pulled his arm back from the man's grip. "My chief, this is the girl. The one you sent orders to intercept. She is Tiann of the Iceni. Although, it seems the orders differed, depending on who received them."

"I sent? What orders? What would I want with an Iceni girl?"

Cartimandua seated herself on the couch on her dais, arranging the folds of her gown. "Venut, I was not expecting you back from the hunt until tomorrow." She wrinkled her nose. "Why don't you go wash yourself, and we can discuss this matter as we dine."

"No, I think washing can wait until I hear about the orders I gave without my knowledge."

Tiann studied the man as he stalked to a stool, set it on the dais with a thump, and sat down, glowering all the while. So this was Venut, Cartimandua's husband. His hair and beard showed streaks of gray, though he moved with the vigor of a man in his prime. He was not tall, but his shoulders were broad and his forearms knotted with a warrior's muscle. Tiann knew he and Cartimandua had reconciled after the split over their views about the Romans, but at this moment they did not seem in accord.

Cartimandua shifted, pouting. "As you wish, my dear. You were away touring the farms to the north, when word came that the Iceni and Coritani were ready to make a peace treaty, with an exchange of hostages. Cerialis happened to be here . . ."

"Quintus Petillius Cerialis? The legate who is commanding

the Ninth? What was that brother of a snake doing here?" Venut jumped up from his stool and paced.

"Sit down, dear. It was just a friendly visit among allies. His brother Nasica isn't even in Brittania anymore, let alone with the Ninth."

"He is fortunate I was not here. Nasica slaughtered half my men only a handful of years ago."

"Yes." Cartimandua's tone was sharp. "And aren't *we* fortunate that I have smoothed over our relationship with Cerialis so that they don't hold us to account for your stupid rebellion?"

Beside Tiann, Costri let out a hiss of outrage. Venut stopped pacing and gave him a sharp glance. "Costri, come and walk with me. I need to see to some things, but I want to hear your account."

Cartimandua sat up straighter. "The man has only just arrived, husband. Surely we can allow him a meal and some rest."

The chief paused, looking at her with a muscle twitching in his jaw. "We will return shortly. I assume you can have no objection to my own man talking with me in private?"

"No, of course not." The queen's voice sounded like honey, but her eyes narrowed. Tiann's pulse quickened in reaction to tensions she didn't understand. When Costri followed Venut out of the hall, Tiann felt oddly abandoned. She bit the inside of her cheek. She must not make the mistake of thinking of Costri as an ally. Perhaps he showed more courtesy, but he still led the party that kidnapped her and murdered her men. She would not be lulled into thinking anyone here was less than a mortal enemy. Only her value as a bargaining tool and her own wits would keep her safe.

Cartimandua returned her attention to Tiann, pursing her lips. "I also have things to attend to. I will have someone send you food and drink. You will sleep in the hall, but I suppose we can curtain off a corner for you. We move back north in three days. Once there we can provide you a chamber, as befits your station."

The queen clapped her hands, and an attendant scurried forward. "See to the girl. But first make sure all is ready for the ritual."

The servant bowed and exited the hall.

Cartimandua descended from the dais, turning toward a door in the rear of the hall, presumably leading to the royal apartment. Tiann stepped toward her on shaking legs. "Please . . . Lady. Does my family know where I am? May I send a message to them? My men—can I let the chief know where they fell so their bodies can return to the Iceni for burial?" The plea caught in her throat, but she forced it out, determined to speak for her men. For Devyn.

Cartimandua laughed. "Ohhhh. She's a do-gooder." Around the hall, accompanying chuckles sounded. "I met your mother once, you know, when we were girls. She was a self-righteous little thing as well. She didn't like me having a bit of fun with some idiot village waif. Got me in trouble, and I had to sit in my chamber during a feast night." She wound a loose curl around a finger. "No, I will send my own message. Having you in my hands doesn't do much good if Boudica doesn't know it. But I will wait until we have reached our northern stronghold. We wouldn't want her to be tempted to come after you. Meanwhile, she can sit in her own chamber—and wonder."

THREE DAYS. In three days, they would move deeper into Brigantian territory. Tiann paced the small space in her curtained corner. Step, step, step, step, turn. Her makeshift chamber contained only a sleeping pallet and her saddlebag. She had concealed a flat, round loaf of bread and a short knife from her dinner at the bottom of the saddlebag. Her chances of escape or rescue would only diminish the farther north they brought her. Tomorrow she would try to get a skin for water and more food. She would test out how closely they watched her.

Listening and watching, she gathered that this was the first night of a three-day ritual. The queen's servants busied themselves with preparations until sundown. Many of the household lit torches from the central hearth and filed out into the night. Cartimandua, resplendent in a dark cloak, led them. If tomorrow followed the same pattern, perhaps Tiann could slip away and get a reasonable head start before anyone noticed she was gone.

Sighing, she settled herself onto her pallet. The torchlight from the hall penetrated the loose weave of the curtain, and she could see her formal tunic hanging from the peg on the wall. She wished she had not worn such an impractical garment, regardless of the confidence she had needed to meet Cartimandua. Her worn and comfortable traveling clothes, now packed somewhere in the wagon, would have served her better. Not to mention ankle wraps and laced boots. She couldn't count on obtaining a horse. Could she make an excuse to recover some of her belongings?

She peered out into the hall. Venut and some of his men sat on stools around the central hearth, which flickered with only a small fire, for the night was warm. Costri sat with his forearms on his knees, leaning toward his chief and talking earnestly. Tiann could not hear his voice, but his posture spoke of entreaty. Venut rumbled a reply and gave the man a clumsy pat on the shoulder. Costri sat back with an air of relief and lifted a cup to his mouth for a long drink.

Why were they here instead of at the ritual? Boudica and Prasudoc always observed the seasonal festivals, warrior ceremonies, and marriage bondings together. The procession following Cartimandua out of the hall included men, so it couldn't be a ritual for women only, as Tiann knew some tribes practiced. Their presence worried her. Guards were one thing, but trying to escape under the nose of the chief himself was another.

FIFTEEN

Tiann crouched in a muddy stream bed, shivering. The clouds had cleared, and the stars now revealed her mistake. The stream she thought flowed southward actually ran eastward. By the position of the moon, she gauged she had wasted almost half the night stumbling in the wrong direction. She needed to leave the water to strike south, but hounds howled in the distance. She scooped handfuls of mud to coat her skin, clothes, and hair, hoping to mask her scent.

Standing, she stretched her ankle, stiff and sore from the hours of hard walking. With a deep breath, she clambered up the south bank, fixing her gaze on a guiding star. Her saddlebag, fashioned into a crude pack, shifted on her back and chafed at her neck with every step. She focused on this irritation, willing herself not to give in to hopelessness.

Tiann continued to plod, stopping to rest only when her body forced her. When she came to another small stream, she removed her boot and makeshift ankle wrap—a strip from the hem of her now ruined green tunic—to soak her foot and ankle for a few minutes. Movement downstream startled her into grabbing her boot and saddlebag and pushing her way into a hedge. A fox, silver in the moonlight, bent his head to drink, then pricked up his ears and sniffed the air. Bolting into the night, he left Tiann with a pounding heart. She made haste to slip her boot back on and continue.

When the stars faded into the gray of predawn, Tiann looked for a spot to hole up and sleep. She ached all over, her eyes stung from sweat, and the mud she had smeared on her skin made her itchy. The emptiness in her stomach cried out for food. A slope where earth had crumbled formed a hollow surrounded by exposed tree roots. Folding herself under the living roof, she pulled the strap of the saddle bag off her shoulder. She dug a bit of moss and pressed it against the raw skin on her neck. She ate half of one of the flat, round loaves she had concealed, and sipped from the waterskin. She could have wolfed down all three loaves and drained the skin, but when might she have the chance to replenish her provisions? She must be careful. Exhaustion pushed away hunger, thirst, and discomfort. Pillowing her head on the bag, she curled into the earthen hollow and slept.

Stirring awake when midday sunlight reached into her den, Tiann eased into a sitting position. She ate the other half of the loaf and drank just enough to wash it down. Standing, she gave herself a few moments to stretch and shake off her grogginess before moving on. Reaching down to remove her boot and adjust her ankle wrap, she examined the sky and trees to get her bearings. Cool air brushed the skin where her boot had been. Tiann stared, uncomprehending, at her bare ankle, boot in hand. Maybe the wrap had shifted down into the boot. She turned it upside down, but nothing fell out except grit. Had she wrapped the wrong ankle? But no, her good foot proved bare as well.

The stream. The fox. The wrap beside her while she soaked her ankle in the cold water. The green fabric of her tunic still lying there, forgotten when she had fled. Waiting to be scented and found. Marking her path.

The sound floated to her on a chill breeze. A shiver scurried up her spine, and it seemed the cold and the baying of the dogs were one sensation. With clumsy hands, Tiann pulled her boots on, concentrating on making her shaking fingers pull the laces tight. She forced herself to chew and swallow one bite after another of a dry, crumbling loaf from her saddlebag. She drank a long pull from her waterskin. There was no reason to be so careful with her rations now. Then she sat down to wait.

The sun had barely tipped toward the west when the baying sounded again close by, accompanied by the unmistakable noises of men and horses. The Brigantes men followed the dogs, who sat quivering in front of her. Tiann rose and showed them her empty hands. One man dismounted and boosted Tiann to the horse's back, binding her hands to the pommel and her feet to the girth strap. The men accompanying her were stoic and rarely addressed her, although they untied her at intervals to eat, drink, and attend to her private needs. Their assignment to track her down and fetch her back did not seem to irk them, except for some grumbling about missing a night of the ritual.

They arrived back at the stronghold in deep night. After greeting the guard and rousing a sleepy youth to care for the horses, the men dispersed. The guard unbound Tiann's hands and feet and helped her, not unkindly, climb from the horse. He rummaged in her saddlebag, removed the small knife, and handed the bag to her. He kept a hold on her upper arm as he led her into the quiet hall and to her sleeping pallet. The curtain had been taken down.

Sick with failure, filthy, hungry, and exhausted, Tiann lowered herself to the pallet. Sleep came swiftly, but dreams chased her until morning activity stirred in the hall.

～

Tiann sat on her pallet, watching people helping themselves from the large cauldron of porridge keeping warm at the central hearth. Those who had already eaten busied themselves with breaking down looms for packing into wagons or tending to bridles and boots for the journey.

Cartimandua came to stand several feet away from her. "Aren't you a sight? I'm inclined to just let you remain in your filth. It's no more than you deserve for your stupidity. But since you must come to the stones tonight—we can't leave you here, clearly—you will have to wash." She gestured to a sour-faced serving woman. "Accompany our Iceni guest outside and guard her while she bathes. We don't want her getting *lost* again."

Tiann did her best to ignore the woman as she stripped off her mud-stiffened clothing in the rough bathing enclosure. She rubbed her skin with a wet cloth until it glowed pink with scrubbing. She didn't bother to unbraid her hair, afraid her hidden coin pouch would be noticed, but she ran the cloth down the plaits. When she was done, the woman handed her a bundle of clothing in the Brigantian style and gathered up the dirty clothes Tiann had discarded. "I will wash them." The woman's voice sounded irritated and weary.

The day passed with dull slowness. Tiann had nothing to do, and no one spoke to her. At mealtimes, a servant handed her a bowl with meat and broth and a hunk of bread. The sour-faced woman returned her clothing clean but wet, and Tiann draped the pieces to dry over a stool. The organized bustle of packing up continued until the hall was nearly bare and the flow of people dwindled. Neither Cartimandua nor Venut appeared.

At last, dusk cast shadows over the day. The household, silent and subdued, congregated in the hall. They lit torches and stood in little knots, waiting. Cartimandua swept in from her apartment, wearing the same dark cloak as before, but now with a headdress fashioned of gold and exotic plumage. Her eyes, pupils huge, gleamed from the middle of exaggerated black outlines. A servant held out a torch for her and backed away, bowing when she took it without breaking stride.

Tiann caught sight of Venut in the shadows, watching the proceedings. He stood with his arms folded, leaning against the far wall. So once again he would not take part in the ritual tonight.

One of Cartimandua's warriors came to where Tiann sat on her pallet. His torch wavered, obscuring the details of his face. "Come." He reached, hauling her to her feet by her upper arm. So she had not been forgotten. Resigned, she went without resisting, although she pulled her arm out of his grip.

The procession wound its way through a path in the forest, wide enough that moonlight penetrated to glint off the queen's headdress. There was no mood of festival, but neither did Tiann sense the calm reverence of some of the rituals Shal had conducted at home. Awe, certainly. But awe heavily tinged with fear. The boy who had taken care of Stadder the first night walked a little ahead of her. The whites of his eyes flashed as he swung his head to look over his shoulder. His steps stuttered while he searched the darkness of the woods.

The path turned upward, and the trees crowded, closing out the moonlight. The torches threw wild shadows. Tiann's unwrapped ankle ached with the climb. She stumbled, and the boy's head snapped around at the sound. She smiled a reassurance at his wide-eyed expression. "Perhaps you would allow me to take your hand? I am unfamiliar with the path."

The boy put a finger to his lips but nodded. He wiped his palm on his tunic before holding out his hand to her. His hand was cold and clammy, trembling slightly. The poor child was terrified. She wrapped her fingers around his. The trees thinned out as they approached the summit of the hill. A wind sighed, prickling the skin at Tiann's nape and carrying a sound not of the forest, but like distant warriors battling with wooden staves. The boy shuddered and looked up. Following his gaze, Tiann found the source of the sound. Tied to branches and swaying in the breeze, hundreds of bones clicked against one another.

The hilltop stood bare of trees but not empty. Four great stones loomed upright, casting long shadows in the moonlight. Another lay flat off to one side. Standing beside it, a druid held the halter of a dark-coated horse. The creature shifted his hooves, nostrils flaring. His wide eyes caught the torchlight. The boy gripped Tiann's hand tighter and whimpered. Tiann looked down at him, and he seemed stricken, tears making tracks on his cheek, his gaze fixed on the horse. A wind lifted the wisps of Tiann's hair that had escaped her braids, and with it came a whiff of stone and old blood. The scent spoke of power, but so different from the scent of green and water at the oak circle at home. This was a darker, harsher power, intent on consuming, not nourishing.

A low chanting pulsed across the hilltop. Cartimandua stretched her hands to the moon, the tuneless words of an ancient language running from her throat. The sound swirled with the wind, coiling around Tiann's mind. The crowd of people stood silent and still. The queen's chanting rose, echoing off the stones, and Tiann's heart beat faster.

Hands still raised, the queen strode to the flat stone where the druid waited. The wind buffeted her dark cloak so it billowed like a raven in flight. She lifted a curved blade from the stone and held it aloft while her chanting climaxed in a screeching frenzy. The sound cut off like a doused flame, the echo eddying in the air like smoke. With a tug on the halter rope, the druid stretched the horse's head over the stone. Cartimandua drew the blade across the creature's neck. A dark fountain sprang from the deep gash, pouring over the stone and spraying the queen and the druid. The horse's legs quivered, then buckled under him.

Next to Tiann, the boy choked back a sob. She put her arm

around him, sickness in her stomach. She kept her attention on the boy, who shook with suppressed tears. She tried not to see as Cartimandua and the druid bent over blood spatter on the stone, trying to discern a sign. They ignored the horse lying in an unnatural position at their feet.

Tiann pressed her eyes shut and held the shuddering boy closer, but she could still picture the poor horse's head twisted against the side of the stone as he had fallen. Heart hammering, she gave the boy a squeeze around the shoulders, then walked forward. Paying no heed to the shuffling and murmuring from the people, she approached the stone. Kneeling beside the horse, she attempted to shift him.

The druid reared back from his contemplation of the blood, screeching in protest. "Get away! How dare you approach the sacred mysteries?"

Hot anger flooded through Tiann like a fever. "How dare *you*! How can you destroy one of the Maker's creatures for your filthy prophecies?" She stroked the horse's head, cradling it in her lap.

The druid hovered over her, uttering curses, his breath fetid.

"Leave her be." Cartimandua's cool voice cut across the druid's indignation. "She is royal—her presence will not disturb the ritual. She is a nuisance, no more. Finish your work."

Tiann opened her mouth to speak again, but the queen made a sign in the air with her hand and the words shriveled in Tiann's throat. A trickle of fear threaded through the burning flood of anger.

"Now you understand." The queen's round face wore a malicious smile. "Do not meddle with power, girl." She turned her attention back to the stone with its gore and the druid. Tiann caught snatches of their conversation.

"... attack successful, then?"

"... must warn your allies ..."

"... and the governor will stay in the South? ..."

"...move in the spring..."

Tiann tried to connect the fragments into understanding, but her mind felt as choked as her words. Moonlight glinted from a drop of blood congealing on the side of the stone. The color expanded, covering the stone and her hands, where they still smoothed the forelock of the dead horse. Tendrils like spilled wine met with the leaping torchlight until the hilltop pulsed with a web of red. Sickness roiled in Tiann's belly, and she gasped for breath, suffocated by darkness and scarlet.

Great Light, help me!

In the distance, thunder rumbled. A warm wind rushed between the upright stones. The red receded, resolving again into torchlight and the sordid ugliness of spilled blood. Clouds blew in, obscuring the moon, and with them, rain. Tiann's breath loosened, and she lifted her face to gulp in new air, flavored with life and growth.

"Hurry!" Cartimandua demanded. "It is washing away."

"It is too late, Lady. The signs are ruined."

"Fool! You swore this night was auspicious!" Cartimandua slapped the druid across the face and stalked away.

The humiliated druid scuttled after, whining in self-defense. The people, wide eyed, hurried to follow their queen down the mountain. Tiann rose, laying the horse's head down so that the obscene gash was less noticeable.

The boy waited for her with a torch that sputtered in the rainfall. "Thank you for helping him."

Tiann nodded. They trailed after the others down the hill. "What will happen to him now?"

The boy gestured to the trees with their grisly decorations. His pace increased. Tiann matched him, eager to be off the hill and far away from the darkness there.

∼

THE PARTY that moved en masse northward kept quiet and subdued, steering clear of the queen's foul mood. Although no particular orders had been issued, Costri seemed to have appointed himself to continue in his role as Tiann's guard. Whether he intended to protect her or prevent her escape, she was unsure. Either way, Tiann was grateful to be more among the faction that gathered around Venut than among the cowed sycophants around Cartimandua.

Deep summer clung to the valleys, the scent of lush vegetation rising from where feet, hooves, and wagon wheels crushed it. When the way rose into mountains, higher and more frequently as they continued, the air quickened with cool, and hints of gold showed in the trees. Every step farther from her family increased Tiann's grief. What was she doing here? She had only meant to protect Mara when she'd impulsively volunteered herself to be the diplomatic hostage. Instead, Devyn and her tribesmen lay unmourned in a nameless clearing by a stream, her family was certainly frantic with worry over her fate, and she might never return to her blood sister.

Like a small crack in a clay pot, her decision had spread into a web of destruction until everything shattered. Tiann careened between self-blame and anger. Anger at Bultur, who had forced Boudica's vow. Anger at the Iceni queen herself for listening to the dark druid. Anger at Shal for delaying his return for so long. Anger at Shinoc, who had marked her down with his eyes even as he'd shared her meal. Anger at the gods for failing to protect her, and especially at Shal's new God, with His confusing messages. Did He care about her, or didn't He?

Dusk gave way to the indigo of twilight as they reached the northern stronghold. They entered the earthen ring fortification two horses abreast, riding between the concentric mounds to the next opening. The wooden stockades loomed above Tiann, set on a hill within three sets of the protective circular barriers. At the top of the winding way toward the gate, a sturdy wall reaching taller than three men blocked her view of the settlement within. An unfamiliar smoky scent drifted in the air, and Tiann sniffed.

Costri caught her glance and inhaled deeply. "Peat smoke. It smells like home."

"Not to me." Tiann pressed her knees to Stadder, edging him closer to where the glow of torchlight spilled from the opening gates. Despite her sharp words, she was eager to be inside, for the smoke mingled with the aromas of baking and meat. A great weariness stole over her limbs, and she longed to huddle in a corner with a hunk of bread and a bowl of stew, eat, and then sleep.

As Cartimandua had intimated, the royal settlement within the hill fort proved far grander than the stronghold they had left. Roundhouses, granaries, animal enclosures, and more crowded the area within the stockades. People thronged around the gate, hurrying to take charge of the horses and to unload the wagons. Costri took Tiann's elbow and swung her saddlebag to his own shoulder. He steered her farther into the village and ushered her into the large longhouse in the center.

Impressions of light and heat and activity dizzied her, and she was grudgingly thankful for Costri's steadying hand. He settled her on a bench along a side wall. "I will find you some food."

Tiann leaned back. The walls were made of stacked logs, and the rounded shapes pressed into different spots along her spine than the wattle and daub walls at home. The central hearth, busy with travelers warming themselves and greeting friends and family, could, if she squinted, look like Boudica's and Prasudoc's hall. Maybe she could keep her eyes half-closed and pretend that at any moment she would hear Aife's brisk voice. That Mara would soon slide next to her to regale her with a tale of her latest mischief or her funny commentary about the latest courtships. That Devyn might take her hand in his warm one.

But the scent from the fire, so unlike the familiar woodsy smoke she knew, would not allow her to escape into her fantasy. Sighing, she stretched out her feet in front of her, rotating her stiff ankle.

Costri returned with bowls of stew and bread. "Are you injured?" He sat beside her and handed her food.

She sniffed the bowl, appreciating the steamy savor of herbs and venison. Dipping her bread, she considered whether to answer. This man had no right to her story. Still, he had protected her at the Roman castra and in small ways had tried to make her journey north more comfortable. If not a friend, perhaps he was not wholly an enemy either. "It is not a recent injury. It happened when this was done to me." She lifted her scarred arm. "Sometimes it troubles me." That was enough. She would not offer more.

Tiann dozed on the bench after finishing her meal. Eventually a serving girl shook her shoulder and led her to a tiny alcove off the main hall. The space was barely five paces across, but it had a curtain at the entrance for privacy, pegs for her saddlebag and cloak, and a thick pallet with wool blankets. Tiann pulled off her boots, wrapped herself in the coverings, and slept.

THE NEXT MORNING she woke disoriented. Sounds of people beginning their day came from the hall. Her fingers reached for her smooth bed covering but found the rough log wall. She blinked and sat up, looking around the small chamber, aware of her need for a privy. Standing, she straightened her clothing, slid on her boots, and smoothed her hair. With a deep breath, she squared her shoulders and pulled the curtain aside. Laying her hand on the arm of a girl passing by with a basket of uncarded wool, Tiann asked for directions.

In the gray morning light, the village within the stockade hummed with activity. After using the privy, Tiann set out to explore. She first searched out the stables and paddock. She found Stadder placidly eating oats from a feeding trough. He looked to have been brushed, and she checked his feet. Reassured he was well-tended, she stroked his neck and spoke soft words to him.

Spotting the boy who had cared for her horse previously, she picked her way across the muddy paddock to him. "Hello. Do you care for the horses here too then?"

The boy paused from shoveling a pile of muck. "Yes. I do the cleaning chores." He held up his shovel with a rueful grin. "But I also groom and feed the horses. I am learning to train them and also to help with foaling and healing." He ducked his head. "I still have much to learn. But I work hard because, well, the horses." He made a helpless gesture, as though words failed him.

Tiann warmed to him. "They are lucky to have you. Will you keep an eye out for Stadder? He is not as fine as some other horses, but he has a good heart, like you. And"—her throat tightened—"he is the only companion from home I have left."

The boy looked up at her, eyes wide and solemn. "I will show him every care, Lady."

Resting her hand on his shoulder, Tiann nodded, blinking moisture from her eyes. "What is your name?"

"I am Fein, Lady."

"Thank you, Fein. I am Tiann." It was the first time she had given her name to another since the ambush in the clearing. Something loosened in her chest at this small connection, this tiny glow of friendship.

With her stomach reminding her she had not yet eaten, Tiann made her way back to the hall. She retrieved a spoon from her saddlebag, then helped herself to a bowl of porridge from the cauldron at the central hearth. Settling on the same out-of-the-way bench as the evening before, she ate and observed. Yesterday's sense of unreality clung to her perceptions. In most ways, the scene resembled the Iceni hall, but with jarring notes of unfamiliarity. The Brigantians' dress and way of wearing hair and beards. The design of a loom. The roof made of timber instead of thatch, holding in the strange-smelling smoke.

She was just scraping the last bits from the bowl when the doors swung open to admit a string of heavily laden servants. She sat up straight, setting the bowl on the bench beside her. Those bundles and chests were from the Iceni wagons. The servants carried in the goods so painstakingly assembled by Boudica to serve as diplomatic gifts, Tiann's household goods, and attire fit for her ambassadorial role. The porridge in her stomach congealed into a stone when she thought of it all going to Cartimandua.

After depositing everything, the servants lingered. "Did he say where to put it?"

"No. Who is to take charge of it?"

"Ask the steward."

"He's not here. He's gone with the shipment of lead."

Tiann jumped up and hurried over to the group. "Ah! Thank you for bringing in my things." Good. She sounded almost like Aife, bossy and sure of herself. She pointed to the chests with her personal items. "Please bring those to my bedchamber at once." She spied a plain wooden box. Inside, she knew, wrapped in waxed leather and padded with washed wool, lay an intricately decorated gold and enamel casket. This costly container held the broaches, arm bracelets, and torcs intended as gifts to the members of the Coritani royal family. She picked it up. "This is extra tack for my horse. I was about to check on him, so I will bring it to the stable. Which way is it again?"

She found Fein in the farthest stable, mucking out a stall. Was she presuming too much on their brief connection? Asking too much of a child? "Fein. Can you help me with something?"

He leaned his shovel against the wall. "Yes, Lady. What do you need? Shall I saddle Stadder for you? He is out in the paddock."

"No. Thank you. I have this box. It is . . . personal. Do you know a safe, private place I can store it?"

His gaze fell to the box, then lifted to her face, searching. Tiann squirmed, knowing he saw through her.

Then he nodded. "I'll show you." He led her to an unused stall. Cobwebs shrouded the corners, but the floor was swept clean. "This stall belonged to the old king's favorite mare. After she died, he ordered it to remain empty." A tack box was built into the back of the stall, and Fein opened the lid. He lifted out a fine saddle and bridle and a woven horse blanket. A box, not unlike the one Tiann held, lay at the bottom.

Fein flushed. "I keep some things in here too. Nothing special, except to me. Just private, like you said. Things I want to keep safe."

Tiann set her box beside his. "Thank you for sharing your hiding place with me." She helped him reload the old horse's tack into the bin. "If anyone asks, I brought an extra bridle for Stadder. Just an everyday one. It probably got mixed in with all the others. Would that get you into trouble?"

Fein grinned. "I'm not in charge of sorting the tack. And the boy who is never knows who belongs to what. Plus, he is rough with the horses." His tone made it clear he thought a little trouble in that direction would be a good thing.

Tiann grinned back.

She spent the rest of the day unpacking her clothing and bed coverings. She commandeered water for washing and sent her traveling clothes to be cleaned with the same imperious manner she had used to take charge of the goods from the wagon. The servants were unsure of her status, and she took advantage of their uncertainty, dredging up every ounce of confidence she had.

She would act like a royal guest until someone told the household otherwise.

Her tiny bedchamber felt even smaller with two chests in it, but she arranged the space as best she could. The pallet she pushed against the wall farthest from the curtained entrance. Once she had hung her clothing on pegs and smoothed out her own familiar bed coverings, she repacked the chests. The more luxurious garments she left stored away in one chest, which she placed against the side of the pallet, forming a barrier between her sleeping self and anyone coming through the curtain. In the other, placed at the head of her pallet, she put the things that mattered: the small objects that reminded her of home and Mara, a dagger, the comfortable clothes and stiffened boots she used for training. She laid her saddlebag in it too, stocked with flint, extra bandages for her ankle, the coins Cattia had given her, a water-skin, and a length of waxed-wool cloth that could serve as ground cloth or shelter. She would try to scrounge up some dried meat and grain. The prospect of escape seemed unlikely, and navigating her way home unlikelier still, but if the chance came, she would take it.

When she was done, she lay back on the pallet. Eyes closed, she twined her fingers in the soft covering, remembering the day she had first felt it under her hand. Her body in agony from the Romans' brutalization, the touch of the silk had held a glimmer of the promise of comfort. Today, it was her heart that felt cut by knives, crushed by hobnail boots. But somewhere, her mother, who had wrapped her up; her bossy older sister, who had stitched beauty into the softness; and her blood sister, who had curled up beside her and shared her pain—somewhere, they were loving her and trying to get her back. For them, Tiann would not give up.

SIXTEEN

The days blurred by with a numbing sameness. The hours of sunlight grew shorter and the ground in the morning glittered with frost. Mountains to the north and west, now wearing a cloak of white, sheltered the hilltop settlement from the worst winds. Still, Tiann dug into her chest for her warmer clothing, made with felted wool and lined with fur. At night she snuggled into the secure nest she had made, her bed covering under her hand and the sachet of herbs under her pillow. She could almost pretend she was home. During the day, the household was polite but not deferent. Word had gotten around that she was a mere captive, albeit one valuable to the queen. Mostly, everyone ignored Tiann.

She tried to combat her boredom by joining training exercises but was rebuffed. No one wanted to put a weapon in her hands, even for practice. She ran circuits around the inside of the stockade and did what she could to keep strong and limber. The horses provided the best distraction, although they lacked the quality of the Iceni herd. She was allowed to ride outside the settlement if she took the slowest mount and warriors accompanied her.

Of the queen and chief, she saw almost nothing. Venut kept himself busy traveling to the far reaches of Brigantian territory. Tiann suspected he would just as soon never return to his wife, except he needed to stay aware of her activities and wield what influence he could.

One day Venut returned from one of his many patrols with his core of warriors, Costri among them. They burst into the hall, bringing a swirl of cold air. From her bench, Tiann watched as they lingered around the hearth. Venut called for mead, and a serving man put clean stones in the fire, ready to be dropped into the flagons to warm the drink. The chief had his arm over the shoulders of a man Tiann did not recall seeing before. But as he raised the mead cup to his mouth, something about him niggled at her.

Cartimandua entered the hall from her apartments. She approached the men at the hearth, wrinkling her nose. "Welcome home, husband."

Venut inclined his head to her. "Lady."

"I will have the cookhouse delay the evening meal so you can make yourselves presentable."

Venut's brows snapped together. With a deliberate gaze, he surveyed her Roman-style gown and heavy cosmetics. "We have traveled hard and are hungry. We are ready for our meal now." He turned his back on her, bellowing, "Tell the cookhouse to begin serving."

The household moved to obey him, with hushed voices and nervous glances at the queen. Cartimandua retreated to her seat at the high table to glower. The chief's men brought the flagons of mead to a table the serving boys dragged from the side. Venut sat with them, and wives and children joined them.

Tiann helped move her bench into its position for the evening meal. She caught the stranger watching her. He leaned over to Venut and said something. The chief also looked at her as he answered and jerked his chin toward the queen. Costri, scowling, paused from eating and spoke. The stranger rose and crossed the hall to where Tiann sat.

She wished she could crawl beneath the table and hide. She would rather be ignored than examined as a curiosity.

"Lady. I believe we have met." The stranger nodded his head with respect.

Tiann stood. "No. I have met few from outside my tribe before now."

"Ah, but I think you would remember me. We were introduced through my wrong behavior at your special feast. You shared a cup of mead and your story." He took her hand and pulled her sleeve back a few inches.

The memory bloomed in Tiann's mind: the belligerent man shouting of cowardice and collaboration from his bloodied mouth. His tears as he told them of the treachery within his own tribe. The wild night filled with feasting, music, and defiance. The night she gained her blood bond with Mara and her new family.

"Yes. Yes! I remember. Teth."

The man's forehead crinkled. "I am sorry to see you here. Sorry that once again you suffer separation from your family. If the chief had known . . ."

"I have observed that the queen and chief do not always confer on their decisions," Tiann said.

He laughed and turned to call across the hall. "Chief! Do you remember the summer you sent me south? This is the girl Boudica adopted the night I nearly got myself killed at an Iceni feast." Turning back to Tiann, he wriggled his eyebrows ruefully. "I am still grateful your queen and chief spared me. I am less hotheaded these days."

Venut approached and pounded the man on the back. "Less hotheaded. Ha! Just a moon ago, you charged a bear, one spear in your hand and none of your companions near enough to help."

"But whose skin was carried back to the hall, my chief? Mine or his?"

A lump rose in Tiann's throat. To remember that night, so full of happiness, when she felt secure among the people who'd claimed her. "Much has changed since the feast that celebrated my adoption."

The two men sobered, glancing at each other. From the high table came the sound of a chair shoved, crashing over.

"What did you say?" Cartimandua's voice penetrated the hubbub of the hall, silencing every voice. All eyes turned to where the queen stood, shaking, pointing at Tiann. "The feast that celebrated *what*?" She swung her finger to Venut's warrior. "The girl Boudica *what*?" Her voice rose to a shriek.

Tiann drew herself up tall. "The feast that celebrated my entrance into the royal family of the Iceni. My adoption by my noble chief, Prasudoc, and a truly great queen, Boudica. A royal family who deserve their position because of their honor."

Cartimandua flew down the length of the hall to where Tiann stood. "You wicked girl." She lashed out, backhanding Tiann's face and leaving a bloody streak from her enormous ring. "What good is some foundling to me?"

The queen's fawning druid advisor sidled up and whispered in her ear. An ugly scarlet flush suffused Cartimandua's face. "The ritual—you defiled the ritual with your common blood." She raised her hand again, but Venut grabbed her arm even before Tiann moved to defend herself.

"Control yourself, wife."

She turned on him. "How dare you manhandle me! Warriors!"

Around the hall the warriors who attended the queen laid hands on their daggers and moved toward her. Several positioned themselves by the knot of Venut's men, who still stood by the hearth. Tension thickened the air as the queen and chief stared at each other with naked animosity. Venut's eyes flicked around the hall.

Tiann followed his gaze. The queen's men outnumbered the chief's by more than twice. Would they actually engage with one another? Warriors from the same tribe? Venut seemed to think so, for he dropped his wife's hand and shook his head at Teth, who had sprung to readiness.

"Apologies, Lady." The terse words appeared to cost the chief.

Cartimandua tossed her head. "Perhaps you are tired from your journey and your thinking muddled, husband. But just to be clear, my hostage is my concern." Her eyes narrowed. "Of course, now that I know she isn't royal, I will need to decide what to do with her."

Anger shook Tiann's body. "I am a fully adopted member of the Iceni royal family."

Cartimandua snorted. "Adopted. That's no better than a pet dog. Boudica and Prasudoc may miss their little pet, but it's not the same as if I held one of their own. I promised the commander I could guarantee cooperation from the Iceni." Her fists clenched, and she whirled around to scan the hall. "Where is Shinoc?"

Shinoc emerged from a group near the doors, shoved forward by the queen's warriors. Shuffling, bowing, and revealing his yellow teeth in an ingratiating smile, he crossed to his mistress.

She regarded him with rage. "You promised me a valuable hostage from the royal family. You said you had inside knowledge. How did I end up with this?" She flung a hand toward Tiann.

Shinoc fell to his knees. "Please, Lady, I did my best. How could I know? Perhaps the Iceni used a decoy. But I would swear she was treated as royal."

Cartimandua lunged at him, clawing his face and kicking him when he cowered away. "It doesn't matter how she is treated. It only matters what she is. I will see you flogged for this! Take him away." Her warriors dragged Shinoc, still protesting, from the hall.

"And what am I supposed to do with you now?" Cartimandua leaned so close that Tiann could see a pulse throbbing in her forehead.

Tiann planted her feet, ready to tell the woman in no uncertain terms that she was royal, with the same status as Boudica's natural-born daughters. Even as she opened her mouth to let the hot words flow, a burning on her arm stopped her. She looked to where Teth had pulled back her sleeve. Her scars glowed a faint gold.

Remember the wounds.

She had not been wounded because she sought status. She had taken the punishment because she loved Mara. Because she wanted to protect her tribe. The Romans had seen her as a slave. It was not as a royal daughter that she had kept her family safe, but as a nobody.

"You are right, Lady. You have found me out. I am just a servant who Boudica sent. I was not even born in the royal household. I came to them as an orphan." The burning on Tiann's arm subsided to a warm rush that swept through her body, soothing her anger like a balm. The tension flowed away from her.

Cartimandua's expression twisted with rage. Her mouth flapped open and shut, but she appeared beyond speech. She stalked off toward the high table, her druid advisor trailing behind her. When she came to a sudden halt, the man plowed into her. Shoving him aside, the queen turned and fastened her gaze on the curtained entrance to Tiann's alcove. She crooked a finger to her warriors, and a handful of them followed her as she wrenched the curtain aside.

"Empty it."

A moan escaped Tiann as she watched them drag her belongings into the hall. The warm peace still held her, but a darkness pushed at the edges, threatening to crack her. They heaped everything by the central hearth, dumping out her chests and piling her bedding. The queen poked through, pulling out the fine garments and handing them to one of her women. When she shook out the embroidered wrapping holding Tiann's few ornaments, she threw the fabric to the floor and viewed the slim torc and plain brooches with disdain.

"Your so noble queen didn't bother to send anything valuable with you, I see. Well, they can be melted down for coins. A very few coins."

Tiann silently apologized to the Iceni goldsmith, who had crafted her jewelry with exquisite care. This woman could only see big and flashy, not quality. The pang in her heart grew to an ache when Cartimandua shook out the silken bed covering.

"Now this. This can be worked into a fine gown. Too bad it is marred by this stitching. Hold the edges taut and bring me a knife." She sliced off the embellished edges, which Aife had worked with Iceni symbols. The scraps joined the embroidered cloth on the floor, and the stripped fabric disappeared into the queen's chamber in the arms of a serving woman.

"Bring the girl to the steward. He can arrange for her to work. If she cannot prove herself, then we will kill her. Put the rest of that mess in the fire."

Two of Cartimandua's warriors moved to seize Tiann by the arms.

Teth stepped in front of her. "I will take her." He stared them down, and the other two backed off. Putting a hand under Tiann's elbow, he steered her out of the hall. As she went, she caught a fragrance of herbs, first crushed, then burning, the scent mingling with the peat smoke that lingered in a haze near the timber roof.

"Why did you do that?" Teth asked once they were outside. "You are certainly valuable to Boudica and Prasudoc. I saw it with my own eyes."

"I said nothing that is untrue. I am not Boudica's natural-born daughter. I did come to the royal family as an orphan."

"But the Iceni view adoption differently than the Brigantes. You have lost any power you have here to ensure you are well treated."

Tiann stopped. "No. I have taken away Cartimandua's power to control or threaten my family. I have kept my power to do as I have promised—to protect them, even with my life, if necessary. I will not hold on to my status at the cost of harming them." The warm security inside her gave sureness to her words. "You're right the Iceni view adopted children as full members of the family. Cartimandua can only see things her way. And she does not even know there is an even stronger bond between Boudica's daughter Mara and me. A blood bond. A vow." Tiann continued walking toward the steward's quarters. "If treating me as a slave prevents Cartimandua from using me to hurt my blood sister, then I am satisfied."

ONCE AGAIN THE days faded one into the other, but now edged with discomfort and frustration. In the mornings, Tiann woke aching and cold in the hall's corner farthest from the banked hearth. She was glad she had been wearing her warmest garments when her chests were ransacked, for she wore them through the night. When she could, she bathed herself and washed her underclothes. She shook off the secret shame of going without them while they laid out to dry in the hall. She tucked her possessions —reduced to a thin bedroll, a wood comb she had begged off one of the serving women, and her spoon—under a bench during the day.

Her duties kept her indoors, and she chafed at the physical inactivity in the close, smoky atmosphere. When she was sent on an errand or got permission to use the privy, she took the time to duck into a hidden spot and move her muscles. She stretched, jumped up and down, or lifted something heavy over and over. Still, she worried she was losing her readiness for action. If the moment came for escape, could she rise to the challenge?

Tiann also took every opportunity to examine as much of the village as she could without raising suspicion. She pretended Mara was there with her, sneaking around, looking for hiding places and spying positions. She held conversations with her blood sister in her mind, imagining how Mara would see things.

The day the wounded young acolyte stumbled into the compound, Tiann was helping with the endless weaving. She sat before the loom, moving the shuttle back and forth, noticing only several rows too late that she had not switched colors at the prescribed time, marring the traditional pattern. She considered pulling out the work to correct the mistake, but wrath against her captors rose in her heart and she left the errant stripe in place. She peeked around to see if any of the other women had observed. That was when she saw two of Cartimandua's warriors half carrying, half dragging the druid into the hall.

She watched from behind her eyelashes as they laid the young man on a bench. The warriors conferred for a moment, then one headed toward the queen's quarters. Tiann's attention sharpened. What could be so important that they would risk Cartimandua's ire at being interrupted? Murmuring to the old crone in charge of the weavers of a need to visit the privy, Tiann slipped out of the hall. Conscious of watching eyes, she walked toward the privy until out of sight, then doubled back toward the hall. Edging with care around the prickly gorse bushes next to the outer wall, she squatted, hidden by the brush. Prying loose a sliver of wood and shading the telltale opening from daylight, she peered into the hall.

The injured man lay only a few feet away. She could hear the rasp of his breathing. If they brought the man to the queen, she would lose her opportunity, for she had not yet discovered a way to spy on the royal rooms. But she was counting on Cartimandua's curiosity and need to be in control. In a few moments Tiann's gamble paid off.

"Where is he? Is that him? Can he walk?" The queen's harsh voice rose over the murmur in the hall. "Very well, let him stay where he is. I'll speak with him there. No, there is no need to guard me—what can a wounded priest do to me?" Why did Cartimandua want privacy to speak to this traveler? The rustle of the Roman-style dress broadcasted her approach. "What is it? Did you come from Mona? What has happened?" Near as she was, Tiann had to move her ear even closer to the opening to hear the druid's ragged reply.

"Sent . . . find Iceni girl . . . my master, Shal . . ."

Tiann clamped a hand over her mouth to prevent a gasp from escaping. Shal! He had discovered her whereabouts. He must have traveled to the druid enclave in the West and heard news of her. Did he send a message to let her know they were coming for her?

Cartimandua's breath hissed out. "Never mind that! Tell me what happened. Did the Romans take the enclave?"

There was a momentary silence, filled with the rough sound of the young man's labored breathing. "You knew? How did you . . . They came to Mona not half a moon ago. No one escaped . . . I only because they thought . . . already dead. With Shal when he died . . . said find girl . . . say Boudica has sent out . . . war call . . ."

"Wait! What? Boudica is gathering a war council? Why would she do that when the druids have been destroyed? Is her husband with her on this? Surely not." The queen's tone turned musing, "He has always tempered her with his caution."

"Prasudoc died. Romans would not . . . recognize her daughters. Boudica . . . flogged. Daughters . . . raped . . . before her eyes."

Shocked tears sprang to Tiann's eyes, and she pressed her hand to her mouth until she tasted the blood of a cut lip. Shal. Prasudoc. Boudica. Aife. And Mara . . . oh Mara!

"Fools!" Cartimandua spat. "If they had left her alone and followed the plan, we could have had the whole South without a fight."

"Plan, Lady? No plan, only a message. Find Iceni girl . . ." His voice trailed off.

Tiann could almost feel Cartimandua's fury through the wall. An abrupt rustle indicated she was moving off. "Someone move that body. He died before he could tell me any news of import."

Tiann slumped against the wall, trembling. With shaking hands, she fitted the bit of wood she had pried free back into place. *I must get back inside.* But the urgency did not penetrate her stunned haze. She drew a deep breath and felt a wail rising in her throat. No. No! She must think, must be calm. But her body reacted without consideration of her wishes. Horror clutched her. She squeezed her eyes shut.

Red. Scarlet red running from stripes on white skin. Rose-red tongue and throat open wide in rage and agony. Mud red pooling next to lifeless warriors. Flame red from torches illuminating cruel, lustful, laughing mouths. Virgin red dripping . . .

A white light, merciful and stern, covered the images. Tiann hauled herself to her hands and knees. She remained, panting with her head hanging, her eyes, nose, and mouth pouring a torrent of pain onto the frozen ground. *Mara. Mara. Mara.* She must get to her.

"Chief of chiefs." Her whisper rasped her aching throat. "Are You real? Shal said You are. I'm calling to You for help. I need help now—I need to get to my family. I need to escape. Tell me what to do if You are real."

Tiann's lungs suddenly expanded past the tightness in her throat. Her legs and arms stopped wobbling. Pushing up to her feet, she passed her sleeve over her wet, mucous-sticky face. She emerged from the brush and made her way back to the hall. She was sure her turbulent emotions would be visible on her face, but the other women ignored her when she sat again at the loom. Her steady hands resumed the hated task, and she was amazed at the clarity of her mind.

All right. Good this far. Now what? She formulated and discarded plan after plan—too reckless, too time consuming, too many supplies needed. All afternoon she kept her eyes cast down and her hands busy as she wove scenarios more intricate than the pattern in the cloth.

As evening fell, she was no closer to a solution. Frustration reawakened grief, and she welcomed the increasing shadows that both ended the workday and hid her countenance. She needed an answer. She seethed, angry at herself for being having been fooled into believing in Shal's unseen God. *If you are real, you will have to do more than send me back to do more weaving—you will have to give me a way to escape.*

When the time came for the evening meal, the looms were pushed aside to make room for benches and tables. The head serving woman supervised and made a circuit, inspecting the day's work. Reaching Tiann's loom, she paused, eyes rounding. "What is this?" She pointed at the mistake a third of the way down the length. She turned on Tiann. "You stupid girl! This is ruined! Can't you see it is wrong?"

"I beg pardon. I am unused to your Briganti patterns. They are so strange."

"This is unusable. You have wasted most of a day and have set us back."

Tiann had enough. "I will cut it out." She pretended to reach into the pouch at her waist for a knife. Everyone carried at least a small one for everyday tasks and eating. The woman probably didn't know that Tiann's blades had all been confiscated.

The serving woman grabbed Tiann's wrist, digging her nails into her flesh. "Can you be so ignorant? It must be carefully unwoven, or we will lose all the work to spin the thread too." She cuffed Tiann's ear and thrust her aside. "No. You will not be near the looms again." The woman marched to the steward, pulling Tiann with her.

As the serving woman put her complaint to the steward, Tiann tuned them out. It didn't matter what happened to her. Despair crept around the borders of her thoughts. Why, when Mara most needed her, was she here in this foreign northern land? Why had Boudica insisted on acting as though everything was normal the day of her leave-taking? Maybe she could have had more time with Prasudoc. Maybe she could have helped him get well. What if Bultur had never come, with his dark ways and fanatical advice?

She watched the low flames in the central hearth while the two discussed what to do with her. She could almost see the figure of Bultur as he had been the night he'd extracted Boudica's promise to send Tiann as hostage. He had stood, arms upraised, head thrown back, a part of the red-tinged darkness. The flames flickered, and the figure shifted to Cartimandua as she had been on the hilltop among the stones.

One hated the Romans. One allied herself with them. Both served the dark, the power that long ago had beckoned Tiann with the deceptive call of friendship. That night by the sea she had chosen to turn away, to listen to Elior, to ride wild and free on a golden mare. But he had warned the way would be grievous. If she had chosen the other path, could she have had the power to protect Mara? Despair circled closer.

Dark did not care about sides. Iceni, Briganti, Roman — dark was only a hunger. What else had Elior said? "The path will be grievous, but do not fear. The dark does not overcome." Tears poured from Tiann's flame-dazzled eyes. *But it feels like dark has overcome. I feel overcome.*

A hand slapped her cheek. "Stop your blubbering. Don't think you can wheedle your way back into easy work with a sad face. Get your things." The serving woman stalked away.

Tiann blinked and focused on the steward. "My things?"

He sighed. "Haven't you been paying attention? Yes, get your bedroll. You'll be serving with the livestock. You need to ask where to sleep. Hurry, before they come in from the paddock and fields."

Could it be true? She hurried to comply. The other women in the hall stared and whispered, following her with looks that were either disdainful or pitying. Tiann understood. To these women, with their tastes formed by their queen, outdoor work was shameful, a disgrace. But walking toward the stable clutching her meager bundle, Tiann felt despair retreating. She entered the dim stable, inhaling the familiar, comforting atmosphere of hay and horseflesh. "Fein? Are you here?"

A shadow detached itself from a corner. "Here, Lady. Can I help you?"

"They have banished me from the hall. I'm to work with the animals. They think they are punishing me." A bubble of laughter welled up in her mouth, but somehow, when it came out, it was a sob.

"Oh, Lady, don't cry. It can be very nice helping with the animals. I know you care for them, the way you look after Stadder." Fein put his arms around her, bundle and all.

Tiann lowered her head to rest her cheek on the top of his head. "Thank you, my friend. I'm not sad to be sent out of the hall to the stable. It's something else. I am missing my family." She took a deep breath and lifted her head. Fein let her go and patted her arm. She held up her bundle. "I need a place to sleep."

~

THE DAY dawned clear and icy cold. Tiann rolled up from her burrow of hay and hastened to pull on her boots. She missed her custom-crafted footwear that supported her ankle so well. Like everything else, those boots had disappeared the day Cartimandua stripped her of anything she was not wearing. She wrapped the ankle up tight with fingers that turned clumsy as soon as they met the air. She tucked her hands under her arms on the way to the hall for bread and broth. Over the weeks since her shift to outside work, she had learned that the trick first thing in the morning was to keep moving. Soon enough the exertion of her chores would warm her. Tiann felt like she could breathe again, spending her days outdoors and expending her energy in physical labor.

As she waited for her turn at the communal cauldron, a voice spoke at her left in a hushed tone. "Don't look up. Just listen."

Tiann recognized the voice of one of the elder warriors who kept company with Venut. She bent her head, busying herself with pulling her spoon from her pouch while the man continued.

"Venut wants to talk with you. He will meet you by the rock outcropping to the north of the horse paddock. Go now—I will cover for your absence."

Tiann did look up at him then, wondering if she could trust this warrior in the royal inner circle. Venut and a party of his men, including Costri and Teth, had been on another of their patrols when the fiasco with the weaving occurred. They had returned a few days ago, but as far as she knew, none had inquired about her absence in the hall. Relations between the chief and queen appeared to be peaceful for now.

The old man glanced down, then away. "Not all of us are the queen's men. I rode with Venut against Cartimandua when he tried to break away. Now we are biding our time. To throw off the Roman yoke."

Tiann nodded once, then stood and walked out of the hall without meeting his eye again. Out in the frigid morning air, she took a deep breath and headed toward the strange appointment with Venut.

Cartimandua and Venut had spent several years fighting with each other. After Caradoc sought refuge with the Brigantes, Venut had wanted to join the fight against the Romans. Cartimandua had been more interested in the wealth and opportunity that came from being a client ruler of the empire. She treacherously surrendered Caradoc to the Romans. Venut was furious and rebelled against his wife, making two failed attempts to wrest power from her hands. The Romans had come to her rescue, and eventually Venut gave up and reconciled with the queen. That had been three years ago.

But now? The queen and chief obviously found each other's company unpleasant. What about their political positions? Was the old warrior being truthful when he said Venut still planned to make a move against Rome?

Stopping in the shadow of a tree with the outcropping in sight, Tiann considered the cryptic message Venut had sent. Did he know what the dying druid had told the queen? Was he trying to trap her into admitting she wanted to escape? Or was it possible, just possible, that he meant to help her? In the clear air, the breeze blew against her skin, seeming to urge her on. Perhaps this was the answer from the unknown God. Straightening her shoulders, she allowed the wind to push her toward the meeting with the Brigantian chief.

CHAPTER

SEVENTEEN

Venut stirred as she approached, stretching a leg as though it were stiff. Just like Prasudoc used to stretch his old wounds. "I wasn't sure if you would come, Tiann." She gazed at him, still wary, but noting his use of her name. Here in Cartimandua's stronghold, she was often "girl" or "Iceni girl" and most often just an indifferent "you."

"I wasn't sure either," she replied.

His lips twitched.

Tiann stared at him. *This amuses him? The queen would have slapped me.* She must not be a fool, rushing headlong into schemes. The chief and his men might have shown some respect and even kindness, but after all, she was still here, captive.

"I know what message that acolyte brought." Venut scratched at his beard. "He wasn't quite dead when my merciful wife had him thrown into the midden pit." His eyebrows lowered with distaste. "Those Roman dogs have wiped out the sacred enclave on Mona—they struck during the Gathering." Venut watched her face, and she struggled not to reveal her thoughts. "A word of advice. If you are going to spy, you must learn not only how to not react but also how to react with surprise to news you are not yet supposed to know."

She flushed and looked down, chagrined at her mistake.

"Does the young man still live?" she asked, wondering how to find out if Venut had learned the rest of the message.

His lips twitched again. "Yes, I have one of my young cousins hiding him in a shelter in the west woods. He will probably not survive—his wounds are rotten, and there are no healers here I can trust—but if he does, I'll move him to my lands in the North. Meanwhile, when he is not delirious with his fever or unconscious, he is giving us valuable information. He is a good lad."

Tiann warmed to him. She had feared he had become an appendage of his ruthless wife, the fight gone out of him, almost a shell of a man. But she had underestimated him. He still had the fight in him, but it was tempered by caution and strategy and, remarkably, kindness.

Venut laid a hard hand on her shoulder and cleared his throat. "He also told us about your family—what happened to your foster mother and sisters. I want you to know that you have friends here, those who are appalled and angry. Ready to act. I am working on a response, including getting you to those you love, where you belong. But we must be careful. It's not just the queen. She is allied with the Ninth Legion, friends with the commander there. I'm asking you to trust me and wait for my arrangements. Will you do that?"

Tiann looked up at his world-weary face and searched his eyes. "Yes, I will wait for your plan." Grasping his hand on her shoulder once, she turned and slipped back to the hall.

As the days went by, Tiann thought it would have been easier to flee into the unfamiliar forest, with no plan and no supplies, than to continue the daily pretense of ignorance and dull servitude. She was grateful for the work with the horses, sheep, and cattle. The variety during the day kept her mind from conjuring up the terrible images of assault on her family. Exhaustion at night allowed her instant, dreamless sleep. The hard labor toughened her muscles back to shape.

It also gave her a natural reason to converse with Venut under the pretext of orders regarding the care of the animals. In this way she received reassuring updates on his plans for her escape. Despite the frustrating pace of progress, she grew to trust his judgment. Also, the young acolyte Nuallen was, against all odds, recovering from his wounds and fever. When one of the men told Tiann this news, she sought Venut just after dusk at the horse paddock.

"I want to see him." They examined the hoof of one of the mares. "I want to hear what Shal told him from his own lips. It's not that I don't believe you. Shal was as a father to me, almost as much as Prasudoc, and Nuallen was the last to be with him. I want to honor Shal's memory."

Venut nodded as he dropped the hoof and sent the mare off with a light slap to the withers. "It is fitting. I am just not sure how to arrange it. We must give you a reason to be away from the compound for at least two days. I think the young man is no longer in danger of dying, although he is weak. If we wait a half a moon, he will be stronger and the lambing will have started. Staying out with the breeding ewes in the field could be an excuse for you. I will tie a white cloth to the sheepfold gate when it is time. Then be on the lookout for one of my men to signal you to follow."

❧

Tiann watched the progress of the moon and waited. The white cloth appeared on the gate. One afternoon she came out of the stable, laden with feed bags for the horses in the paddock. A horse trainer waved her over to where he was conferring with three people she didn't recognize. She set the bags down, careful not to spill the grain, and joined them.

"The lambing has started in the western pastures. They need help and heard there is a young woman with some skills with herbs and such. Do they mean you?"

Tiann glanced at the shepherds, two weather-toughened men and an older woman. Venut must have arranged this. "Yes. At home I often attended during births for lambs, calves, and foals." This was true in the strict sense. She did not mention that she mostly watched Mara when her sister assisted an animal with a difficult birth. Tiann's role involved no more than holding out a cloth or pouring oil on a hand.

The trainer nodded. "Very well. We can do without you for a few days. Bring your bedroll."

Tiann entered the stable. "Fein?"

The boy poked his head out of a stall.

She smiled as she plucked hay out of his hair. "I am being sent to help with lambing in the western pastures. I left the feed bags just outside. Can you get them to our hungry friends in the paddock?"

"Of course, Lady. Will you be gone long? I will miss you."

She put an arm around his shoulders and squeezed. What would she have done without his uncomplicated affection? "Just a few days, I think. Don't forget to keep an eye on that sore spot above the bay mare's front knee."

"I won't. Fair journey, Lady."

Tiann set off in the company of the shepherds, with her bedroll stuffed in a spare sack slung over her shoulder. Her legs burned with the steady climb. She was glad for the conditioning her duties had given her. Could she have made the trek if they had consigned her to weaving in the hall day after day? She would certainly have shamed herself by asking for rest. As it was, she welcomed the chance to travel into wilder landscape. The track was clear, though muddy, but the snow deepened alongside the higher they climbed. The white blanket hushed the world around her, leaving her with her thoughts and the sound of her breath. Eagerness to speak to the young druid spurred her on as the sun lowered into a pale dusk.

The shepherds, who had been almost silent through the hours of their walk, turned off the main trail and led her to a sheltered spot like a bowl scooped out of the hillside. Nestled in the curve of the mossy cliff sat a bothy, surrounded by a fenced area dotted with snug pens. Ewes in various stages of pregnancy populated the area, and the sounds of active labor resounded from one of the pens. The shepherds took their leave, nodding acknowledgment to her thanks and ducking into the pen where the ewe was giving birth.

Venut emerged. "I'm glad you arrived when you did. That ewe is having some trouble with twins, and Beathas is the expert at sorting out which limb belongs to which lamb." He headed to a water trough and scrubbed his hands and arms up to the elbows. "It is not just that her hands are smaller. She seems to know them by touch." His skin looked red and cold. "Let's get inside. I am chilled through, and I'm sure you are hungry and tired. And certainly Nuallen has heard your arrival. If we don't hurry, he will disobey me again and rise from his bed."

Inside the bothy, a fire crackled on a small hearth, enough to create a cozy warmth. The young man sat propped on a bed of sheepskins. The quick glimpse she had caught of him when he'd entered the hall had shown a ragged, skeletal frame, sickly gray skin, and matted dark hair. Now he had color in his face and live-liness in his eyes. His hair was clean and neatly braided back from his cheeks. Startled, Tiann noted the blue designs running from his temple to his jawline. Did the wild tribes in the far North have druids?

"Yes, a painted man who seeks training with the druids is rare." The man grinned up at her, revealing even, white teeth.

Tiann jumped. Had she spoken out loud? Or had he heard her thoughts?

Nuallen laughed. "I assure you, I am only hearing what I have heard a hundred times from people who look at me with the expression you currently wear."

Venut grunted. "He says he does not hear thoughts, but his insight can sometimes be quite uncomfortable." He took the sack from Tiann's shoulder and indicated a low bench, also padded with a sheepskin. "Please rest. I'll bring you some food."

"I am so happy to finally meet you. I am Nuallen."

She sank to the bench, wincing at the stiffness in her legs. "I am Tiann. I am pleased you are healing."

"Shal talked about you a great deal. He had vast sorrow when he learned of your disappearance. You were very special to him."

"He was like another father to me. I wish to hear the telling of his last days."

Venut handed them bowls of porridge with cheese and dried meat. Nuallen set his to the side and leaned back. "I met Shal on Mona. I had come to the island in search of a teacher, but none had taken me. The Gathering was to convene at the next full moon, and druids arrived daily from all over the two islands, even from Gaul. No one talked of anything except what the Romans were doing. In the West they continue to mount campaigns against the remnants of Caradoc's people. In the South they establish cities with a flood of trade coming and going from the rest of the empire, more than Albion has ever seen. In Gaul they absorb the tribes into their government system and suppress the druids and cut down the oaks. In the East they press their power on client kings and steal the land and the people to build colonies for retired Roman soldiers."

Nuallen paused to sip some water from a clay cup. Tiann, who had been captivated by the rhythm of his telling, spooned some porridge into her mouth. The first taste awakened her belly, and she realized she was ravenous. She kept eating as Nuallen took up the tale again.

"No one wanted to talk to me about taking me on as a pupil. And no one wanted to talk to Shal about a man across the world who the Romans had killed. One day, discouraged, I walked to a far rocky point where I could sit alone and ponder. Shal was already there, but he was not sitting and pondering, as I intended." Nuallen's grin flashed out into the darkening room. "Actually, I called it pondering, but I was just planning to sit and feel sorry for myself for a while."

Tiann laughed. She set her empty bowl down and accepted a clay cup of water from Venut. "Please don't stop. What was Shal doing?"

"He stood on a rock with his arms raised, talking to the sea, or so it seemed to me. I could catch snatches of it. Sometimes it sounded like he spoke to a friend, and sometimes he was reciting. But then he would stop and extend his arms, like this." Nuallen held out his hands, palms up. "And he just waited. He fascinated me, but after a while I felt embarrassed to be watching. I was just about to go find another lonely spot to be sorry for myself, when he turned around.

"He looked at me as though he didn't realize he had been observed, but at the same time, he did not seem surprised. He invited me to sit with him, and we talked. My apprenticeship began that day."

"And did you become a follower of this Man too?"

"Yes. In Shal's words over the next days, I found the wisdom I left my home to seek. And as the Spirit of Light filled me, I came to know who Shal spoke with and who he heard."

Venut cleared his throat. "Forgive me, Tiann, but if you allow him to continue on this trail, we will find that the night and tomorrow have both vanished with many other things left unsaid."

Nuallen shrugged and smiled. "He's right. I love to tell the stories of the Man. But our time is limited, and you want to hear about Shal, of course.

"The island's shelters filled with visitors, and the shoreline and fields glowed with the fires of those who slept under the stars. News trickled in with each new arrival. We heard of your disappearance first. Shal spent a night on that lonely rock by the sea. I went with him and built a fire and laid out blankets in the cleft of a rock nearby, out of the wind, but every time I woke, he was still there, talking to the Maker. Two days later we learned of Prasudoc's death. Your chief had collapsed while training with his men. He was gone before they could even get him to the hall.

"At this Shal wept but did not spend the night by the sea. When I asked him why, he said he knew he could not have helped Prasudoc, so he did not need to wrestle with guilt."

Tears trickled down Tiann's face. "On the day I left, my father's heart showed a weakness. Shal was able to treat him then. Ever since I heard of his death, I have wondered if I could have done the same if I had been there."

Venut stirred then, putting a new brick of peat on the fire. "It sounds like it was too sudden for anyone to help. And if Prasudoc was the chief he was reputed to be, he would never have sat inactive in his hall. He would always have been a leader, a warrior." His voice held respect and sympathy. He handed Nuallen the neglected bowl of porridge and sat again.

A burden lifted from Tiann. Her grief still flowed, spilling out onto her cheeks, but the bitter tang of it was gone. The two men sat silent, Nuallen eating and Venut poking at the fire, while Tiann wept. The flow diminished and dried, Venut refilled her cup, and she drank.

Nuallen continued. "Shal turned his face toward his Iceni home then, deciding to leave as soon as the Gathering ended. He spent every moment either teaching me or going to his brothers with the good news that burned in him. The first morning of the Gathering, after I had collected some bread and filled a waterskin, we came upon a large crowd murmuring with excitement and alarm. At the center stood a druid in a dark cloak, shouting. When Shal saw him, he pushed his way to him and seized the man's arm. They exchanged words I could not hear, and then Shal stumbled back. His brothers made way for him, some trying to speak to him, but he ignored them. He seemed dazed. I followed as he walked for a long time."

"It was Bultur. Bringing the news about my mother and sisters. Yes?"

"Yes. He came to convince the brotherhood to support Boudica as she called the tribes to arms. The debate completely hijacked the Gathering. Many who followed the path as Bultur does gave their immediate support. Soon even the more cautious and moderate of the fellowship leaned toward war. But Shal took no part. He prayed and mourned, not eating, barely sleeping. He told me about your red vision when you were a child, Tiann. He said he had always feared it held a wider meaning.

"But then one more bit of news spilled from the mouth of a newcomer, and Shal rose to action. We heard you were alive, here. The weight of his losses lessened. Shal was determined to reunite you with your family. He knew your presence would be healing for Mara. He thought perhaps if Boudica knew you were safe, it would help her think clearly. We packed up our things and secured provisions and a boat to the mainland, intending to leave the very next day after addressing the Gathering about the Man of Light."

Nuallen stopped. He picked up his cup and sipped, then tilted it back and forth in his hands. Though Tiann longed to urge him on, she held her tongue. This part of the story belonged to him.

At last, the young man cleared his throat. "That very morning we woke to shouting and calls to arms. Everywhere people strapped on swords and snatched up bows, every inhabitant of the island. Clusters of druids streamed toward the shore with torches, crying out with incantations. Shal and I hurried to see, and there on the mainland, a large Roman force prepared to invade. They were already crossing with shallow boats and swimming the horses across.

"Shal grabbed my arm, and we ran toward where our boat waited for our journey. Perhaps we could still escape. But then we saw a knot of Romans heading toward a woman. She was not one of the warriors but a woman holding a child and trying to hide behind a rock. Shal pulled out his dagger and stood between them, yelling to the woman to run. What could I do? I also drew my dagger and joined him. There was no chance we could win against them. We could only give the woman time. At the end we lay speared through, and the soldiers moved off, grumbling about their lost prize."

Tiann closed her eyes, picturing Shal's tenderness to children, to her. His gentle hands when he'd soothed her grief at the death of her father. His patience and affection while he'd advised and taught.

"My wound burned and made me gasp from the pain, but eventually I could lift myself up and crawl to where I heard Shal moaning. Blood covered his chest, but his eyes were clear. 'Get to my Iceni girl,' he said. 'Tell her all that has happened. Tell her to follow the Light.'"

Nuallen's voice choked. "He spoke a charge and a blessing

over me. Then he could not speak anymore. His hand, though weak, pushed me in the direction of the boat."

The three of them sat silent, honoring Shal's passing. After some time, a soft voice called for Venut. He opened the door to reveal that night had fallen. Tiann heard Beathas inform the chief that the ewe was safely delivered of two healthy lambs.

Venut thanked the woman and returned to his seat by the fire. Nuallen smiled at him. "Chief of a tribe, yet you still care about each small lamb. Remind me to tell you a story about that later."

"I will. But for now, I think it is time for rest. You are still mending and building your strength, and Tiann has trekked up from the valley today." Venut opened a chest and pulled out another sheepskin, which he arranged with the one taken from Tiann's bench to make a sleeping place for her.

She had just pulled up her blanket and closed her eyes when something heavy and warm was draped across her body. "That's Teth's bearskin. He thought you'd need something warm up here in the mountains." The weight pressing down on her felt like an embrace—like Shal's love coming to her or maybe even like the kindness of his God.

The next morning, Costri and Teth arrived. They brought with them bundles, which they handed to Tiann. One was her old saddlebag, still packed with the stash of items she had stored in it for her escape. The other sack contained her boots and the embroidered strips of fabric from her bed covering and old tunic.

Tiann clutched the ragged cloth to her face. "I thought it was all burned. Why did you save it?"

Costri shuffled his feet and looked at the sky. "Teth remembered the stitching from the garment you wore as a child at your feast. And I remembered how carefully you always laced up those boots on your journey north. You told me you had an old injury. I thought they would be useful."

"Thank you." Tiann's voice choked over the words. Eyes swimming, she brought the bundles inside.

Venut welcomed his men and ushered them in behind her. A shepherd joined the group in the bothy. Once they were all settled with warm drinks, Venut laid out his scheme for Tiann's escape. Once he described the broad idea, Nuallen lifted a hand, stopping the chief before he launched into the details.

"Will the plan need to be altered if I go with Tiann?" At Venut's immediate frown, he added, "I know you intended to move me to a safer place in the West. But my heart is calling me south, to provide some of the support Tiann would have had from Shal. I cannot replace his wise counsel or fatherly love, but I can at least be a friend so she does not have to journey alone."

Tiann leaned forward. "I thank you for it. But the way will not be easy. Are you strong enough?" She could not bear the thought of Nuallen suffering from hard travel, scanty food, and rough nights in the open. Or even worse, if he became unable to go on, preventing her from getting to her family.

Nuallen laughed. "That is the only difficulty I did not consider! After all, I crossed the width of Albion with a spear hole in my side."

"Yes, and you were so close to death, they threw you out with the garbage!" Teth interlaced his hands on his head and stretched his feet toward the fire.

"But I did not die. I am tough. My wound is healed, and I am rested." Nuallen rose from his pallet and knelt before Tiann. "I promise you, if you allow me to come along, I will not slow you down. I have many skills for traveling unseen and living off the land. Remember, I am from the far northern tribes, known for making trouble and then vanishing."

Venut grunted, his mouth twitching with amusement. "Sit

back down, young painted druid. You can go, if Tiann will allow it."

"Yes, come with me. A friend would be welcome."

The chief looked at each person. "Then let me tell you how it will work."

CHAPTER

EIGHTEEN

Tiann laughed at Fein's antics as they brought hay to the horses in the paddock. A pale warmth released the scent of the armfuls of dried grass. She lifted her face to the early spring sun. The touch of its light brought energy and hope. Soon the signal would come, and she would be on her way to Mara. Meanwhile, Fein's combination of mischief and shyness reminded Tiann of her sister when they were children. She would miss the boy.

Dumping her load of hay, she gave herself a long stretch. She froze, catching sight of Shinoc standing on the path coming from the cow's winter pasture, looking at her with loathing. He too had been banished from the hall, and he looked the worse for it: thin, unkempt, and ragged. He uttered a foul word and spat. Collecting a shovel from an outbuilding, he shuffled back toward the pasture.

The man's hatred dimmed the shine of the day, but Tiann shook it off. "Come, Fein. Let's check on the lambs." Most of the sheep roamed farther afield and lambed in shelters built close to their pastures, like the one where Tiann met Nuallen. However, the shepherds brought laboring ewes from the nearest pasture here. Day after day since coming back to the valley stronghold, Tiann took Fein to the sheep pen. Although his beloved horses remained first in his affection, he loved to cuddle the newborns, only setting them down when the mother ewe's bleating grew anxious.

The early spring warmth continued, and the snowcap on the western slopes retreated. The sounds of melting and thawing filled the air. After morning chores one day, they went to visit the sheep as usual.

Fein hung over the side of the pen. "Look, there's a new ewe. And she has twins, but I think they are older. I wonder why the shepherd brought them in."

Tiann's heart thumped. The sign. Today.

"Fein?" Her voice was unsteady. She tried again. "Fein, I just remembered something I forgot to do. Why don't you stay here while I finish it? It may take me quite some time. But first let me pet one of the lambs for a minute."

Fein scooped up a lamb and carried it to her. She stroked the little animal's soft fluff for a moment, then put her arms around the boy, taking care not to squeeze the creature between them. "You are a good friend." She planted a kiss on his head, then on the lamb's hard skull. She walked to the stable, checking each stall to be sure no one was there. Working quickly, she emptied the feed box in the back stall and opened her box. She took the smaller pieces of jewelry from its casket and stashed it in the pockets she had sewn inside her clothing. The gold items weighed her down, dragging on her garments, but did not hamper her movement too much. She had decided there was no way to bring the heavy torc, arm rings, or elaborate gold casket itself. She wrapped them back up in the wooden box and returned everything to the feed box. Maybe Fein could use it someday to make a good life for himself.

Tiann stopped at the paddock to stroke Stadder's nose for a

precious moment. She had no time to spare, but she allowed herself the space of three long breaths to whisper a farewell. She forced herself to step away and take the path toward the cow pasture without looking back. This was the tricky part. She was forbidden to leave the compound unaccompanied, but less and less attention had been paid her over time. She carried nothing and tried to walk with assurance but not haste.

Where the path curved out of sight, she plunged into the woods, following the markers Venut had made her memorize. The lightning-split tree. The sound of ice melt rushing to a small brook. A boulder as tall as a man, with a peculiar stripe halfway up. Clouds blew in, obscuring the sun, so she had to rely on the directions she had recited to herself during the waiting nights. At last she reached a steep hillside, where sparse trees grew at impossible angles. Searching under the brush at the base, she found the bundle Teth had planted there for her. She changed into her sturdy boots. Her old saddlebag had been fitted with an extra strap so she could carry it securely on her back. She checked the contents. Flint, extra wrappings for her ankle, a full waterskin and packet of food, the waxed-wool cloth, a plain but serviceable dagger, even the little pouch of coins Cattia had given her. At the bottom, in neat rolls, lay the embroidered strips of fabric rescued from the fire. She divested herself of the jewelry in her pockets, wrapped it in the fabric, and repacked, putting her discarded shoes away too. Nothing left behind would betray her this time. She drew the bloodied cloth from her dagger sheath. She held it to her lips for a moment, then tucked it away in the bag. The dagger took its place.

Sliding her arms through the straps and settling the bag on her back, she surveyed the hill. She gave herself time to map a mental route, then tackled the climb. Scrabbling as much with her hands as her feet, she clawed her way up, using the scrawny trees to brace herself. She dug into the hillside with fingers that soon grew raw. Once she slipped on a muddy spot and lost two body lengths of progress. She reached the top just as the sun touched the horizon.

Not daring to pause to catch her breath, she paced five steps and marked the spot with two fallen branches. Maintaining that distance, she walked parallel to the edge, scanning the trees above the third branch. Finding nothing in one direction after several minutes, she went back, marking where she turned around. From her starting point, she walked in the opposite direction, still scanning. The sun sank lower, and Tiann fought down panic. She turned around once again, passed her starting point and where she had first turned. This time she went farther and was rewarded. There, a marking newly carved into a tree: a spiral. She marked the spot and hurried back to remove her other markers, returning to the carved tree as the sunlight cast its last glow from its place below the horizon. She struck out straight away from the steep edge of the valley, following the spirals, over which she wiped mud as she passed. Just when she was sure she would have to stop and spend the night in the open, she came to a heap of enormous boulders. They looked like someone had thrust them up out of the earth. In dusk's blue shadows, Tiann found the shelter formed by two massive overlapping stones. She crawled in, feeling her way. Her hands met a torch, which she pulled out into the gray twilight and lit. Crawling back in, she found a stand for the torch, a loaf of bread, and Teth's bearskin. She ate, drank from her waterskin, doused the torch, and slept.

THE CLOUDS PERSISTED the next day as she pushed on, turning to a dreary, persistent drizzle. Midmorning she stopped to pull out the waxed wool, draping it over her head and around herself and her pack. Occasionally she backtracked, having missed the next marker. Venut told her she should reach the next stopping point by midday. It was hard to mark the passage of hours in the rain, but her complaining stomach let her know the day was wearing on.

At last she saw the mark she waited for—her own spiral alongside Nuallen's flame. Over the days while Tiann waited and Nuallen worked on strengthening himself, Teth and Venut had marked out trails for each of them. Besides intimate knowledge of the landscape, their constant patrolling duty had given them reasons to range far without particular notice given to their comings and goings. This mark was where the paths converged. Tiann settled down to wait, huddling under low-hanging branches while water dripped from her makeshift hood. She ate just enough to satisfy her hunger, being frugal with her food, but drank deep. Studying the pattern of the rain off the trees, she fashioned a funnel to refill her waterskin where droplets met in a steady trickle.

She fell into a fitful doze, leaning against a tree with her knees tucked up to her chest. A hand on her shoulder caused her to leap up, swinging wildly.

Nuallen ducked her blow, grinning. "And that's why you need a companion. Sleeping away where anyone can sneak up on you."

Tiann gave him a quick, hard embrace. "I am glad to have a companion. And glad to see you. Venut and his men have returned to the royal stronghold?"

"Yes. They left the morning the shepherds came back from delivering the ewe and her lambs. How could they be helping you escape if they are there, disturbing Cartimandua's peace? If they played their parts well, they caused enough commotion with their feasting and the chief's bickering with the queen that no one had time to notice your absence for a good while. Maybe they still don't know."

"Sit and rest for a while. Are you hungry?"

"No. I ate as I went. If you are ready, we should continue. The next way point will give us proper shelter. We need to go hard and fast tomorrow, so we should get there as soon as possible and sleep."

Tiann collected her waterskin and put it in her pack. After obscuring the telltale signs of her presence and the mark on the tree, they set off. Although the drizzle continued its monotonous discomfort, Tiann's mood lifted. It was working. They were away. Every footstep carried her closer to Mara. And she didn't have to do it alone.

Their shelter that night was an abandoned hut, derelict and reclaimed by the forest. But once they located it and pushed their way through the brush to duck through the entrance, Tiann saw that just like the rock shelter, the inside was prepared for them. A small fire pit with well-seasoned oak gave welcome heat with little smoke once lit, and another loaf of bread supplemented the food in their packs. The roof showed signs of having been patched, and they spent the night warm and snug.

Dawn just pearled the sky when Tiann and Nuallen left. They needed to reach the estuary by low tide. They spoke little, though Tiann sometimes heard Nuallen singing or humming. The rain had stopped overnight, and they made good time. The sun was still high when the wide waters came into view. As arranged, their side was barren of boats. No one could follow them or wait on the other side to ambush them. In the planning, Venut, Teth, and Costri considered how pursuers would go about catching fugitives, then set about cutting off those possibilities. Tiann lit a torch, and Nuallen fished a small, polished bronze mirror from his pack. They signaled several times and soon saw a boat coming across the river to them.

Relieved, Tiann shrugged off her pack and sat on the grassy shore to wait. Surely, once this wide water lay between them and Cartimandua, they would be safe. She stretched her legs out, leaning back on her hands. The sun cast a weak warmth. Closing her eyes, she lifted her face to it. She listened to the water and Nuallen's absent humming.

She almost ignored the faint vibration under her palms. But the sensation thrilled through her, and her eyes snapped open. "Nuallen, hush." Lying prone, she pressed her ear to the ground. Hoofbeats. She sprang up, pulling out her dagger. The boat was less than halfway across.

"Tiann, what . . ."

"Someone is coming on horseback. I can't tell which direction." She swung from east to west, scanning the banks of the river and the woods behind them. She could hear it now, and a moment later her ears pinpointed the sound, coming from the inland direction, beyond a curve in the estuary. The boat's progress was agonizingly slow.

The rider came into view. Tiann could tell when he spotted them, for he kicked his horse into a gallop. He wore Brigantian dress and held something in front of him on the saddle. With a buzzing in her ears, Tiann recognized his ungainly posture. Shinoc. *Disgraced and blaming me. Desperate to regain Cartimandua's favor. Somehow, he had known.*

"Tiann, do you know him?" Nuallen stood at her side, dagger drawn.

"Yes." Her mind raced. "He is a clumsy rider. It shouldn't be hard to unseat him." *Does he mean to ride us down? How else could he expect to disarm us?*

"He probably thought you would be alone."

Tiann decided to wonder later if Nuallen was hearing her thoughts. "Maybe, but he would know he is still outmatched. He will use the horse." *How can I use the horse's momentum to our advantage?* "I will run at him and seize the bridle to slow and turn the horse. If that doesn't throw him, you grab his leg and pull him down."

"You can grab the bridle of a galloping horse?"

A chariot thundering by, a leap to grasp a hand. "Oh yes. I am Iceni."

Shinoc was only two hundred paces away, and the horse slowed. The burden Shinoc held must be heavy. *Why carry something that hinders his attack?* One hundred paces.

Tiann crouched, ready to spring forward when Shinoc was close enough that he could not pull up to avoid her. She sensed Nuallen's tension, and in her peripheral vision his knuckles whitened on his dagger.

Fifty paces away, Shinoc pulled hard on the reins, thwarting her plan. "Greetings, Iceni girl." His yellow smile leered. "Surprised to see me? My queen will be delighted to have you back. I heard her say just the other day that a powerful sacrifice was needed. You should do nicely. And won't she be grateful to the man who provided it?" The bundle in his arms wriggled and moaned.

The air whooshed out of Tiann's lungs, and she struggled to draw another breath.

Shinoc laughed. "What, no fierce words? Something to do with this?" He dumped the bundle on the ground and dismounted, standing over it.

Nuallen hissed, "Tiann, the boat is nearly here. Let's grab our packs and run for it."

She kept her eyes on the bundle at Shinoc's feet. "No. We can't."

"Then let's attack him and get it over with." Nuallen's voice rose.

"Oh, I wouldn't do that." Shinoc bent and pulled the sack off the bundle.

Fein lay bound and gagged. Shinoc drew a short sword and pointed it down at the boy. He threw a rope toward Tiann. "Have your apostate druid friend—or is he your lover?—have him bind your hands. And do it right, or the boy will pay. Maybe he would like a mark to match yours, Iceni girl." The point of his blade edged to Fein's arm.

"Nuallen, get the rope." Tiann's voice was hoarse.

"Tiann, no . . ."

"Do it."

Nuallen held his arms wide and walked toward the rope. "God of rocks and hiding places, shield us from evil schemes. God of truth and faithfulness, deliver us from treachery."

"Keep your incantations to yourself, druid. I have already invoked the power of the gods."

Nuallen picked up the rope. "God of stronghold and fortress, defend us from the trapping net. God of all times and this time, shelter us from the contempt of the proud."

Yes. Yes. Great God, rescue us!

Shinoc's scream echoed off the water. "Stop talking or I will cut him. I will take his ear. I will take his hand."

The boat reached the shore, and Costri leapt out, running through the shallows to reach them.

"Tell him to stay back!" Shinoc's screech rose in pitch.

Costri came to Tiann's side. "We can overpower him."

"Not before he hurts Fein."

Nuallen began to sing, his voice rising in the language of the North. The melody was the bard's song, the tune from Devyn's pipe, the music of the Maker's pattern.

A cloud formed in the blue sky, casting its shadow over Shinoc. He lifted his sword with a shaking arm, pointing it at Nuallen. "What are you doing?"

Fein turned his head toward Tiann. His eyes shone wide and fearful.

Words poured from Tiann's mouth. "Maker, give me help, though I don't deserve it. We are in trouble. Do not let the darkness add this grief to my heart—I cannot bear it. Shine on us, Great Light. I am calling on You." She knelt, stretching out her hands to her young friend. "It's all right, Fein. It will be all right."

A dazzle filled her vision. The place where Fein lay disappeared into a blinding light. Shinoc dropped his sword and threw up his arms over his face.

"Now, Tiann," Nuallen called.

She rushed forward into the light and scooped Fein into her arms. She ran, stumbling, toward the boat with Nuallen on her heels.

"No!" Shinoc's enraged shout sounded behind them.

Costri tossed their packs in and held the boat steady. Tiann and Nuallen climbed in, hauling Fein with them. The warrior pushed, face red, the sinews of his arms straining. The boat floated free. He stepped out after them to climb in, as Tiann and Nuallen seized the oars.

Costri's mouth opened in a wide grimace. Behind him, Shinoc withdrew his Roman gladius. Blood pooled in the water. "Go," Costri gasped. "Get to your family. Tiann, I'm sorry." He turned to face his attacker.

"Tiann, row." Nuallen's voice broke.

She tugged on her oar, and their boat surged away from the two men. She kept pulling, watching the two combatants. Just as the retreating tide caught them and sent them westward toward the sea, Costri lifted his dagger for the killing blow. Then he sank below the water.

TIANN SPREAD her waxed-wool cloth over the fresh bracken she had cut to soften the rocky ground. They had brought the boat to land in a tiny shallow bay just south of the estuary. She sat, motioning Fein to join her. She had foraged healing plants, crushed and soaked the leaves in a curved piece of bark, and concocted a paste. This she spread over the places on Fein's wrists and ankles made raw from Shinoc's binding. She rummaged in her pack, finding the cloth stained with Devyn's blood. She laid it aside. Using the strips of embroidered cloth from her bed coverings, she bandaged Fein as best she could. He snuggled close, and she put her cloak around both their shoulders. Nuallen tended the fire and the fish cooking over it, handing around the tender, smoky flesh as soon as it was ready. Fein fell asleep the moment he swallowed his last mouthful. Tiann laid him down, but he kept a fistful of her tunic, like he was afraid to let her go.

She hugged her knees, watching the rippling reflection of the moon on the water. Her heart ached for Costri. She found she had no more anger at what he had done in taking her captive. What more could he have done to prove himself a friend? Despite her sadness, and the difficulty of the journey ahead, a contentment settled on her. She was on her way to Mara. Really and truly on her way home. She cupped her scar. During their blood bonding, Shal had said her scar became not one of shame but of honor and love.

"Nuallen, when the Man came alive again, did His wounds disappear?"

"No. He has chosen to always bear the wounds. They are the signs. They show He became one of us. They show His great love. And they show what He has overcome. It is His wounds that bring healing to our spirits."

"Today His light overcame the dark."

"Yes."

Tiann's fingers touched the bloodstained cloth. "But it doesn't always."

"Shal told me there is a great war. It is not between Brigantes and Iceni, or Romans and the tribes. It is the powers of darkness against the God of Light. Darkness still fights and sometimes wins a battle. But darkness does not know what we know."

"What?"

"That Light has already overcome. Darkness cannot win the war. The Man has already secured the victory."

Tiann laid down next to Fein's warm body. She looked up at the stars. There was so much more darkness than stars, and yet the stars kept their light. As she looked, they seemed to swirl and turn, dancing to the Maker's song.

"Nuallen, will you tell me a story about the Man? How His light brings healing?"

"Once the Man traveled with His friends, and a great crowd of people journeyed with Him. A person met Him along the way. Now this person was sick—no one wanted to be near him, or hire him, or have a family with him. His tribe cast him out because of his sickness. But he gave the Man a greeting of honor, and said, 'If You want to, You can make me well so I can return to my tribe and have a life that is whole.'

"And the Man stretched out His hand."

AUTHOR'S NOTE

First-century Britain captured my heart and mind with the incredible stories written by Roman historians. But what truly lit the fire for me as an author was the history combined with all we don't know about the time period from the point of view of the native tribes. What a treasure for a writer who loves history but also loves a bit of world-building. While I tried to be faithful to what is known about events, people, and places, I also filled in what is unknown with how I pictured it in my imagination.

Many years ago on my first trip to England, I spent hours at the Museum of London and the British Museum, examining every artifact and reading every placard related to the early years of Roman Britain and especially Boudica's remarkable rebellion. The story simmered for a long time on the back burner. Sometimes during the years of homeschooling my kids, and teaching literature, writing, and history, I threw in some ingredients and gave it a stir.

When the time finally came to move the whole thing to the front burner, I talked one of my now-adult sons into coming to England with me for another trip to research. We tramped around paths in the Iceni ancestral lands, visited more museums, went to the Norfolk coast, and checked out the remains of the Camulo-dunum temple foundations deep underneath the Norman castle in Colchester, which now serve as a museum.

The story of *A Hand Outstretched* unfolds against the backdrop of historical events furnished to us by Roman writers, mainly Publius Cornelius Tacitus and Cassius Dio. The main outlines of their accounts are similar, but I have leaned more heavily on Taci-tus. Though he was a child during the time period, he was at least a contemporary, while Cassius Dio was born a hundred years later. In addition, Tacitus had the benefit of his father-in-law, Gnaeus Julius Agricola, who was a participant in the events preceding and following Boudica's rebellion.

The Romans considered the Iceni rulers—Boudica, and her husband, Prasutagus— client rulers who cooperated with the empire. I chose to portray that relationship as less straightfor-ward, based on the fact that the Iceni had previously resisted Roman rule and, of course, ended up staging a full-blown revolt against the occupiers. The rebellion itself is well-attested not just in the histories but in the archaeological record. For example, a distinct layer of ash found in both Colchester (Camulodunum) and London bears witness to the devastation of fire at the hands of Boudica's army. The stormy relationship between Cartimandua and her husband, Venutius, including the betrayal of Caratacus, comes from the Roman historians, as does the Romans' attack on the druids on the isle of Mona (present-day Anglesey).

The real people in the story (indicated on the character list with an *) come to us through Roman chroniclers. However, their names, if accurate, are certainly Latinized, and we have no record of what the tribes used as names for these people. I chose to tackle this problem by "un-Latinizing" names. So Venutius becomes Venut and Caratacus becomes Caradoc.

As for Boudica herself, there is disagreement about the spelling of her name (you can find Boudicca, Boadicea, and others), and even if that was the queen's name at all. It may have been a title or a descriptor.

I named the fictional characters with an ear to Celtic languages but was not dogmatic about it. Again, we just don't know how first-century British sounded or how similar it was to the languages that descended from it. A few names are still in use, like Aife or Mara. Other names I invented from words that sound like them and describe the character. For example, the word *còmhstri* means "struggle" or "conflict" and became Costri.

Tiann came to me fully herself, name and all.

As with the names of people, the names of places come to us from Roman sources. Where I reference places the Romans named themselves, like Camulodunum (present-day Colchester) or Lindum (present-day Lincoln), I used their Latin names. For everything else I mostly refrained from using names, as we don't know what the tribes called them or even exactly where they were. For example, we know present-day Thetford in Norfolk was an Iceni settlement, but was it Boudica's home base? If so, what did she call it? It may have been primarily a military stronghold, with the rest of the royal household living somewhere less fortified.

The Roman road carrying Tiann and her captors north, now called Ermine Street, was mainly complete to Lincoln (Lindum), but the castra where they stopped for the night is fictional. I based it on descriptions of many such facilities throughout the empire and the likelihood of such a place existing.

As far as I know, there is no real tunnel and cave with neolithic carvings under an Iceni archaeological site in Norfolk—but who knows what future discoveries will reveal?

Archaeological finds demonstrate robust trade between Britain and the rest of the world and especially the lands around the Mediterranean, starting even before the Roman occupation. Where goods travel, news also travels. The early church was spreading through the Roman empire in the AD 50s and 60s. I chose to speculate whether stories of Jesus might have made their way to the Britons and particularly the religious leaders. The systematic attack on the druids by the Romans and the Boudiccan revolt could have interrupted an earlier spread of Christianity.

Readers may notice I took portions of the Bible as inspiration for songs, stories, and prophecy. The bard's song is based on Psalm 65. Elior's words to Tiann on the beach are drawn from Isaiah 60–62. The original story Shal tells about Jesus healing a man who could not walk can be found in Matthew 9. Nuallen's story at the end of the book is told in Luke 5.

The people of ancient Britain would not have the written Hebrew Scriptures, but they may have heard some of the songs and stories. I imagined how the message of good news might be delivered to people with no Jewish or Greek cultural context. Stories told by missionaries who have traveled to people groups unconnected to Western culture sometimes speak of dreams or angelic encounters, which prepared these people to hear about Jesus. Tiann's spiritual sensitivities and meetings with Elior grew from that seed.

The triple spiral, or triskelion, is a symbol found in many cultures. I believe all truth is God's truth and see the triskelion's use as an echo of a knowledge that sounds through humanity. The mystery and wonder of the triune God still calls to us.

Do you want more information and conversation about ancient Britain, Romans, the spread of Christianity, or historical fiction? Do you want to know what happens next to Tiann, Mara, and the other people in the book? Visit my website Kirstenp.com to read blog posts, sign up for my newsletter, and get updates on the next books in the series.

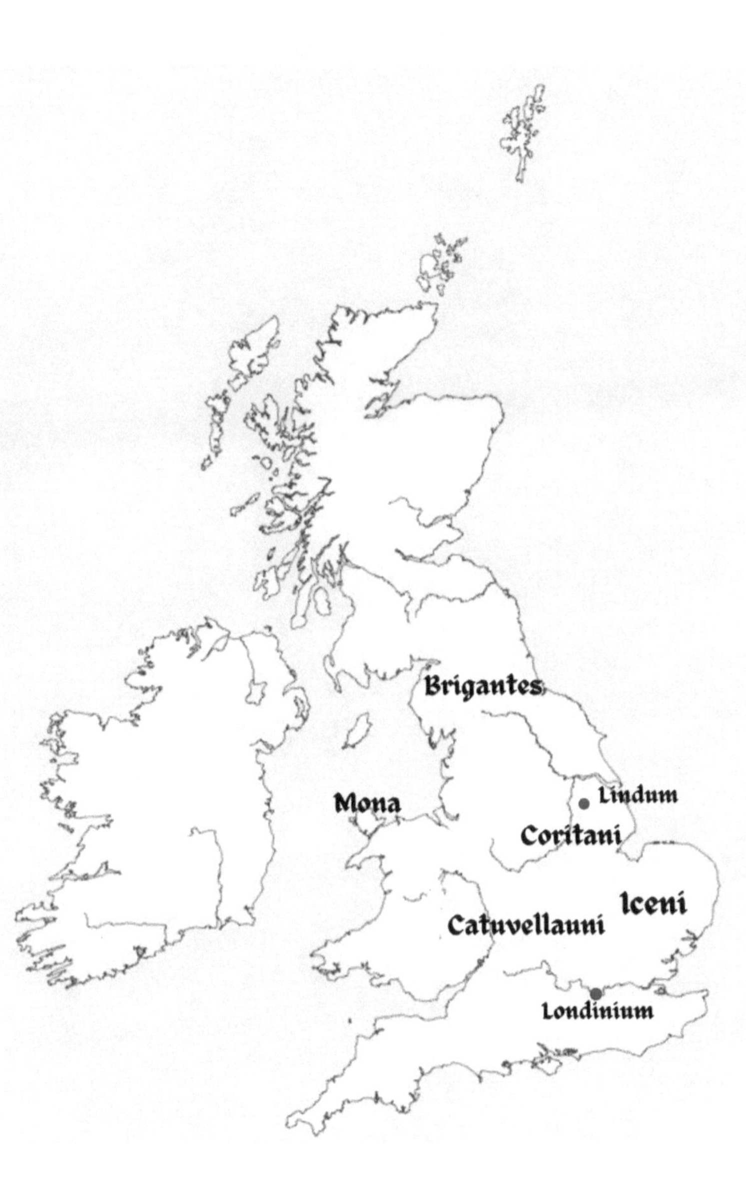

Brigantes
Mona
Lindum
Coritani
Iceni
Catuvellauni
Londinium

ACKNOWLEDGMENTS

I have years' worth of thanks to give people who helped me bring this book into being.

My friends and family who have encouraged me, especially my sister Linda: you are too many to list, but if you ever patiently listened to me talk about ancient Britain, writing, or this story, then you know it's you.

My writing friends in workshops, seminars, and critique groups, especially my faithful Word Weavers Page 24 women Alynda Long, Judy Ducharme, Teresa Lasher, Dena Hobbs, and Lynne Tagawa: this book is so much better because of all of you!

My former literature and writing students, including my own kids: teaching you challenged me to up my game and become a better reader and writer. Thanks for your enthusiasm and for keeping me on my toes. I learned so much during my time with you.

My editor, Dori Harrell: your attention to detail and insightful comments saved me from mistakes and polished up the manuscript. Thanks for your expertise delivered with gentleness.

My beta readers Sue Case, Stacie Capone, and Dee Brennan: your willingness to read an early draft and meet with me to discuss it improved the final manuscript immeasurably. What a treasure to have dear friends who are also gifted critical readers!

My sons Nicholas and Alex and my bonus daughter Victoria: you have been part of this journey from the very beginning. Sash, thanks for discussing character development with me and going on the research trip. Sorry I got us lost that day. Nicholas, thanks for your cheerleading and hugs when I'm discouraged or stressed. And Victoria, you came into my life a little later, but I can't imagine my family without you. And you even joined my launch team. I love all of you.

My husband Dan: travel companion, patron of the artist, proofreader, excellent cook, runner of all errands, pray-er, friend, lover. I'm so grateful you are my partner to work with, laugh with, and build with in this life. Adventures!

And most of all, the Man who changes everything: Jesus, I'm profoundly thankful that Your hand reaches out to pull me into Your light.

COMING NEXT!

Footsteps on the Way
Light At Empire's Edge Book 2

The red of fire and blood sweeps over the land as Tiann races to find her family. Can she reach them before disaster overtakes them all?

For updates and other fun stuff, sign up for my newsletter at kirstenp.com

ABOUT THE AUTHOR

Dear Reader,

Thank you for traveling ancient Britain along with Tiann and me!

You can find behind-the-scenes material on my website kirstenp.com. Newsletter subscribers also receive exclusive updates, first looks, and peeks into the messy life of a writer.

For the curious:

I have a pretty typical author origin story: scribbling tales in blank books as a child, melodramatic short stories as a teen and young adult, and lots of lyrics as a singer/songwriter. I also fell in love with history as a child, enjoying living-history museums and reading through the history shelf in the children's library. In sixth grade, passions intersected and produced a sixteen-stanza ballad for a school project ("Eleanor of Aquitaine, Born into a duke's domain..." May God bless you for your patience, Mrs. Haynes.) My first crushes were Daniel from *The Bronze Bow* and Johnny Tremain.

The first season of my adulthood involved homeschooling my kids, developing and teaching Bible studies, doing some speaking, and writing just for myself. After my kids graduated high school, I got serious about a writing career, first with nonfiction books for parents of kids with mental illness, and now with my first love, historical fiction.

When I'm not writing, I love to travel, hang out with my family, ride rollercoasters, read with a cup of tea, hike, run, and swim outdoors (forward motion athletic endeavors only - I'm not very coordinated), nap, watch movies and tv series with compli-cated plots and strong female protagonists, and daydream. Except for the napping and tea drinking, these are all fueled by coffee.

I believe exploration of the human experience makes fiction compelling. When I read or write a character in an unfamiliar setting, I sit with her wounds and loves. Then I ask: what do I know now - how has my vision widened? What do I feel – how is my heart more open?

I hope that fiction does that for you too. I'd love to hear what you think. Get in touch at kirsten@kirstenp.com.

HOW TO HELP THE AUTHOR

I hope you enjoyed *A Hand Outstretched*.

If you're willing to help, I'd really appreciate a review on Amazon. Reviews are the best way to help authors spread the word about their books.

It doesn't have to be long or expressed in fancy words - just a little of what you thought of the book or how it made you feel.

Please leave a review for *A Hand Outstretched* on Amazon.